THE LIGHT OF DAY

TRENA CHRISTIE-MacEACHERN

The Light of Day
© 2023 Trena Christie-MacEachern

Cover image: Rebekah Wetmore
Editor: Andrew Wetmore

ISBN: 978-1-990187-82-7
First edition November, 2023

2475 Perotte Road
Annapolis County, NS
B0S 1A0

moosehousepress.com
info@moosehousepress.com

We live and work in Mi'kma'ki, the ancestral and unceded territory of the Mi'kmaw people. This territory is covered by the "Treaties of Peace and Friendship" which Mi'kmaw and Wolastoqiyik (Maliseet) people first signed with the British Crown in 1725. The treaties did not deal with surrender of lands and resources but in fact recognized Mi'kmaq and Wolastoqiyik (Maliseet) title and established the rules for what was to be an ongoing relationship between nations. We are all Treaty people.

For my mom,
Margaret I. Christie
One of the strongest women I know

This is a work of fiction. The author has created the characters, conversations, interactions, and events; and any resemblance of any character to any real person is coincidental.

The Light of Day

Prologue

Trena Christie-MacEachern

"Here. Stretch out your legs."

Mary Ellen tucked the blanket taut around my swollen calves, the way I like it. She fluffed up my pillow, too. "Is that better, Gran?"

I blinked in acknowledgement, sat back, and waited for the kettle to whistle. It was nice to have my youngest granddaughter here spoiling me. My family seemed to think I had difficulty now with even the simplest of tasks.

"The whisky's in the cupboard, dear. And the honey. A table-spoon of each," I called out. Sat back. "Make it two." I still enjoyed a good cup of tea. Strong and hot. It would feel good on my parched throat.

She retrieved the silver tea set from above the fridge. A small luxury I allowed myself to take here. There wasn't room for any-thing much. The apartment was a small one-bedroom with kit-chenette, but at least all the rooms were on the same floor.

"It's what you call downsizing," they said.

When Mary Ellen was younger, we'd wear paper crowns and costume jewellery and drink tea from the silver tea pot, polished bright and shiny. I made homemade cookies then, buttery short-bread with dollops of pure, white icing and slivers of maraschino cherries on top. Or thick molasses cookies. Mary Ellen loved those. Everyone did.

I had a package of store-bought today. Gingersnaps.

"The butter's in the fridge, dear."

"You should leave some out on the counter, Gran, so it spreads easier."

"Gets too soft on the counter."

"Yeah, but it gets too hard in the fridge. It breaks the cookie when I try and spread it." She made a face.

"Doesn't matter. All goes down the same way."

She laughed and nodded.

I watched her as she poured the cups. She was sixteen now and so lovely. She looked so much like her great-grandmother. It was the hair—that beautiful, deep auburn, with a slight curl—and those dark brown eyes like a rich chocolate.

"You look like so much like my mother," I said.

"I know," she said. "You tell me all the time."

"Do I?" I thought for a moment. "Did I tell you where the butter was?"

Her cheeks turned rose-pink.

I stared, admiring her. "I bet you and your sisters have lots of boyfriends."

She brought over the tea on the matching silver tray. The cups rattled but her face remained calm as she concentrated on her delivery. She walked carefully around the living room chairs, and placed the tray on the side table.

"Very good. No spillage."

"I hope I didn't make it too strong," she said, as she passed me the cup.

I took a sip, then stuck out my tongue, jokingly showing my dismay. "It's fine, dear. Just perfect."

"So." She cleared her throat, wrapped her hair behind her ear. She poised a pen in her slender fingers. "Should we start?"

"What's this for, again?"

"For school, mostly. But I'd like to learn, too. You never really talk about what life was like back then. When you were little."

I tried to smile. It was so long ago and there was never much to say. "Well, we were poor."

Mary Ellen rolled her eyes. "You've said that before."

Then she stuffed the cookie into her mouth and stood up. "I almost forgot."

She rushed to her book-bag and dug out a blue folder, studied it for a moment and then presented it to me. "Looky here."

Inside were photos. Old ones.

"My my." I brought my wrinkled hands to my lips.

The first picture showed my father standing in front of the barn. The pictures were black and white, but I could see every line and detail on his face as if I was just there staring back at him. "This was your great-grandfather."

"He looks cross," she said over my shoulder.

"He was."

The next picture was of me holding a small boy. I didn't look much older than Mary Ellen was now.

"Is that my dad?"

I nodded and ran my finger over the glossy print. "Where did you get these? I haven't seen them in ages. I forgot I even had them."

"I found them in your old house. In a box. When we were there last summer."

"Ohhh. I thought I threw them out by mistake or someone took them. Put them away."

The last one was blurry. A head shot. Half exposed film. It was of my mother.

My breath caught and my cup rattled as I choked on my tea. "Where—?"

My eyes blurred. I placed the cup on the side table and dug through my pockets, pulling out a balled-up tissue.

"Awww, Gran. I'm sorry. I didn't mean to make you sad."

She wrapped her warm arms around me and we stayed that way for a few minutes, staring at the fuzzy black and white. "She's beautiful."

"Yes. Yes, she was. I miss her still." I couldn't take my eyes off the photo.

"I wish it was clearer. You think she looks like me?"

She held the picture beside her face, tilted her head just as my mother used to do. Then she placed the picture back down on my lap. "You can keep these. I made copies."

I nodded.

"Ready?"

I nodded again.

"Where did you live when you were growing up?"

"In Port Hope. In the place you call 'the old house'. My father called it *àite mòran de na craobhan*, which means 'a place of many trees'. Port Hope was more 'the town'. We lived on the outskirts, near the woods."

"By the way, Dad says they are going to turn the old house into a cottage for everyone. Won't that be nice?"

"Ohh," I said. "Yes, that would be nice."

"Okay. Sorry. That was off-topic." She laughed. "Tell me about your first memory."

"I doubt I can recall that long ago."

"Okay, tell me something that first made you happy. A happy memory."

Without hesitation, I blurted, "When Momma came home."

"Your mom was sick for a while. Oh, that's a good start. You must have been happy."

"We were. We were all beside ourselves, cleaning the house, and preparing food. Even though we had very little then, compared to now."

Mary Ellen pressed a button on the machine. It clicked. "Gran? Are you okay with this?"

"Sure, Mary Ellen. Anything for you."

"Anything you don't want to talk about is okay. Dad says you don't like to talk a lot about the past."

Mary Ellen was right. I didn't like talking about my childhood. Life was good when I was married and we were having the children, but the earlier years, growing up.... I shook my head. Things happened that we simply didn't talk about. The past needed to stay there. Let sleeping dogs lie as they say.

No, I wouldn't talk about those things. Couldn't. About any of it. It's too shameful. What would my granddaughter think of me? Or any of the family? I cleared my throat, brought the tissue to my eyes.

"Gran?"

I pressed my fingertips to my lips. *Should I? Unlock the demons from long ago?* I lay my head against the high back of the chair and rocked, took a good sip of my tea.

"What would you like to know?" I whispered.
"All of it."
"You're sure?"
She nodded and smiled.
"I had just turned seven and Momma was coming home..."

Trena Christie-MacEachern

Part I – Sarah

Trena Christie-MacEachern

1: A weak heart

October 26, 1946

"*Tha i dhachaigh*," he said. The snow thick on his head like he wore a white hat. It was late October and the winter had arrived early.

"Momma's home?" Sarah, my second oldest sister had asked. She was standing at the entrance of our house, relief in her eyes. "For good this time?"

Papa nodded.

Our youngest sister, Mary, bolted from behind upon hearing her horse. "Papa!" She screamed, "Leela needs water. Look at her. She's thirsty."

Mary narrowed her eyes as she moved towards her chestnut horse, patting her belly and chest. Leela snorted as she talked to her gently.

Papa grumbled under his breath but paid Mary no mind. He didn't like the idea of Martha giving away their horse to them. He didn't want their pity. He didn't need their charity and by no means did he want anything from the McFarlands. Period. But Martha made it clear it was Mary's horse and he had needed to borrow her to take our mother home.

"Mary," a voice croaked. "Is that you?"

Mary hopped up into the wagon and hugged Momma right quick.

When I walked toward our mother and saw her, my smile disappeared. What was left of her? I furrowed my eyes as I studied her. Her face was pale and thin. I peered up at the woman who was supposed to be our mother.

She smiled in a sad way and called me by my name, "Maggie."

Papa startled me; barked for me to get out of the way. Mary did a little curtsy as they entered the house. She ran back to Leela, grabbed the reins, and led her down to the barn to spoil her with her supper, fresh water, and apples she stole from the cold storage.

~

Even though our mother had told us she had been born with a weak heart, and had been in the hospital for months, I expected things to be the way they were before she left. I expected it to suddenly be summer with the sun bright and warm, the breezes gentle, the fireflies flickering their intermittent glow at nighttime. I thought I'd see Momma in the kitchen baking and cooking again, wiping her hands on her apron. See traces of flour in her hair. I expected to see her eating freshly picked strawberries or raspberries with warm milk.

I wanted to smell the aroma of fresh, baked bread, sliced thick with butter or molasses. Have swims at the brook, and games of chase while our father made hay and came in too tired to do anything else but eat his supper and go to bed. On those evenings, Momma would let us stay up late, and she would tell stories of when she was a girl, and tales of her sisters and brothers, and of her parents. Sometimes, on good nights, she'd tell us of the people she danced with at the ceilidhs before she met and married our father.

We sat and listened. Our legs folded onto themselves, while our oldest sister, Joanne, braided hair. Mary rested her cheek on Momma's lap, falling asleep right then and there.

This was what I expected. But maybe I imagined it all—what life was like before our mother left us.

Papa had Momma propped up on his daybed with pillows and blankets, her feet extended past the cushions. This did not look like the mother I remembered. Her hair was no longer the beautiful shade of auburn but was wiry and grey. The skin around her chin and neck drooped, and her eyes sat in dark pools. She looked like the stiff doll Mary had received one Christmas. It was a small, pretty thing with a blank stare. Its legs wouldn't bend.

Papa placed a book beside her so she could rest her teacup on it. He ordered Sarah to make a fresh pot even though Momma said she didn't want any. I noticed her hands shook.

He hovered over our mother like a nervous rabbit, staring, twitching his mouth, moving swiftly away only to swing around again and check on her. It was almost comical. Every time Momma sipped her tea, he'd check her cup and signal for Sarah to refill it.

Finally, Momma raised her hand. "If you make me drink any more tea, John, you're going to have to bring the bedpan right here." Her voice was raspy. She laughed quietly, though, so we all laughed with her, but this seemed to make Papa uncomfortable.

He took away her teacup. She just looked up at him, and then at me, and smiled.

I wanted to say something so bad, but the words just got stuck in my throat. Every time I opened my mouth, my tongue froze and my heart pounded. Instead of words, I'd cough and cry.

Mary, on the other hand, asked Momma one hundred questions.

Sarah, however, came to my aide. "Maggie? What's wrong with you? Are you alright? Momma's home now. Can't you see? You don't need to cry anymore."

I knew our mother was home because she was lying right there before us, but it was different. It wasn't right. She was so thin and didn't look the same. She had been away far too long and I wanted everything to be the exact same as it was before.

Deep down, these strange feelings gnawed at me even though I didn't really know what was going on. How come Momma looked this way and why didn't Papa explain it?

"They're happy tears. Aren't they, Maggie?" Joanne said. I looked at her and she smiled.

Momma just stared. Her frail arm rested on her lap. Joanne hugged me tight and I let her. I pressed my nose into her chest.

Papa cleared his throat. He stood outside his bedroom, leaning sideways, his arm bent. He was as tall as the door frame, his spiky, grey hair elevating his height. We had forgotten about him. He stared first at us, but then for a long time at Momma. It halted our talk.

"Time for bed," he said. "Your mother needs her rest."

We scampered off without question. That was how we were raised.

2: Gone

Momma's voice wheezed and gasped as she steadied herself to bring forth her words. "Promise me you'll look after them. That you'll be good to them and love them always." I didn't hear Papa's words but I saw him nod and take her hand in his own.

She made him promise. And I saw him. I saw him nod.

~

Momma lay still in her bedroom with Mary curled by her head and Sarah at her feet. I stood by the door, watching. Joanne and Momma's sister, Martha, stood behind me. The room felt cramped and hot.

"How come she's so tired?" Mary asked, stroking Momma's face. She lifted her hand, brushed her own long hair out of her eyes and hopped off the bed.

"You need sleep when you heal," Joanne offered, turning her gaze upward. "Right, Aunt Martha?"

But by now Mary was in the other room, buzzing about. She'd found something else of interest to entertain her thoughts.

Aunt Martha and Joanne were whispering and Momma's eyes flickered open. She stared at them. She lifted her arm as if to say something but no words came out.

Aunt Martha squeezed Joanne's cheeks and touched Momma briefly on the hand. "It will be alright, dear, you'll see."

She breezed out of the house as quickly as she had come in. I walked to the living room and watched from the window as she climbed onto the wagon and snapped the reins. The leather cracked against the saddle and the horse pulled away.

I returned to the kitchen. It smelled of woodsmoke and cigarettes. I wanted to go back to Papa and Momma's bedroom, but Papa had stretched out his legs. He bowed his head, like he was praying. I was scared to walk by in case he got angry with me, but Joanne gave me the nod and shooed me in.

I tiptoed very carefully over his feet and peered into Momma's room. She lay limply in the bed, her eyes closed. Sarah was beside her, trying to talk to her. She stroked Momma's thin, sleepy face.

My gaze turned back to my father. The peaceful expression he wore days before had changed. But what was that look? Fear? Disappointment? Anger?

Sarah came out of the room, crying. "Why won't Momma talk to me?"

"Stop it." Papa didn't like the drama, the noise.

Sarah cried anyway, sobbing for most of the afternoon and into the night. Eventually, her wailing ceased, but so too did our mother. Come morning-time, she was no more.

~

Papa left early that morning. Earlier than usual. He went to get the undertakers. He took Momma out of the house before we got up so we wouldn't see her like that. Sarah said she watched the wagon pull away with Momma on it and said, 'Papa didn't even cry.'

After he got home, he went down to the barn and did his chores and came up for his tea like always. He pointed a finger and said we were not to mention what happened and not to talk about her, 'So help me God!'

I looked at Sarah, dumbfounded.

When Mary finally came down for breakfast, she opened the door to Momma's bedroom and asked where she was.

"Close the door," Papa snapped.

Mary looked at us and at Papa, her face a wrinkly pout. She opened the door again to see the unmade bed with no Momma in it. "Where is she?" She blinked, her eyes widened, her face expressionless and calm, as she hung on to the door knob, peering in.

"Gone," he said.

Like an unwanted grain of dust that was tossed outside.

Sarah muffled her cries as best she could, wiped her face with her sleeve. Then Mary started. They clutched each another.

"I want her back, Papa," Mary cried.

"Enough! Enough. Be quiet."

He stared into space, drank his tea, ate his biscuit, then shooed them away from his daybed where he sprawled out. He placed one arm behind his head and closed his eyes. It was like she never existed.

To him.

To us.

Ever.

~

We waked her at home. They brought her back and we laid her in a simple, wooden coffin our neighbour had made. Aunt Martha picked out a blue dress for Momma to wear and she thought she looked beautiful. I didn't think she looked beautiful and we could only see her dress from the waist up. I wanted to see her toes.

I wondered if it really was Momma in the coffin. Maybe she really just left us like Papa had said—escaped somewhere, and he placed this impersonator in her stead. I thought she would come back for us. Maybe when it was summer and the weather was warmer. She never did like the cold.

This person's face was pale. Her mouth rigid, her face wrinkled, her hair really grey. I touched her, placed my finger on her cheek and nose. She felt hard. I was scared this person would open her eyes and tell me to stop touching.

Then the people came, like Old Art, our neighbour from down the hill, Miss Morrison, our teacher. She looked at us with sad, tearful eyes. There were people from our church, and Mr. Bouldry from the store. Mary recognized him.

They moved in single file, walked from our kitchen through to our living room, whispering. Some tried to talk to Papa, but he just grunted. Some tried to shake his hand, but he just sat in a chair with his arms crossed.

Sarah, Joanne, Aunt Martha, and I had placed our dining room chairs in a row right beside Momma's coffin. Papa would often get up and leave us, disappear somewhere alone. Then he'd come back, stare at the casket and at Momma lying there, and mumble silent words.

Mary flitted back and forth from room to room like a butterfly, eating the treats that the neighbours brought. We weren't used to such delicacies. She nibbled on slices of bread, and homemade cheese. The white crumbs peppered her mouth.

She'd try and sit on Joanne's lap. "There's no room for me, Jo-Jo. You're getting fat."

Papa's ears perked up and his head swivelled like an owl's. Joanne went pink.

I wasn't sure who to look at. Joanne, because her face glowed like a wild rose, or Papa, because his dark eyes burrowed holes into my sister? He muttered in Gaelic.

Aunt Martha leaned over and whispered in Joanne's ear, tapped her on the leg. Joanne, although she kept her head down, nodded.

Then they came and took our mother away again. For the last time.

I envied Joanne. She got to go to the church, but I had to stay home with Sarah and Mary. How I wanted to go. Not to say good-bye to the woman who didn't look like our mother in the coffin, but to pray for my mother, wherever she was, in church where prayers mattered.

And pray for us too, for me and my sisters—for we all knew something had changed forever.

3: We'll talk after

The snow swirled and danced around the small porch. A man, with his head bent down, sent snow flying when he shook off his hat. He combed his fingers through his hair, stomped hard on the hardwood step, shaking off more snow like a tree in a November wind. It was Old Art, our bachelor neighbour, Papa's friend.

Art had a short frame and bulging gut, and his wiry hair stuck out the same as Papa's. He let off an odour because he never washed. He had a bulbous nose, and his cheeks were red like he was continually sunburnt or frostbit. His lips were thin, surrounded by thick whiskers. Long hairs escaped his ears and nose and one front tooth had gone missing ages ago. We called him Old Art because he was.

"Girls," he said, "How're you all holding up?" No one said anything. "G'day to you, John." He nodded to our father.

"*Latha math,*" Papa said with a returned nod. He got off the cot, took a seat at the table, and pushed the other chair out with his foot for Art to sit down.

"I was in your barn," Art said in his scratchy voice.

"That so. And what were you doing there?"

"Well, I saw a light burning. And this one," he pointed to Mary, "hanging out in the stables, talking away. You feeding that horse of yours?"

"She's not mine," Papa said.

Art twirled his fingers and puckered his lips. "Well, she's looking awfully thin, John."

Papa stared down at the table and then looked over in Joanne's direction. Without his having to say a thing, Joanne went to the water bucket and proceeded to fill the pot to make tea.

"You want tea?" she asked over her shoulder.

"I got something better than tea."

Art pulled a jam jar out of his pocket. It had white, clear liquid, like water in it. He unscrewed the top and placed it under his nose. "Whew. That's holier than water." He slammed his fist on the table, laughing.

We surrounded our guest, happy to have the company. We didn't see many after our mother had died as the weather had been so terrible. The roads had not been cleared since the last storm.

Art took a sip, winced, and passed the jar to our father, a liquid smile creeping across his face.

Papa held the jar to his lips and gulped down a mouthful. He coughed and his body twisted and squirmed, and Art laughed the whole while, watching.

Joanne made the tea anyway. It seemed Papa didn't care much for the watery liquid, although Art certainly did.

As they drank their choice, we sat and listened to them talk about the weather, the prices of things, the local news. About how the Rory boy was very sick and the MacLellans' cow had twins, which was early in the year for cows to be calving.

Papa kept drumming his fingers on the table, looking at the time. He'd shift in his chair and lift the cold tea to his lips and stare at Joanne. She thought Papa wanted more tea so she tried to offer more but he'd place his hand over it to block her pouring.

We stood there, listening, while Art kept talking and getting louder with each sip. Whenever he thought he said something funny, he'd slam his fist down on the table.

Finally, after what seemed like a couple of hours and when the liquid in the jar almost gone, our stomachs gurgled for supper. "Well, we better be going. I suppose it's getting late." He looked at Joanne.

"Who's we?" Sarah asked. "Are you going somewhere with Art, Papa? At this hour?"

Papa opened his mouth but Mary squeezed in beside us at the table and poked her finger at the jar. "Can I have a taste?" She stretched out her nose and sniffed and reached for the drink.

Joanne's eyes widened but Papa paid Mary no mind. Instead, he stood up and walked to the back room, called for Joanne to come.

Art nudged Mary with his arm, winked at her, and, as quick as a rabbit, she brought the jar to her mouth. After one sip her face twisted and her lips curled. She stuck her tongue out and coughed.

Art slammed his hand down on the table, his mouth opened wide, exposing his blackened teeth. Then he grabbed Mary and gave her a squeeze.

"Get away, Art," she said, pushing him. "You smell like old cows' farts."

Art howled with laughter and let her go. That's when Papa and Joanne came back to the table. He looked at Art, his expression sombre.

"I like this here one. Can I have her instead?" Art said with a chuckle.

Papa shook his head. "Mary, Sarah," he ordered, pointing to me, too, "go in the living room for a moment. "I need to speak to Art."

Art's eyes gleamed more than when he had first arrived. He stood and staggered, held onto the back of the chair and laughed. "I think I had a wee bit much," he said. His face flushed red.

"Papa?" Joanne asked in her most assertive voice. "I don't want to. Please don't make me." Her eyes were full of water.

Papa turned to the rest of us. "Out, you three. Go say your prayers."

"That's why I don't have me a wife," Art said with a strange smirk. "Not only do they get old and fat, they talk too much." He jabbed Papa in the arm.

"Well, you'll have no use for Mary," Papa said in Gaelic. "She doesn't stop talking."

"What about Maggie?"

I felt a heat come to my cheeks when he mentioned my name.

When he saw I was still standing there, Papa raised his voice. "Didn't I tell you? Get in the other room!"

Sarah pulled me by the hand to leave them alone, so I wouldn't get into any more trouble. We stayed there until we heard the door open, and felt the cold chill come in from the outside. We looked out the window and saw Art trudge through the snow and get in his wagon, but he wasn't leaving.

I rushed back to the kitchen despite Sarah's pleading. Joanne mewed like a small kitten as Papa asked her questions.

"And the money? Where did you get it?"

"Aunt Martha gave it to me."

In the days when Momma was home, Joanne had extra duties. For one, having to go into town to get things for our mother. A few of those times, she had come home and given us a surprise: a small piece of candy. A rarity. We weren't sure how she got it. We didn't ask, but we savoured that treat like it was something special. Because it was.

"It was a bribe," Papa stated, clenching his fist.

Joanne looked so incredibly sad. Like she was lost, confused, and in pain all at the same time. I'll never forget it. "Papa. please," she whispered, tears streaming down her cheeks.

He squeezed his fingers. "What would your mother say?"

But Joanne said nothing more. Her face was so white.

Papa stood, although his shoulders stooped, and he opened the door. She stood too, rushed out ahead of him.

"Where you going, Jo?" I asked, standing on the threshold of the porch door. Joanne didn't look back. She couldn't say out loud what was on her mind.

"Papa?" Sarah stood behind me now.

"Never mind," Papa snapped, "asking all these questions. Never mind. Get the supper on the table."

But we didn't. We stood watching as Joanne descended into the darkness and the swirling white. And when he closed the door behind her, he locked it.

We ran to the window in the living room, then to the front of the house, where we watched in horror as Joanne got up on the back of Old Art's wagon and they slowly rode away.

No one said anything for what seemed like a very long time. We just stood and watched; Sarah breathing deeply behind me, her hands cupped my shoulders. She opened her mouth but Papa silenced her by staring hard, his black eyes burrowing holes into her.

I cowered by the wood box, picked at the bark with my fingernails.

Finally, Sarah sighed and went to the cupboard. She started the process of dinner by taking the bowls out of the cupboard. I ran and got the spoons and placed them around the table. Papa grumbled, took his seat, stretched out both arms and bowed his head in prayer. He blessed himself and looked up. The scars on his face seemed more pronounced when he was tired or upset.

Sarah tried lifting the hot pot of broth from the wood stove and grunted. She managed to lift it a couple of inches from the stove before it slammed back down. "I can't Papa. It's too heavy and too hot. I'll either spill it or I'll burn myself."

The chair scraped across the floor as Papa pushed it with the back of his legs, muttering all the while. He grabbed hold of the pot with his large mitts, practically swinging it in an arc 'till it landed with a thud on the table.

"I'm sorry, Papa, I'm not as strong as Jo—"

"Quiet!" His voice reverberated off the walls.

He flipped the cover off the pot, plunged his bowl into it instead of using a ladle. The broth sloshed down the sides and all over the table. He grabbed one of Sarah's fresh biscuits from the plate, dipped it into the hot liquid and stuffed it in his mouth. Sarah and I didn't move an inch when Papa ate.

Then he barked, "Call Mary to come to the table and be quiet. I don't need the three of you chattering and whining. You hear me?"

We both nodded. But Mary never came to eat and Sarah and I ate with trepidation.

We sat in silence while Papa finished his meal. He lay back down on his daybed and I caught him staring off into space. He was looking at nothing, muttering to himself. Words that I could not understand.

When he saw me look at him, I turned away.

He closed his eyes, rested his head against the wall and drifted off. As long as we were quiet, he was quiet. Most times anyway.

As Papa slept, Mary sauntered into the kitchen and popped down into the root cellar in the corner of the room. She grabbed a couple of limp carrots and proceeded to put her winter gear on.

Her sole purpose, it seemed, was to spend as much time as she could with her new pet.

"How long do you think Joanne will be gone?" I whispered to Sarah, standing at the sink. She looked down at me, the grey water up to her elbows.

"Shush." She looked over at Papa. "We'll talk after."

She placed the bowls and the cutlery in the sink and my arms tired as I reached for them. We silently agonized over the monotony of our duties. I had to take several breaks and yawned and wondered how much more work we would now have because of Joanne's absence.

I could sweep and fold clothes, but who would go to the store? It was Joanne's job to go and get the items on Papa's list. Joanne made the meals, too, and did most of the baking. We wondered what to do next without disturbing our father's slumber.

We heard Mary before she entered, and braced for it. She had thrust the door open, startling Papa.

He jumped up, one foot hitting the floor. We thought he was going to land on his backside.

Sarah stifled a nervous laugh and I found it funny too.

Mary sang Happy Birthday and Papa looked annoyed. "Be quiet. Be quiet. What are you going on about?"

"Oh, Papa." Mary sniffled, rubbing her runny nose with her soggy mitt. "You're always so grumpy."

"Where were you, you little rat?" He swung the other foot on the ground, bringing himself to a sitting position, arms rested on his knees.

She took off her coat and wriggled out of her boots. Like everything else in the house, our clothes were either too big or too small.

She coughed a bit. Her small eyes closed and she brought her fist to her throat. "Hurts," she said, "when I swallow."

"You feeling all right?" Sarah asked. She went to her, held her face in her hands, touched her forehead. "Your cheeks are just red from being outside, but you don't feel warm."

Mary smiled at Sarah, then tip-toed over to Papa and stood in front of him. She placed her hands behind her back. "Papa?" she asked, staring at him without blinking. "Why'd Jo-Jo go?"

Sarah and I stole a quick glance at each other. We knew when Mary started asking questions, she wouldn't let up.

Papa shook his head and scratched the back of his neck. "Too late to be talking about that."

"I want to know, Papa. Tell me." She crossed her arms in front of herself, and hopped back and forth on her little feet while loose strands of hair swung across her sweet, pouty face.

"That's enough. That's enough." He waved his hand in the air like he was swatting away a fly. He stuck out his tongue and rolled it around his lips. "Gimme some water there." He pointed toward the pot of water Joanne had melted from snow earlier in the day.

Sarah grabbed a glass and scooped up the water and gave him his drink. He lifted his head and downed it in one gulp.

"Papa!" Mary whined. "Where is Jo-Jo?" Papa ignored her. "She takes me to bed at night because Momma isn't here, and now she's gone, too."

He waved the glass back to Sarah for another drink, took a sip, and said, "Settle down, Mary."

Mary kept bumping into his knee, kept asking where Joanne was, swaying back and forth, as her eyes got droopier and shinier. Her face flushed pink. "Papa! Tell me!"

But Papa said nothing. Instead, he placed the glass on the floor beside his foot, stood up, and sauntered off to his bedroom, closing the door behind him.

Mary started to wail. Her little mouth opened wide and her head fell back. Her arms fell to her waist, defeated. She was so tired. Tired and lonely.

Sarah scooped her up and whispered into her ear, talked softly while Mary let out little bursts of sadness. Her tears ran down her pretty cheeks and onto her thin shirt.

Sarah dropped her down and took her by the hand, guiding her to walk in front as the two of them made their way up the back staircase. There was nothing left for me to do but to follow.

The chill set into my bones instantly once I left the warmth of the kitchen. The dining room which we never dined in was cool, the living room, colder, and when we ascended the last step at the top of the stairs, our teeth were clacking. Joanne called this place the Antarctic. 'Penguins could live in our bedrooms,' she would say.

Sarah undressed Mary quickly. She pulled her dress over her head in one swoop and threw on her pyjamas. Mary instantly turned to her side, stuck her thumb in her mouth, and closed her eyes. Sarah laid down beside her. She placed her arm around her tiny waist, and nestled her close.

I stood at the foot of the bed watching them. My whole body trembled like I had just come from outside without a coat. I could even see my breath in the dimness of the room. Clutching my arms, I wondered if I should take Sarah's bed (as it was empty) and looked over my shoulder.

"Maggie." Sarah had read my thoughts. She lifted her head off the pillow. "Hurry. Jump in," she whispered. "We'll all sleep together."

It was exactly what I wanted, needed. I needed all my sisters.

I undressed as quickly as Sarah had changed Mary, throwing off my day clothes. My teeth continued to chatter as the cold cotton brushed against my skin and the mattress squeaked under the weight of my body as I slid in beside my sisters.

"Holy Gosh, Maggie. You're colder than ice."

I was. My feet felt like solid blocks and I buried my frozen face and nose against Sarah's warm back. I dug my hands under her right rib and she spasmed, squawking out loud.

"Maggie, can you move them until you warm them up a little?" Her body began to tremble.

"How do I do that?"

"Rub them together."

I held my hands against my chest under the heavy quilt. I squirmed back and forth, listening to Mary's steady breathing, a whistle emitting from her delicate throat telling us she was dreaming in the land of make-believe and fairies.

My body began to warm beside my big sister. How I wished she slept with us every night. I breathed in Sarah's scent, smelled her hair, felt the softness of her night dress, her long braid. Its texture, a smooth weave. I played with it, running my fingers up and down, finding the process soothing.

"Sarah?" I whispered. "Are you asleep?"

"No," she sighed. She wiggled around 'till she was lying on her back, staring up at the ceiling. I stayed on my side. My hands had warmed so I placed my left arm around her waist.

She placed her hand on top of mine. "I can't sleep," she said. "I'm thinking about Joanne."

I had actually forgotten about Joanne for a moment, the cold lulling my brain to a deep fog. I wished she hadn't mentioned our older sister because now I thought about her too. "What do you think she's doing right now?" I asked.

Sarah shrugged and stroked the top of my hand.

"Do you think she'll come home soon?"

"Don't wake Mary," Sarah whispered.

Then she turned to face me. I could feel her warm breath. "I hope Papa lets her. And soon."

"I hope he didn't marry her," I said.

Sarah gasped. "Who? You mean to Art? No, Maggie! God! He's too old!"

I tried to get thoughts of Art and Joanne out of my head. "What about you, Sarah? Will you marry someday?"

"Maybe. But to someone who is nice and has a little house and we can raise our own chickens and cows and we can plant a garden."

"Could I come and visit?"

"Of course. Maybe you'll live with me. All of you. And the house will be warm and there will be lots of food."

It sounded wonderful. "I hope you get your wish, Sarah."

We stayed quiet for a few minutes while I imagined Sarah's little house and the white, fat chickens running around and all of us holding a crisp apple in our hands. I didn't know what her husband looked like but I knew he would be nice and handsome.

"And Joanne will be there." I said it a little too loud.

Mary coughed and moved around, the bed squeaking as she flipped over.

Sarah let out an 'oof' when Mary's arm smacked her on the cheek. She started to snigger and I joined in too because I couldn't help it.

I laughed out loud but Sarah shushed me, even though she was laughing so much that the whole bed shook and quivered and squeaked. Tears ran down our faces and my belly ached from laughing.

Then we heard him. "Quiet up there!"

We froze. Sarah poked me to flip over so the three of us slept on our left sides, holding onto each other as we drifted off, dreaming of what we hoped our future would hold.

4: Nimble as a field mouse

March, 1947

Papa lay stretched out on his daybed. His arm rested behind his neck. He had one leg bent, the other lying straight. He still had on his work clothes: dark pants and shirt.

We fixed him a meagre supper because we had run short of flour and baking powder for biscuits. He didn't even have his tea. It had been over a week since Joanne had left us.

A voice called out, jolting our father from his slumber. "John? John, you here?"

Martha entered holding a large pot. "Did you have your tea and supper, John?" Her voice was loud and authoritative, unlike Momma's, which was soft and silent.

"Ach." He sat up, blinking, pulling his suspenders to his shoulders.

"Did you eat yet, John?" Martha looked at the table littered with crumbs. The molasses pot sat in the middle where the thick, dark syrup pooled in a sticky mess.

"I'm not deaf," he barked.

"I didn't ask if you were deaf. I asked if you ate. Where's the girls? Oh!" She smiled upon seeing us. Sarah and I stood side-by-side by the wood stove, quiet-like.

Papa grumbled something incoherent.

"What are you saying, John? Speak up. I can't understand you. That awful language."

Papa got up and walked to the sink, then back to his bed and sat down again. He rested his hands on his knees, stared at the floor, shook his leg.

"Pffft. You can't make your own tea? Come now, John. Relying on these girls. So? Where is Joanne? You send her to town again? On foot?" she tsked. "That's what the horse is for, John."

Papa's cold eyes stared at Martha before he turned his gaze to me.

"Well, I made soup. The girls need to eat."

She lifted the heavy pot onto the stove. "Sarah, get me one of your mother's and I'll pour this in. Can't leave you with my good one now, can I?"

Papa growled when Sarah went to the cupboard. Sarah froze mid-step.

"Leave her be. Honestly." Martha gave Papa a staunch stare. "These girls work just as hard as you do, probably more so. I'm sure Mary can milk the cows herself. What exactly do you do all day, John?"

As Martha spoke, she signalled for Sarah to retrieve the pot. Sarah tiptoed to the cupboard and brought out Momma's biggest and handed it to Martha.

Martha fished around for a spoon and used it to transfer the soup. She placed the pot on the table.

"Now come on, John," she said forcefully. "Get that into you. Maybe then you won't be as cranky."

Without another word, Papa walked to the table and set about eating.

Martha took the loaf of bread she had made, sliced him a piece, spread her butter on it, and placed that beside him. She put water on for tea and took out two of her cookies to put in front of him as well.

My mouth hung open. Papa behaved like a scolded dog, doing everything that Martha told him. I saw a hint of a smile on Sarah's face. Maybe this was why our aunt was not welcomed at our house.

"The girls are thin, John, and that horse! Dan is down at the barn now giving her some fresh oats."

Papa stopped moving, the spoon held in mid-air. I could almost hear him thinking.

"Now girls. When do you expect your sister back?"

Papa slammed his hand down on the table, his mouth set in a grim line. Sarah and I jumped but it didn't faze Martha.

"She's at Art's, Aunt Martha," Sarah said, her voice low.

Martha stopped what she was doing for a moment. "I see," she said, and went back to wiping down the counters and busying herself around Momma's kitchen.

When Papa finished his supper, she whisked his dishes away and washed them. Then she swept the floor and shook out the mat.

Papa didn't even say so much as a thank you. He just grumbled and went back to his daybed, stretched out and closed his eyes.

Then Mary burst in. "I smell something yummy," she shouted.

Papa didn't acknowledge her, even though she had been gone most of the day with the horse.

"Is your Uncle Dan almost finished?" Martha asked Mary.

"Uh-huh. Said he's ready when you are."

Martha walked to the back of the house and we all followed her like ducklings. She pushed back the curtain to see her husband, Dan, sitting on the wagon, a dusting of snow covering his head and shoulders.

"Oh my, girls. I'll have to go," she said. "Can't leave Uncle Dan outside. He'll catch his death." She pulled her gaze away from her husband and looked at us.

"Won't he come in at all?" Sarah whispered. "I could put a chair in the porch for him."

Martha chuckled. "You're too kind, dear. No. Uncle Dan is best where he's at."

She grabbed Mary's cheek and pinched it. "Your horse doing okay in the barn?"

Mary nodded with a wide grin.

"But don't be riding her in bad weather, Mary. You know the two of you could have a bad fall. Or worse."

Mary shrugged and started hopping and dancing about like she hadn't really heard.

"All right, girls, it's time for me to go. I hope there's enough there to keep your belly full."

Martha narrowed her eyes at our father. "Be sure and get some of that to your sister, too," she whispered. "She needs it more so."

We stared at the preserves she put on the counter: relish and pumpkin, jams of raspberry and strawberry, apple sauce. There were two loaves of bread, Fat Archies, her big pot of chicken soup, butter, and tea.

And then she was gone. We watched as she and Dan pulled away in the darkening evening and seeing them leave made me lonesome. I realized then how much I missed my mother.

"What's the matter?" Sarah asked. She touched my cheek. A tear spilled down onto her finger.

"I don't know," I said.

Sarah wrapped her arms around me and I hugged back. We walked back to the kitchen and that's when we saw him.

Papa paced back and forth from the table to the stove. Suddenly, he shoved all the preserves to one side of the counter until one tipped over the edge. Glass and apple sauce splattered across the floor.

Sarah immediately went to clean it up but Papa cussed and growled and then rounded on her, his fists clenched. "That woman! Should never be here! In this house! And Sarah! You were never to tell her about your sister!"

Sarah had backed to the counter, her hands pressed behind her. "But why, Papa? What's the secret?"

But he ignored her. "Look at this stuff! This nonsense!" he roared. He was pacing back and forth, agitated like a caged animal.

"But, Papa. It's for us. For you and Joanne—"

That's when Papa struck her. Right across the face.

We both felt it. My mouth fell open and Sarah's hand went immediately to her cheek, and she sobbed openly.

I sobbed, too, and Papa turned around. His black eyes were on me and, before I knew it, he was shaking me, hollering.

A loud shriek emitted from Mary's tiny body. She kept screaming until everyone stared at her, till she couldn't scream any longer. "Papa!" Her little hands cupped her face. She commanded him and he stopped.

Papa took deep, raspy gulps as his arms dropped away. *"Duilich,"* he said, his voice low. He scurried to his room and closed the door behind him.

Mary bolted back outside, back to the barn and her horse.

My body felt loose and shaky. Sarah started picking up the shards of glass with her fingertips. I helped even though my hands shook.

Sarah continued cleaning the kitchen, swept the floor, and lined the remaining preserve jars on the counter.

We didn't talk about what had happened. The damage was clear enough: the red, swollen welt on Sarah's cheek.

~

"Say a prayer for Mary today," Sarah had asked, after she put the biscuits in the oven. She said it so casually and it came from nowhere, I wondered why she asked it at all. Mary had come home three nights before with a cough. The night she ran off after Papa got angry at us.

Then I heard it. A loud, rattly bark came from the living room where Mary was. Not the slight, pretend cough I had when Momma first came home. It was hoarse and deep.

My eyes widened. Sarah blessed herself. I knew what she was thinking.

"She'll be all right," I said. "She's a trooper. It's just a bit of a cough. Like when I had it."

"I'll go and check on her," Sarah said, perturbed. "You keep an eye on the biscuits."

I remembered the stories Joanne had told us a thousand times whenever we weren't feeling good. Papa would be away working in the mines. It was just Momma and us then. She did what she could to manage the farm—the animals, the gardens. Joanne told us that Papa wanted a house full of boys because he thought girls were trouble and always getting into things.

"We are a bunch of troublemakers, aren't we, girls?" Joanne had said and she'd laugh.

Papa thought boys were stronger and could work harder, plough the fields, build the barns, make the hay. But Momma couldn't make boys. She had Joanne and Sarah, then me and Mary.

But Mary was different. She wasn't a boy but acted like one. She was brazen and bold. She didn't take guff off of anyone and she was pretty to boot. Prettier than all of us put together.

And I heard once somewhere—maybe it was when Momma died when people came to her wake—'God picks the loveliest flowers first for his garden.'

But Mary wasn't a flower. She was a stone. Hard and tough and resilient.

She was so tough that she had run wild for a while. After Momma died, she ran to the fields and everyone let her. She would go in the barn and take Leela out alone. She often stayed with him, too, long after the sun went down. We'd hear her creep into bed way past her bedtime, her body as cold as frost.

She was as nimble as a field mouse and as quick as a bunny. Papa used to chase after her, growl at her to be careful when she'd be riding. But then he stopped. Nothing seemed to matter. So, Mary got away with things. How jealous I was.

Old Art's message to Papa about how thin Leela was bothered Mary. She knew that the summer work would be hard on her horse. So she'd steal carrots and apples from the root cellar and lead Leela down to the brook to feed her in hiding.

It was late when she got home. Later than usual, and her little body shook although her forehead burned. Her small eyes shone like glass and so we took her to bed.

The first night she coughed and sweated and so Sarah threw on extra blankets. Her lips turned blue and she said she wasn't hungry.

"We have to take her the hospital," Sarah pleaded.

But Papa wouldn't hear of it. "What they do for your mother?" he said, his eyes cold. "All the money we spent on her medicine. Money we didn't have and it did nothing. Give her the broth. It will pass."

Sarah glanced in my direction.

Before he nodded off, he said, "Good enough for her. Taking the horse down to the brook this time of year. Serves her right."

"Papa. You knew she went there," Sarah said, exasperated.

But he didn't reply.

She stood over him, willing him to open his eyes and respond to her, then she threw up her hands and stormed off.

Sarah and I decided to sleep in the opposite room and let Mary sleep alone. Deep down we were scared we'd catch what she had.

We stayed up, though, taking turns with her. Changing her sheets when she threw up, tossing on extra blankets when she got cold.

Finally, we lay down together, listening as she moaned in her sleep. Then everything fell silent and still. I smiled. The coughing subsided. The fever had passed. We all drifted off easily, because we were so exhausted.

Then I heard Sarah's voice the next morning. "Paapaaa?" His name moaned into a question.

The fact he ran up the stairs, his heavy feet slamming hard on the stair treads, told me something was up. I ran to where Papa was. He stood silently as Sarah screamed Mary's name.

I wouldn't go in the room.

The funeral was solemn. We stared at her lifeless body, disbelief in our eyes, sorrow in our souls. We didn't think she would die. How could she? She was as tough as a trooper.

And when we buried her, when that little coffin was taken away, it was like Momma's funeral all over again. A knife in our hearts.

Then, the day after the funeral, he took his gun out of the porch. I saw him swinging it, mumbling and cursing in Gaelic. He cast his dark eyes downward, and he rubbed his stubbled chin with his free hand.

I noticed his hair. It had turned whiter and whiter with each passing day since Mary had left us.

He headed towards the barn.

"No," Sarah gasped, her fingers at her lips.

He disappeared inside. The shot sounded and Sarah's body tensed. Her eyes stared straight ahead. I looked up to the sky.

We hoped without speaking that Leela was with our Mary and Momma. Somewhere up in the heavens, where the air was warm, the grass was green and the sky always blue.

42

5: Are you marrying him?

April, 1947

Papa would surely disown us if he knew Sarah and I were going. But we had to.

It had been a little over three weeks since we buried Mary. The quietness in the house without Momma, and then our little sister, was intolerable. Everywhere I looked, I saw them. Their voices, their images. They hung about like smoke from a fire. It clung to you.

"We'll just go for a quick visit," Sarah said. "Our chores are done and Papa is sleeping. But we've got to hurry."

Papa would be up soon enough, looking for his tea or his supper, or for us to bark at. It seemed nothing we could do was good enough lately.

Sarah pointed to the back window and she and I snuck out. We would go to great lengths not to disturb our father.

"If he asks, we'll just tell him we went for a walk." She winked at me and took off at a run, sliding on the icy patches in the field.

Martha's house looked grand, with all its windows, the smoke sailing from its stack like it had been hand-drawn with a pencil. Icicles glimmered in the sunlight while patches of teal-shadowed snow covered the hills and trees behind.

The driveway was fully cleared, which gave us ample room to walk side by side, and there was wood perfectly split and piled standing at attention to the right.

Before we had a chance to knock, Aunt Martha met us at the door. "My, look at you. I'm so happy you're here." She opened her arms and squished us into her soft flesh.

We entered into the warmth of her kitchen, which was painted a bright yellow, Momma's favourite colour. White-lace curtains starched to perfection hung in the windows.

"Come in. Come in. Will you have a bite? You both must be hungry."

I stood at the door, not sure what to do next.

"Come in. Come in," she said again, her voice authoritative. "Don't just stand there."

Sarah walked in and grabbed the nearest chair for herself.

"I take it your father doesn't know you're here," she said.

We were silent.

She shook her head and reached for my cheeks. She squeezed them and kissed Sarah on the top of the head.

Sarah could almost pass for Aunt Martha's daughter, with her dark hair and eyes. They appeared almost the same height now, too. Joanne, on the other hand, was tall and slender like Momma, and had her pretty, deep-auburn hair. I was told I took after Papa's side. I looked like his sisters, and had the curse of the red hair.

"You're both looking pretty thin. Are you getting enough to eat?"

Before we could answer, Martha placed a bowl of hot soup and a fat piece of bonnach in front of us. Only then did my belly growl.

Martha's pudgy fingers touched my shoulder. "If your father *is* feeding you, he's not doing a proper job."

I didn't say a word.

"I'm cooking now," Sarah interjected proudly. "Since Joanne has been at Art's."

"That's wonderful," Martha said, as she poured herself a spot of tea and one for each of us in two pretty cups. She sat down at the table. "Eat up, now."

The soup was delicious. I spooned out a piece of chicken and showed Sarah. Aunt Martha winked at me. There were lots of vegetables: potato, carrot, turnip.

Martha took a sip of her tea and touched Sarah on the forearm. "I'm going to put the bread in the pans soon. I can show you, Sarah, if you have time? Maggie can help Uncle Dan in the barn."

Sarah smiled. I did, too, and swung my feet as I ate.

Martha took it all in. Her head swung back and forth between us as we spoke and ate. She seemed delighted we were here and that we were enjoying her food so much.

"This is so good, Aunt Martha. Thank you," Sarah said.

"Oh, you're welcome, dear. And you're so polite. You're a star," Martha gushed, patting her on the arm again. "I don't get to see you girls much. It's the least I can do."

She sat back in her chair and smoothed out her apron, then took another sip from her tea. "Of course, I'd like to see more of you girls." Martha closed her eyes. "but your father and Uncle Dan don't see eye to eye on a lot of things. But that will all change soon."

Sarah looked at me.

Martha continued, squaring her shoulders, "Your father doesn't see eye to eye with a lot of people."

When I finished my soup, I placed my spoon in my bowl as quietly as I could. I didn't want to appear rude when Aunt Martha was talking.

"I especially don't think it right that he sent your Joanne with that crude man...especially now...after everything's that's happened. She should have come here." Martha crossed her arms.

"She *would* be better here." Sarah said with confidence.

Martha tilted her head to one side.

"Papa's mean," I said.

Sarah's cheeks tinged pink.

Martha's lips turned up at the corners and the skin around her eyes crinkled. "He's a hard man, your father, and truth be told, I don't understand him or his ways or why your mother—"

The conversation ended with the door opening.

"I thought I heard voices," Uncle Dan said, walking in. He ducked under the casement because of his large frame. He smiled with kind eyes and a gentle face then turned and looked at me.

Martha met him in the doorway, and placed a peck on his lips. Sarah and I giggled, my cheeks hot as the tea.

Martha laughed. "What?" she asked. "You girls not seen a wife kiss her husband before?"

Sarah and I replied, "No, ma'am."

"You go on now, Maggie, and help your Uncle Dan. I'll show Sarah how to put the bread in the pans. And we'll send some good-ies for you to pass along to Joanne." She winked.

Uncle Dan offered his hand and I took it. It was warm.

~

The sun was disappearing behind the clouds and the dampness and cold had begun to set in. I shivered. Fine snow started to fall and, if I closed my eyes and thought really hard, I could imagine it to be Christmas.

We would just be coming home from church with the anticipa-tion of what Santa had brought. It would be something small, of course: a top or a doll, pencils, an orange, maybe a sugar treat if we had been very good.

"You're awfully quiet, Maggie," Sarah said. "You okay?"

I nodded as we lumbered homeward. Sarah's pockets were filled to the brim with baked goods. She didn't want to run too fast in case they disintegrated in the lining of her coat.

"We have to be careful," she yammered on. "I'll hide these until we see Jo. If we don't eat them all first." She laughed.

I was lost in thought about sneaking off to see Aunt Martha, wondering what kind of trouble we'd get in once we got home. If it was even worth all the trouble.

Sarah obviously had had a great time. She kept talking about what Aunt Martha had taught her in the kitchen. What they ate. When not to over mix, because 'that makes the dough tough.'

I wished I had stayed with them instead of being in the barn. The barn was Mary's special place. Not mine. The kitchen had been Joanne's, now Sarah's.

Where did I belong?

They told us to come back 'soon', and Uncle Dan patted me on the back. He said I was a pretty girl, but I knew that wasn't true. He gave me a candy but I dropped it in the hay.

Our lane was just up ahead and butterflies flitted around my stomach. I would have given anything to be in my room right now, alone, to avoid Papa, and get away from Sarah's endless jabbering.

I sprinted, and left her behind. She hollered for me to slow down but I couldn't. I just ran.

~

Two days later Sarah told Papa we were going to see Joanne. She said it matter-of-factly. Papa watched as we left this time. He stood in the door as we headed down the road towards Art's.

Old Art's place was surrounded by snow-laden trees. It was pretty here, and sheltered, and it seemed Art did a better job of looking after his home than Papa did himself. The roof came down low on all sides, with several gabled windows up top. The outhouse was to the left of the path and the barn had a big fence around it, enclosing a horse and several cows.

He was cutting wood when we arrived. Sarah waved and kept heading toward the house when he hollered for her to come back.

I watched from a distance how he smiled at her. The willies ran through my body like smelts in the river. He laughed, too, at whatever Sarah had said to him. When his mouth opened, it exposed his blackened, rotting teeth.

"Hello," I said, to be polite, and held my arms tight to my chest. I passed him, holding my breath.

He spit black chewing tobacco on the ground by his foot. "You can go in too, Maggie."

I didn't respond and kept walking. Inside, I heard Joanne and Sarah squealing.

"You've come too, Maggie? Get over here. Give me a hug." Joanne waved me in.

I opened my arms and ran to her, feeling her warmth, not wanting to let her go.

Joanne's face was as round as a pie. "Oh my gosh. It is so good to see you," she gushed. "How are you both doing? Are you hungry at all?"

We never turned down food. As Joanne set her biscuits on a plate and sliced them in half, Sarah pulled out the cookies Aunt

Martha had sent.

Joanne's eyes lit up when she saw them. "My favourite." She brought one to her mouth and her body went limp. "Mmmm, I think these are the best I ever had."

She broke off a piece and offered it to Sarah, who swallowed it whole. Then she offered me a piece and I shook my head.

"No? Why, Maggie? What's wrong?"

"Nothin'. I just don't want any, is all."

Joanne looked at me sideways, continuing to eat her cookie. "I should write Aunt Martha a note, to thank her," she said. "Will you two give it to her? You can be my secret messengers."

As she scribbled on the paper, I blurted, "Joanne, when are you coming home?"

She kept at her writing, then folded the paper in half and looked at me with her light-brown eyes. "Soon," she said, looking at us intently.

She patted her stomach. "Those cookies feel good in here."

Her mouth showed a serene expression—no sadness, but her eyes looked lonely to me. Her face was pale but she looked like she had gained some weight. Her cheeks were full.

"Is he mean?" I whispered, searching her face for evidence.

Joanne sat back in the chair, looked over at Sarah enjoying herself. She smiled, but I thought it was a fake one. "What's with you, Maggie? Art is good. There's food to eat and the house is warm. If I need something, he'll take me to the store and get it for me."

"Are you marrying him?" I asked.

Joanne laughed out loud and held her sides. Sarah, on the other hand, pursed her lips together.

"Maggie. Why would ask her such a thing? He's old enough to be our grandfather."

"You thought it too," I said to Sarah.

She shook her head, denying it. I knew Art was as old as Papa, maybe even older. That's why we called him Old Art. But I had to ask it. If I didn't, it meant it could be true.

"I'm here for a reason," Joanne assured me. "When Art no longer needs me...to help, then I can go home." Her nose was raised in the air, like she had practised saying these words out loud.

"But why do you have to help Art?"

Joanne smiled a weak smile, ran her finger over the table.

"Does Papa come to see you?"

"My. All the questions. You're as nosy as a crow."

I let out a small gasp as Art came in, his face shiny from cutting the wood. He had an armload of it and dumped it into the wood box beside the stove.

"Maggie," he said gruffly. "Why don't you come out and I'll load you up with wood so your sister stays warm tonight?" He rubbed his hands together, wood shavings falling off his forearms.

"No," I said briskly.

Joanne's mouth fell open. Art stared hard.

"That's okay," Joanne said. "Maggie's tired. I'll give you a hand, though." She used her hands to help herself up to standing.

"You're walking funny, Jo. Did you hurt yourself?"

Joanne ignored me. She kept to the coat rack and grabbed her shawl.

"I'll help you, Art," Sarah said too sweetly, causing old Art's eyes to squint, his mouth to turn up at the corners.

I didn't like Joanne being here. She should be home with us. Why was Art getting our Joanne to do his chores? It looked like he worked her too hard already. I wanted to take a piece of wood from the pile and throw it at him.

Art walked over to Joanne and leaned close to her ear. He squinted his left eye, said something so low only she could understand. Our sister session was interrupted. We followed Art outside.

Joanne waddled like a duck over to the woodpile and squatted. She loaded up a few pieces of wood into her arms. Art rushed up behind her and knocked it out of her hands. They clinked as they fell to the ground.

"What did I tell you?" he barked, "Don't be stupid. Now get in the house."

He saw me and Sarah staring, our brows furrowed, then waved his hand in the air. "You...go start supper...or something." Then he signalled for us with his forefinger to come to him.

Joanne brushed the wood shavings off her apron, turned on her heel and did what she was told.

I took in what I could of the wood because I didn't want Art to be mean to Joanne. Sarah and I took armload after armload into the house. I had wanted to come visit, not work all afternoon. That's what we did home.

"Can we stop now?" I asked, breathing hard.

Art placed the last log on top of my arms, patted me on the back, then said, "All right. That'll do."

The sky turned nightshade and we knew it was time to get home. Papa's supper would be late and the growling would start.

We kissed Joanne on the cheek and hugged her. "We'll see you again, soon, Jo."

"Sooner than you think," she said, waving.

Art closed the door and we turned and walked away.

~

The sun finally shone after what seemed like weeks of grey weather. It was a welcome sight to see the brightness filter into our room.

The sun's rays caused the frost on the window sill to melt, sending droplets of water cascading to plop and splash onto the floor. Tiny dust particles danced in the air, awakened by the warmth.

Spring was here.

The tip of my nose throbbed, however, telling me that Papa hadn't stoked the fire very well today.

I stretched out my arms and flipped over. The warmth of Sarah's body was long gone, her place covered by a heap of blankets. She always managed to wake before me, always getting out of bed-making duties.

I dressed quickly, grabbing the nearest sweater. It once belonged to Joanne, and to Momma before her. I liked wearing it. It reminded me of them. It was soft against my skin and lavender in colour. The buttons used to be pearls but they had fallen off. Momma had sewed on small white ones, although not all of them matched.

I relieved myself in the bucket beside the bed. The pungent smell of urine always made me choke when I took off the lid. It was Joanne's duty to empty it when it got full, but now that she was gone, it was Sarah's job. We'd go to the outhouse in the summer, but because there was so much snow and ice built up around the door now, we couldn't get to it. The bucket got 'pretty ripe' as Momma used to say, but it beat having to go outside in the frozen air late at night.

"Sarah. The pot needs changing," I hollered. I had told her yesterday and she scowled at me. But putting it off wouldn't make it empty itself.

When I arrived in the kitchen, I felt the chill in the air. Papa cut back on the wood if there was even a hint of a change in the weather. The door, however, had been left ajar, adding another layer of chill to the downstairs. I went over and shut it, shivering.

"Sarah," I hollered. There was no sign of her. Maybe she was hiding? Maybe she snuck out for wood because the house was cold and the porridge sat in the pot, runny. Papa wasn't here, either, but he may have set out early for the barn chores. Yet, why wasn't Sarah back already?

The empty kitchen felt terribly eerie. A place I didn't like being alone. Yet I sat at the table in front of my porridge bowl, waiting.

I looked around to busy myself. The walls needed painting, and the faded, yellow curtains Momma loved so much needing washing or replacing. The broom that she used to sweep with leaned in the corner. All these things that once made our house feel like a home, suddenly made me feel lonely.

My lip trembled but I shook my head. There would be no tears today. Tears would do nothing, change nothing.

I had bowed my head to say my morning prayers when Sarah flew in like a runaway horse. Her eyes were large and searching and her hair hung wild about her face. She panted like she had just run a mile.

"What is it, Sarah? What's wrong?"

"It's Papa and Art. They're fighting. Art came in all haywire this morning."

"What did he want?"

"I don't know. He tried to talk to Papa in private so they went to the barn. I snuck in, heard them arguing. Then Art kicked over the bucket of milk." She made a face. "And then they started punching each other."

"Why, Sarah?"

"I don't know," she shouted.

She moved quickly around the kitchen, braiding her hair, talking so fast. It was like she didn't know what she was doing, her brain thinking at lighting speed.

She grabbed her coat and pulled on a hat. "I have to go," she said, excitedly. "Art said I should go get Aunt Martha."

"For what?" I stood up.

"For Joanne, I think. Art said she was bleeding. Papa said to put the kettle on." Sarah dashed out the door, slamming it behind her.

But how could I? There was no fire on.

~

"We're going to need something stronger than that," Art said, looking at the tea I had just made. I wasn't sure how much to make. The colour resembled raw biscuit dough.

He had a sly, sickening smile like his mouth was full of something he couldn't swallow but enjoyed the tang of it all the same. He rubbed his hands together, then pulled out his jar, took quick sips from it and paced the floor. He stuck out his tongue after he swallowed, and rolled it around his rotten teeth.

His eyes started to swim in his head. His face was bruised and swollen where Papa had hit him. Blood lay crusted on his eye and mouth.

He sat on the chair nearest the porch—his usual spot. He leaned forward, rested his forearms on his knees and spoke to Papa in Gaelic. Papa placed his hands over his ears, grumbled.

Sarah and I were as tense as stray cats before they are drowned in a sack. She obviously knew more than I, but said nothing. She kept one eye on Art, the other on Papa, and was back and forth checking the window for Aunt Martha's return.

Between the fighting and the so-called visit from Art, the day was disappearing. It had been morning and now the darkening evening sky was setting in. It was no later than six o'clock, and Old Art had finished off the liquid in his Mason jar.

Papa remained on his daybed. Sarah busied herself with menial chores, resweeping the floor in front of the wood box, pouring more tea for Papa, emptying Art's ashes from his cup. There was a heaviness in the house. An unusual quietness.

Finally, Art spoke up. "The apple don't fall from the tree, does it, John? But maybe she'll be luckier?"

Papa cleared his throat.

"Eh?"

Papa still didn't answer.

"John? Are you willing to make that sacrifice?"

Papa continued to ignore him.

Sarah and I listened in earnest. We understood some of the Gaelic, dribs and drabs.

"*Tha an t-àm ann*, John."

"What is it time for?" Sarah's voice trembled.

No one answered my sister. Instead, Art slammed his fist on the table. "John! Don't be so god-damn stubborn."

Then, we heard it. The rattle of the wagon. It had to be Aunt Martha.

Sarah rushed to the door and I was happy to see it was her. She looked pale and wide-eyed and tired. Her apron was streaked with red. I waved to her but she didn't acknowledge me.

Art pushed Sarah out of the way, and when Martha stood in front of Papa, everyone spoke in whispers. The porch door was left open, like this morning, and the cold night air sent shivers down my back.

Martha covered her lips with her fingers, touched Sarah on the arm. She left without saying a word to me. The room was so quiet.

"What did she mean, Papa?" Sarah asked. "Art? What did she mean?"

Papa didn't look up. He stared at his hands.

Art stood up, swayed, then walked toward the doorway. He used his arms as support in the door frame and didn't say anything for a few moments. He cursed at Papa in Gaelic and then in English. "You son of a whore."

Then he went into a rampage, tossed the chairs, throwing the teacups. One of them hit Sarah and she squealed.

Old Art tripped and dropped to the floor. That's when Sarah grabbed hold of his pant leg and dragged him to the open door. She rolled him out in the cold, dark night, slamming the door, locking the latch, huffing.

I crawled over to the window. Art lay flat on the snow-covered yard, laughing and crying. He turned on his side and cursed bad things. He flung his hands up in the air as if he was praying, hollering in Gaelic and mixed English. He looked like he blessed himself, although I didn't think he was a holy man.

He flipped over and stood up, going down on one knee before hobbling away—saying things as he made his way back towards his house.

Sarah was in a fit. "It can't be true. Papa? Tell me he's lying," she said, squeezing her hands together.

Papa closed his eyes and covered his face.

Part II – Joanne

6: You know how people talk

March, 1954

Strange sounds emitted from Papa's throat and he mumbled words I could not understand. I sat and played another round of solitaire as Sarah went to get changed to sneak out to the dance. I finished up the supper dishes, counted the seconds on the clock, watching Papa, making sure the coast was clear for Sarah's escape.

He lay there with his mouth open, eyes closed, head facing upwards. His narrow, angular nose made him look even more frightful when he was asleep. His whiskers were shocking white against his dark complexion. They looked coarse, like short needles all over his face.

His hair needed to be cut, but he didn't see the point when he could do it himself. He saved every nickel. He attempted the last cut himself, shaved up the back of his head and above his ears with his razor. The blade became dull so he couldn't cut his bangs. They fell over his eyes which made him look like a sheep dog. Then he'd swipe back his locks with Brylcreem but that made his hair look greasy.

He was a tall man, or maybe the fact he was so thin made him look taller than he really was. He looked over six feet if he took to arguing with you. And no one wanted to argue with Papa. He had a way of intimidating even the sternest men.

It had to be those eyes—dark and menacing, like they could stare into your soul and tear it out. His mouth was perpetually turned down, like the only emotion he felt was sadness.

I shivered even though the warmth of the fire blazed beside me. I got up and took a log out of the wood box and lifted the element.

When I poked the burnt timbers with the metal rod, and made

room for the new stick, Papa grunted, "That you, Mary? Where were you, you little rat?"

He stared blankly at me, rested on his hands, then pushed himself upward. I remained silent as he cleared his throat. It was as if he heard a voice, or something else registered—reality, seeing the inside of his kitchen, me. He mumbled, made his way to his bedroom, and closed the door.

Perhaps the only person who truly understood him was Momma. And when she died, he lost part of himself. Was talking simply too painful for him because it made him remember things? Memories he wanted buried? I hope that will never be me.

I stayed near the fire for a few more minutes, wanting to make sure Papa was fast asleep before Sarah snuck out.

When she left me alone in the house, the pang of loneliness in my heart was palpable—still so empty and raw. Even after all these years. I craved human interaction the way a dying man seeks God's solace, a thirsty man seeks water. And I knew too, once I went upstairs, that was Sarah's cue to leave. There was no winning.

I became Sarah's night watchman, waiting for her return, entertaining myself with thoughts and prayers, dreams, if I was lucky. Then, in the early morning, I'd help her back in after her night of dancing was done.

Quietly, I made my way to the staircase but my feet were reluctant and my steps felt forced. Every time I lay my foot upon the stair tread, my spirits felt heavier and heavier, my heart, lonelier and lonelier.

How I wished I had a place to go like Sarah. Someone to talk to, laugh with. It seemed I spoke more to the spirits lately than my own sister.

Sarah was alone in her own world, nodding, grimacing like Papa. The only time she appeared her old self was when she was readying to go to the dance.

I reached the top of the staircase, looking forward to watching Sarah getting ready, to ask her a few questions. Who she would see and who would play and who would ask her to dance—to at least give me something to think about when I would be alone.

But not tonight. The rooms were empty. She had already left, not even waiting for me to give her the signal this time. Her desire to be with her sweetheart had become too great and any time away from him was 'time lost'.

The window was opened a spec and I lifted it higher so I could stick my head out. I squinted my eyes and strained my ears.

Was that Sarah walking down the road? Or my imagination? I forced my eyes to see.

It looked like a figure in the distance. Was it her? My heart pounded. I wanted to call her name but I was scared.

I didn't want to wake Papa and I most certainly did not want to get her into trouble.

I stood back and the curtains fluttered in the breeze.

Then I heard them. Voices. And they called to me.

"Go," they said. The curtains waved and settled back again.

I contemplated these thoughts and turned to leave. Then I heard them again.

"Go," they said.

With my fingers in my mouth, my eyes darted around the room. I tiptoed to the closet and grabbed a sweater and threw it on. I didn't want to think anymore.

Making sure to close the window just the way Sarah did, but leaving a crack for my fingers, I edged out of the opening.

But it was darker than I thought on this side of the house and I wasn't sure exactly what to hold on to or where to place my foot. Within a split second, my heel-less shoe slid on the roof's frozen surface. Down, down, down, I went like a shot.

With no time to think, let alone shriek, I toppled feet first with a thud into a bank of crusty snow behind the house. My face smashed into the snow pile.

I remained stunned and motionless for a second before sitting up, the hard snow crystals sticking to my hair and nostrils. Feeling for blood, I touched my throbbing, numb nose before pulling one leg and then the other onto level ground.

When I realized I was okay, I bent forward and crept to the front of the house, peering into the living room window.

Had I woken Papa? I searched for his shadow but I didn't see any movement. I walked towards the back again, trying to figure out how Sarah got up on the roof and into the bedroom. It looked impossible. Everything was so dark and unfamiliar at this time of night.

The front door was locked and I cursed myself. If I banged for Papa to let me in now, I would surely give away Sarah's secret life.

I scurried to the front of the house and rested my back against the cold stone. My heart raced and my hands shook. Looking down to ground myself, I gulped in the cool night air and as I turned my head, my breath came out as smoke. Shivering, I pulled my sweater over my frozen hands to help warm them.

What was I to do now? My eyes welled and a lump formed in my throat. I was truly alone.

But when I looked upward, I noticed how brilliant the moon glowed against the dark night. Stars studded the sky like tiny fire-flies. And when I listened, I heard them. The voices in this outside world spoke to me again.

"Go," they said.

They pulled me. They told me not to go back in. They told me to walk down the road towards Sarah. They said I would find her.

Something inside me swelled as I listened to them: forces greater than myself.

I started walking.

I knew the direction of the dance hall because Sarah talked about it all the time. I tiptoed until I was away from the lane of our house, the rocks and dirt crunching under my feet, then I ran. I ran as fast as I could until the house was out of sight. The only sounds were the pounding of my heart, my breath, and my feet as they struck the road at even intervals.

I ran until my lungs felt on fire, then I slowed, taking deep gulps of air. Sweat dripped down my back.

My eyes slowly adjusted to the dark. The peepers squawked from their bogs and water holes; a lowly owl hooted. Branches snapped in the woods along the road and the wind rustled the newly-born leaves.

All these sights and sounds were too much for me and I called out to my sister in hopes she wouldn't be too far ahead.

"Sarrraaaah!"

I rushed ahead again, letting my feet propel me. Everything seemed farther at night.

"Sarrraaaah!" I called again, straining my ears, hoping to hear my name in return. I stood still this time, not allowing any part of my body to move for fear I would miss my name being called.

Nothing.

Hairs began to stand up on my body and my eyes widened. There looked to be a figure moving, its dark shadow approaching.

I didn't stick around and bolted forward. I ran with my arms swinging, hair swaying, lungs heaving. And when I thought I couldn't go any farther, I pushed myself harder.

I ran as far and as fast as my legs would take me. I dared not stop for fear of those cold, spiking fingers would wrap around my wrist or, worse, fangs and claws that would tear my body apart.

What was I thinking? I cursed myself. *How did Sarah do this the first time? What was I doing?*

I didn't feel my legs or even hear my breath. I ran with one thought: to get to the hall before *it* got me. I swore on my mother's grave that I would never, ever, on God's green earth do something so stupid again. Tears filled my eyes but I dared not look back.

"Maggie? Is that you?" Sarah laughed in disbelief but I felt that I had heard the voice of an angel. When she came into focus, I ran and wrapped my shaking arms around her neck.

"What are you doing here?"

For minutes I couldn't talk, even breathing was difficult. I placed my hand on my hip and walked in circles, my body hot and sticky from the pace I had kept.

I removed my sweater and ran my palm up the back of my neck and through my hair, wiped off the perspiration. I took deep heaving breaths.

"Let's walk with her," Colin said. I glimpsed in his direction. He was Sarah's sweetheart. They had met outside church on Thanksgiving Sunday last year, and since Papa didn't believe in courting or romance, Sarah had to sneak out to see him. She had become more like Mary than ever.

He looped his arm around mine and Sarah took my other one and we walked, the three of us, down the dark road towards the dance hall. I finally caught my breath and he asked if I was okay. I nodded.

"Good." he said, stopping and facing me. He removed a jar from his jacket pocket.

"No, Colin. She's too young."

"I'm fifteen," I said.

"She needs it. Look at the state she's in."

Sarah pinched her fingers together to show how much I could have. He unscrewed the cover and held the back of my head and fed me a drink. It went in like water but down my throat like fire.

I coughed and choked for several minutes before he said, "One more?"

I nodded.

"Take a good one."

He smiled at me and winked at my sister before he helped himself, wiping his mouth with his fingers. He shook his head and his shoulders, like a wet dog, before tucking away the jar in his pocket.

My breathing slowed and then it felt like all my limbs loosened. Once the hot-cold liquid was in my veins it made me feel light-headed and happy.

"You left without saying a word, Sarah, and I didn't want to be home alone again." I looked around, feeling frightened, but all that was behind me was the dark sky and trees.

"I told you I was leaving early tonight, Maggie. You must have forgot."

"I never forget," I told her.

"Ladies. We shouldn't be fighting on this fine, spring night. You feeling better there, Maggie?"

I nodded but almost tripped. I laughed out loud and covered my mouth with my hand.

Sarah grinned at me. "This is your first dance, Maggie. You better behave yourself."

I didn't reply. The happy liquid was already doing wonders for my mood.

"Well, I hope you replaced your running shoes with dancing shoes."

I couldn't grin any bigger. This was going to be so much fun I could feel it in my bones.

"Why were you running so fast anyway?" Sarah asked.

I turned around this time facing full on the way I had just come. "There was something out there." I pointed to the dark behind us, squinted my eyes.

"Like what?"

"A deer?" Colin asked.

"I never thought of a deer," I stated.

Sarah laughed, bending over, her head turned toward me.

I made a face and looked up at Colin. I thought he was handsome and he seemed very kind. He was all those things because he helped calm me down, gave me a drink to settle my nerves, and talked to me nice. No boy had ever talked to me before, only when making fun.

"What did you think it was?"

I never answered.

"A ghost?" She raised both her hands in the air.

"Not funny, Sarah."

We were interrupted by Colin's friends, who were gathered outside the small one-story building. The sound of the fiddle tuning made my heart pound.

Colin passed around his jar and Sarah threw her head back. This did not seem like the sister I knew, the one who lived at home, who kept herself busy and quiet doing her chores. This was a different sister—the one who snuck out at night to see her sweetheart.

Would Momma frown upon this? It wasn't the proper way. No. A suitor would have to come to the door and ask to take Sarah out, but Papa being the way he was would never allow it.

I felt bad for Sarah having to seek her own methods.

After looking around, I realized I was probably one of the youngest people here. I really didn't know anyone, but that was okay. The sips Colin had given me made me feel like I could talk to anyone and it made me feel good.

The music moved me and I remembered some of the steps that Momma taught us years ago and I nudged Sarah as I hopped on one foot. "Is this how you do it?"

"Well, looky-there?" an older man remarked as he saw me shuffling back and forth holding my skirts. "She's already to go, boys," he laughed, elbowing the circle of folks that were around him. "Would you like to dance, miss?"

I felt very bold and brave and confidant, even before Sarah could tell me if I was doing it right. I nodded my head and pulled a strand of hair behind my ear.

"Well, let's go, then." He tossed his cigarette away from him, smoke billowing out of his mouth. "What's your name, sweetheart?"

"Maggie."

"You're an awfully pretty gal. I've not seen you around here before. This your first time?"

"How'd you know?" I asked. The heat came to my cheeks.

"I know all the pretty girls and I've never seen anyone like you." He stared at my hair. "Who's your father?"

Without thinking, I told him that, too. He gave me a stiff nod, grabbed my hand and led me into the dance hall.

We took our places in a circle with other couples. There were seats against the wall and folks were chatting, and some stared at the stage waiting for the music to start. The fiddler kept tuning his instrument with the same repetitive motion as he adjusted the pegs, then he started to play.

I held hands with the man, my partner. His fingers felt strong in mine. His palms calloused and hard.

We all moved back and forth into the centre of the circle, keeping time to the music. My partner pushed me to dance with my side partner but I kept my head down. I focused on the movement and the footwork as this was my first real dance and I didn't want to embarrass myself.

The women in our group danced with ease and looked at me with an air of curiosity. I smiled and tried to appear affable.

I had never danced a full set before, but knew there were three figures and a small break in between so the fiddler could change tunes and have a drink. The figures also got faster and there was a lot of spinning.

In the final set, I got mixed up which direction to go and my dance partner turned me about and gave me a quick shove, teaching without talking the correct manner of the square set. It was all in fun though and I laughed at my mistakes and danced my best.

Most of the men could dance just as well as the women and they all bounced and weaved in almost perfect synchronization. Streams of sweat ran down the men's faces. Many had their shirt sleeves rolled to their elbows and the backs of their shirts stuck to their bodies. Even when I danced with my partner, when our arms held onto each other's waists, I could feel the perspiration and heat emitting off him and I was sure he could feel it from me.

When we finished, everyone clapped loudly and cheered, then rushed out of doors to the fresh air to cool down and sip spirits from jars. Already, the next group of dancers were taking their places to start the dance again.

"That was very fine, Miss Maggie John MacDonald. Your mother would be proud."

"You knew my mother?"

"Your mother was a very fine dancer," he said with a nod, "and gone too soon. God rest her soul." He blessed himself and pulled a hanky from his pocket. He wiped his face, but before I could ask anything else, Sarah took me by the arm.

"You told him your name?" she scolded me. I nodded, then grimaced when I saw Sarah's face.

"I-I didn't mean to. He just asked."

Sarah dragged me to the side of the hall where it was the darkest, where she had been standing with Colin and his friends. Sarah badgered me about dancing inside and saying my name.

"I thought that was why you came here?" I shouted. "To dance."

Sarah covered my mouth with her hand. "Would you be quiet? Not so loud."

"She's all right, Sar. She just danced. What harm could it do?"

"No harm, as long as word doesn't get back to Papa. You know how people talk."

Sarah looked up at Colin and he stared back at her. He brushed her cheek with his hand. How I longed for someone to look at me that way, maybe even touch me. Maybe one day I'd be as lucky as Sarah.

But right now, I didn't care. I was outside the hall at my first dance and having a great time. I didn't want it to end.

"Well, no one will talk," I said in a cocky tone. "Now where's that drink, Colin? I've got bit of a thirst."

I danced three more sets. One of Colin's friends asked me to join him. His hands were clammy as a wet rag. I felt as if I would slip away from him like soap in the sink if I didn't watch myself. It was a hard set.

Between the drinks I sipped from Colin's jar, dancing with other men, my head spun faster than the O'Donnells, who intertwined their arms like lover's knots and turned around and around on the dance floor.

Then my stomach felt like it was going to lurch out of my throat. I left as quickly as I could, banging into walls as folks walked around me. I stumbled over a woman sitting on a chair and I apologized. I ran behind the building to get away from as many people as I could.

The vomit forced its way out before I had a chance to do anything. I didn't want anyone to see me. I didn't want Sarah to see me either, or especially Colin, he was so handsome.

I retched up watery acid that burned my throat. I kept walking as I vomited more. I felt ashamed, having behaved so stupidly. I'd never be able to go to the dance again.

I walked until I tripped over a stump, spewing and gagging. The night spun around like a top. *Let it go away. Let it stop.*

I lay down on the cold earth, wishing for sleep to come.

I awoke to the sound of horse hoofs clopping. I was moving but I didn't know where I was going. I couldn't open my eyes, but I heard people laughing, snorting. They were like dreams.

Was I on a wagon? Was I going to church? With Momma and Papa? I smiled to myself and called out to her. How I yearned to see her, to touch her, to smell her sweet skin. "Momma," I yelled. "I'm here. Papa! Don't forget me. Don't leave me."

But no one heard me. Did I even speak? Was I dreaming? The voices kept laughing and the horse hooves kept clopping and darkness came again.

~

My body trembled and shivered and my teeth chattered as I searched for my blanket. I reached out for it but nothing was there.

I tried to turn over but I couldn't; nor could I open my eyes, no matter how I willed them. They appeared glued shut. I craved water and felt I could drink an ocean. I imagined the cool, shallow brook in the summer and I was knee-deep in it.

I cupped my palms and brought the liquid to my lips and puckered for the taste.

His breath was upon me. A stench, like manure and sour, old milk. My stomach spasmed and I groaned.

"You're ready?" a man said, his voice harsh. I was lying on something hard. A bed? A wagon? The ground?

"Sar—" That was all that came out of my raw throat.

I felt hands on my chest. Strong, fumbling fingers pressed hard into my skin. I smelled him again and I twisted my face away. I called out but nothing came. Was this a dream? Where was I?

He pushed up my skirts and placed his hands down there, all over me. It stung. He made strange noises. He pulled my skin, crushed my bones.

"No!" I cried as he forced his weight onto me.

I tried to push him off but he was too strong. He pushed me back and my head hit something hard. My head swam.

I cried out again, and then there was another voice. "What's going on?"

Searing pain with each rhythmic force. He grunted.

There were voices around me. They argued and bodies shuffled. I heard thuds and cracks, crunching of sticks, and gravel. It became quiet again and I whimpered softly.

Then hands were on me again, readjusting, pulling up and pressing down my clothes and then lifting me in the air. I was up and over. Upside down.

I smelled cigarettes and an unfamiliar scent. A voice.

"There, there, Maggie."

My head swayed as tall, wet grass brushed my face.

7: Tainted

I awoke to a smell of lye soap and must. The sun gleamed at me, its rays shouting for me to arise. I had never been in bed with so much heat upon me. I felt like I was on fire and I cried out for water. My tongue was so thick it stuck to the roof of my mouth.

I must have fallen down a huge flight of stairs, or from the hay loft. I moved and the pain ripped across my hips and legs.

When I opened my eyes, I saw that I was in my room, in my bed, alone. The quilts were heaped high on top of me like I had been fighting with them. The door was closed.

I tried to imagine what had happened. How did I get here? Back in my room?

I lifted my head off the pillow, and pain seared through my right eyeball and the side of my temple. Everything throbbed with a vengeance.

I lay still for a few more minutes and listened for movement downstairs. Was I alone in the house? Where was Sarah? Was she too busy doing chores in the kitchen? I willed her to come to me but it was no use. I tried to call her name but talking hurt my throat.

I pushed backed the quilts and saw I still had on last night's clothes and my fingernails were caked with mud. A piece of straw fell from my hair.

"Sar," I croaked.

Then I heard her. Little steps ran up the stairs and a soft knock at the door. She opened it, looked at me with intense wonder. She cupped one hand over her mouth, clutching a glass of water with the other.

I grabbed the glass with trembling hands and gulped it dry.

"More," I pleaded, but Sarah didn't move. She took the glass back and sat on the edge of the bed, concern in her eyes, but other things, too: fear, confusion.

"What?" I asked.

"Maggie?" she whispered my name so low I had to strain to hear her voice. She dropped the empty glass onto the bed and stretched out her body over mine. She hugged me and sobbed. "I thought. I thought. I don't know." She couldn't string any words together that made sense. "I looked. We looked... everywhere."

She raised up on her forearms so she was but a nose distance away. A hot tear dropped on my cheek and ran towards my lip.

"It's alright, Sarah. I'm here. I'm okay."

"No, you're not. Look at you."

But how could I look at me? I couldn't even get out of bed let alone look in a mirror. I grimaced trying to sit up and made a small yelp as I twisted. My hip hurt so.

She hopped off the bed, raised her index finger in the air and came back moments later with a cool washcloth and more cold water. I drank another glass. She tried to wash my face but I winced and pushed her hand away

Her brown eyes looked as sad as the cows before they were brought to slaughter. "Papa knows."

Those two words brought me upright as quick as anything. "He knows?"

Sarah nodded, eyes wide. "I thought you ran home. Oh, Maggie. I'm so sorry. I should have sent you home, or Colin and I should have taken you home, but you were having so much fun. How much did you drink?"

I shook my head and then lifted my hand to my head. It hurt to shake it. Even the thought of spirits made me feel like I was going to throw up again, and I held my hands to my mouth.

"Who took me home?"

Sarah shrugged. "You don't know?"

"No."

"I waited for you at the window, but I fell asleep. Someone knocked at the door early this morning and when Papa got up to answer, that's where he found you. You were in a heap on the step and he took you upstairs and put you to bed. He woke me up and asked all sorts of questions, but he knows, Maggie. He'll find out what I was doing and—"

"I won't say a word about you, Sarah. I promise."

"It's too late. He's been out. It's over."

And then her voice went up an octave. "I'll never see Colin again. Papa will make sure of it."

Sarah shut her eyes and the tears spit out. Her lips were twisted too and her body shook. "He was the only thing that made me happy, Maggie, and now he and I will never be together."

Her voice kept getting higher and higher as she spoke and she rocked back and forth on the bed. The movement made the bed squeak and made me nauseated but I dared not say anything.

I suddenly felt so small. The only thing Sarah had was her sweetheart. She had only been able to see him once a week for a couple of hours and I took that away from her because of my selfishness. There was no reason to have gone to the dance. I was still young and Momma said when it was time, we would be able to go. Sarah was older and deserved to be going with friends her age but Papa was too selfish, wanting us to stay home and keep logs on the fire and wash dishes and play cards while he sleeps.

I had no right to interfere and now what will happen? Papa will punish us until the end of time and then Colin will have found another sweetheart.

My heart felt sad and I held her hands and bowed my head and felt the tears come to my eyes too.

The squeak of the door told me we were no longer alone. I felt him there, staring, his cold, black eyes boring holes in my skull.

"*Èirich*," he said, in a stiff, expressionless voice.

Sarah stifled her sobs at once and whispered, "Get up."

We locked eyes. It was time.

~

He strutted like a caged animal. He paced, his nostrils flared, hands gripped into tight fists like he was holding the reins on a runaway horse. He said little at first. He waited for us to come down and then pointed for us to sit.

"*A dhà,*" he exclaimed, holding two fingers in the air. Sarah and I dared not look at each other. He walked to the wash basin and then turned toward the stove. He did this several times, walked back and forth, back and forth. He was making me dizzy. He said nothing when he paced, and the more he paced, the more nervous I became.

He was wearing his nicer clothes. Not the usual wool pants and long undershirt but the dress shirt and dark pants he wore when he and Momma went somewhere, like church.

My hand flew to my mouth. Church. We missed church! Today was Sunday. The Sabbath.

"*A dhà,*" he said again, louder this time. Sarah touched the fabric on her apron. I knew she was trembling. I could feel the vibrations sitting beside her. "Two of my daughters not at church today. Today!" his voice raised. "Do you know what today is, Maggie?" He stopped pacing and stared down at me. I could not keep his gaze. I stared down at the floor.

"It's the Sabbath," I whispered.

"*Agus?*" He bent at the waist, and I smelled his sour, hot breath. I looked at Sarah out the corner of my eye. She tried to tell me with her eyes, but I couldn't understand. My head was too thick, too full of haze and fog from the night before.

Instead of answering, I shrugged.

He stood tall and I could tell that he was both disgusted and angry. "Tell her, Sarah," his voice boomed.

Sarah's voice was small. "Today was Momma's birthday."

The wind went out of me. I sagged into myself and my body went hot. Beads of perspiration bloomed on my forehead. How had I forgotten? I felt I couldn't breathe and wanted to cry. I could not bring back yesterday nor the mass for Momma. I wanted to crawl under the table and die or at least, pray for penance.

"I'll go to church now, Papa, and ask Father Dunphy for confession and I'll—"

"You'll do nothing!" he screamed. "No such thing. You and your sister have disgraced me. You are following in Joanne's footprints! Sneaking behind my back."

The lines on his face seemed to edge deeper into his flesh. "You've shamed this family."

I muffled a cry.

"You have tainted this house!" He turned away, faced the table and whispered, "What would your mother have said?" His knuckles crushed onto the table as he leaned with all his weight.

I thought the whole table would snap in two. I felt woozy suddenly, and in pain. My face and cheek ached, the back of my head, my side and stomach. "I'm sorry," I blurted.

He extended his right arm, fingers stretched, his head bowed. "I will not hear your apologies."

"I'm sorry, Papa. I'm so sorry." I wanted to die.

Sarah trembled beside me. She buried her head in her hands.

"Now both of you. Get on your knees and pray for forgiveness."

Sarah swooped to the ground with a thud and blessed herself. It took me a few minutes to lift myself off the chair and I let out a groan as I knelt on the hard floor beside her.

We started saying the words to the Lord's Prayer.

Papa turned, stared at Sarah. "And I haven't even begun with you."

Sarah openly sobbed while she kept saying the prayer.

Papa went to his room and we heard him shuffling about, changing his clothes, taking his work pants and shirt off the nail behind the door. We knew he was going to the barn then and welcomed the few moments we would have to discuss what had happened last night. but Papa lingered.

His face twitched and he gritted his teeth. It was as if he was boiling over, the rage couldn't contain inside his body.

He slammed his fist down on the table and Sarah and I jumped, continuing our prayers in unison.

He went back to his room and came out with a mason jar. He unscrewed the cap and took a gulp and wiped his mouth. He shuddered as it went down and I felt a sudden wave of nausea.

His dark eyes narrowed and he lunged at me, pulling me by the top of the head and holding it back. I cried out and he emptied the contents down my throat.

It came up as quickly as it went down. I spewed all over the floor and onto my sister's hair and clothes, but it didn't faze Papa. He drank what was left and continued his rant.

"You snuck to the dance and took your sister with you? What's wrong with you? So she can get drunk and disgrace this house?"

Sarah sobbed. "Please, Papa! Please, I'm sorry." She had her two arms raised towards him, like she wanted to be picked up and held. "I'm sorry. I'm so sorry."

"You're not! You're only sorry you got caught."

He rested his hands on his hips and looked down at us. "I don't know what I did to deserve the likes of you. I never wanted girls. I told your mother that."

He turned away from us, walked toward the door. With his hand on the knob he said, "Finish your prayers and do your chores."

He left for the remainder of the afternoon. He didn't come in until we had long gone to bed.

~

"I can't take it no more, Maggie. I'm leaving."

"You're what?" I asked, dumbfounded.

"You heard me."

"But where?" My eyes searched her face.

"Ontario."

"But how? That's so far, Sarah." I couldn't fathom my sister leaving.

We were sitting on my bed. Since Papa's punishment had rained down on us, over a month ago now, life had changed again. He went from grunts and occasional chatter to nothing at all. It seemed he wanted to avoid us altogether because he didn't know what to do with us.

Yet, he was always in the background, watching us. I was no longer allowed to go to school. We were basically prisoners in our own home.

For the first few days, I welcomed it. Healing needed sleep. I was sore, and black and blue all over. I had scratches on my face, although they were scabbing now. The physical scars started to heal. Those that were inside still felt raw.

Papa said I had tarnished the house and that meant no man would ever have me. It was known by now I had been taken. The 'rumour' had started and no doubt Sarah wanted to get away from it as far as she could, too.

"Colin said people are talking," she said, "and it's not good."

Someone had left me outside on the step. Was it the first man I danced with who took advantage of me? It didn't matter. I didn't want to know. I could barely remember the night.

Everything was dark and sort of a blur. On occasion though, in the middle of the night, I'd see his face, smell his breath, and I'd wake up in a sweat.

Sarah fluffed up the pillow and lay down upon it. She fiddled with a piece of yarn. "I can't tell you all the details, Maggie. And I can't tell you when. I'm just going."

"Can I come with you?" I pleaded, praying that the obvious answer was yes. But seeing her expression and downcast eyes, I knew the answer.

She touched my arm, "Maybe once I get settled, I'll send for you. But I can't, not now. There's not enough fare for you to come."

My body started to tremble. I wanted to die. How could I possibly live here all by myself? I wanted to bury my head in the pillow and suffocate myself. I wanted to scream or punch her. I wanted to run away.

Instead, I lay silent then turned over on the bed and faced the wall. Silent tears streamed down, but I dared not let her see. I took the blanket and rubbed my face.

"I'll be alone, Sarah. How could you leave me?"

Sarah squiggled over to me and brought her arm around my waist. I could feel her warm breath on my ear but she didn't say anything. She just held me. She held me for a very long time, her body warm and familiar.

I closed my eyes and I felt sleep coming. I didn't try to fight it. I was exhausted. Tired from my punishment, tired from all the extra chores, tired from Papa's constant silent treatment and from Sarah's constant state of sadness. My aches and pains had tired me out and I just drifted off.

When I woke, Sarah was not there. She had left like she said she would.

I didn't expect it to be so soon.

8: If you can't beat them

July, 1954

"Well, look what the cat dragged in."

My mouth hung opened when I saw Joanne. She laughed an ugly laugh. "I thought you died. You never bothered to come see me." There was a chill in her voice.

"Uh," I choked.

"Cat got your tongue too?" Joanne regarded me with narrowing eyes while she puffed on a cigarette. The grey smoke blew out the corner of her mouth.

"I didn't know you smoked."

"That all you've got to say?"

I shrugged, lay my small bag by my feet. "Sarah's gone," I offered.

"Good for her," she snapped. I watched her take another puff.

Joanne settled her large brown eyes on me as she stubbed out her cigarette in the ashtray. It was mounded high in butts and grey ash. She caught me staring at the tray and moved it aside. "Want to try one?"

I shook my head.

Joanne laughed, her teeth blackened and stained. "You were always a 'fraidy-cat, Maggie."

I guessed I still was. "When did you start smoking?"

She lifted the cup to her mouth and took a slurp. "Oh, I don't know. After I was here for a while. You know the old saying, if you can't beat 'em..." She gave me a wink.

"What's wrong, Joanne? You seem...different."

She laughed instead of answering me and looked down at my cup. I had hardly tasted it. "What's wrong with the tea?"

But before I could answer, she squinted, pointed a finger. "Right.

You want something stronger. At least, that's the story I was told. I couldn't believe my little sister Maggie was into the sauce and out at a dance. I thought they were talking about someone else. I even argued with them that they had to be lying. But, no. It was true, wasn't it?"

The redness in my face gave her the answer and she laughed all the more. It seemed she was getting a good chuckle out of me being the butt of her jokes at my misfortune.

"Maybe you're not so fraidy-cat anymore?"

It seemed living with Old Art made Joanne a little bitter, frazzled. Even her hair was wild, sticking up in odd angles. "For God's sake, Maggie, sit down. You're making me nervous."

I did as she told me. "You're terribly thin, Joanne. Is Art feeding you here?"

"Yeah, but I've been throwing it up. Almost every day. Must be a bug."

That's when I noticed not just her thinness but the small swelling in her stomach. "Is that why you're here?"

"Papa threw me out, and by the looks of it, you too?" Joanne filled her cup with the steaming hot beverage and poured a bit of milk into it. She sauntered back to the table, the tea taking a dangerous slant. She winked at me.

I sat silent for a moment, wondering what she meant. Was she carrying Art's child? I shuddered. I wanted to ask but didn't. Some things were not allowed to be talked about, even if it was your own family. Your own sister.

I was tempted to take a puff of Joanne's cigarette just to show her I wasn't as scared of things as she might think. But something stopped me. A voice. Taking up smoking would make me turn out like her: thin, bitter, pregnant, unmarried.

No, I didn't want to be like Joanne, no matter how much I loved her.

"Where is Art, anyway?" I asked, looking around the cramped living space of their house. I called it *their* house because she had been here long enough, since Momma passed away. The kitchen wasn't as neat as ours but I supposed Art didn't care. I doubted there was ever a woman in this house before Joanne came.

"He's out."

"Out where?"

She gave me a sly look. "You ask a lotta questions. Who cares, Maggie? He's out and you're here. Are you fancying Art now? That why you want to know where he is?"

I grimaced and my face flushed as hot as the July afternoon. "No," I answered in a whisper. "Just making conversation. That's all."

Joanne was angry but I wasn't sure why. This wasn't the Joanne I really knew. Her hands trembled quite a bit even when she sipped her tea. Nervousness? I couldn't say.

"Can I make something to eat for you, Joanne? Are you hungry? When was the last time you had anything? Maybe...the baby is hungry?" There, I said it.

"I feed it these," she said, holding up her half-smoked butt. "And this," her teacup. "It seems that's all it wants. Food makes me sick."

"Joanne, you need to eat. Else the baby won't grow."

She patted her stomach. "If you don't think this is growing, Maggie," she said in a half-cocked tone, "then I don't know what is."

"Who's the father, Joanne? Is it Art?" I hoped to God it wasn't.

Joanne was taken aback by my question. Her face turned a shade of grey. "Maggie!" she snapped, stubbing the butt with considerable force. "The nerve of you."

"I'm just worried for you."

"That why you left me here?" she huffed. She stood and walked away. "You've exhausted me, Maggie. I'm going to lie down now. You can clean up these dishes and start supper. I guess that's why you're here, isn't it? Or were you too useless even for Papa?"

Her words stung but I said nothing. I watched as she went up the stairs. They groaned with each step. The bed creaked as she lay on top of it and then there was silence.

I started clearing the table. I hadn't expected this. I thought Jo and I would talk and reminisce about the old days and the good times; the funny things Mary got away with; and Momma, and Sarah's new life. I sighed. If I didn't know better, Joanne was turning into Papa. Into Art.

I dumped the ashes in the woodstove and thought maybe Joanne was upset that Sarah left without telling her. They were so close. I used to hear them whispering at night when they shared the same room. Before Jo left us, and before Momma died. Sometimes I heard them giggling too, the bed squeaking and bouncing beneath them.

I envied them, their friendship, their bond. Mary was so independent. She didn't need me. She didn't need anyone. So, when Joanne was sent away, and Mary passed, I secretly hoped Sarah and I would become bosom pals. But no, we kept to our own rooms after our sisters left. Then she found Colin. There was no more room for me.

The door clicked open. Lost in my own thoughts I didn't hear him enter. Art. I startled when he came in and rushed to finish the washing.

He laughed loud. "Lazin' about just like your sister used to do."

He placed his purchases on the table: flour, ginger, jars with red filling, jars with clear liquid, teabags, cigarettes.

"Sorry," I said. "She just went up for—"

"Who?"

"Joanne. She went for a rest."

He raised his hand, palm out. "Okay, Maggie," he said, grabbing his smokes.

"She said she was tired...after being up all morning."

Art remained quiet.

"We were talking so I didn't get time to..." I looked at the dishes.

"Well, you got time now." He gestured to the table. "You can make me up a plate. There are biscuits over there. Put some jam on it."

"Maybe I'll send one up," I said, eyeing the plate.

Art sat down opposite me. "How 'bout give her a wee drink of this?" He shook the jar with the liquid. "No, on second thoughts, best not. I better hide it."

He looked at the table. "The wench will drink them all."

He unscrewed the cap and brought it to his nose, squinted, and took a good swallow. "That'll put hair on your chest."

His laugh turned hoarse and he wheezed and barked, coughed up phlegm which he spat on the floor. A wave of nausea hit me.

I didn't know how Joanne had lived here for so long, but her words came rushing back: *if you can't beat them*. She did what she had to, to survive.

~

I finally heard from Sarah. She sent me a letter which Art brought to me. It was addressed to Papa's house. It was the first time I had ever received a piece of mail with my name on it.

I admired her beautiful penmanship on the envelope and ran my finger over her return address on the front. I smiled. She left me imagining her grand new life which she now lived. I brought the envelope to my nose to see if there was any trace fragrance of her. There was none. Just the scent of the paper.

I then tore it open, eager to hear her news.

July 12, 1954

Dear Maggie:
I hope this letter finds you well. I apologize for the lengthy delay it took me to write to you. I needed to find a place of my own and get settled but as you can see, I finally have.

You would absolutely love it here. There's so much to see and do. There are shops and restaurants, movie theatres, and incredible dances. Even better than the ones back home. I think so anyway.

I'm living in a nice little place with two sisters, Frances and Gloria. You might remember them? They went to school with us but they were older than me. Colin's joining me soon too, because, brace yourself - we are to be married! Of course, I would have loved to tell you this in person but this letter will have to do. We set the wedding for next fall. It will be our one year anniversary since we first met. I'll do what I can and send you some money so you can come. Isn't it all exciting?

How is Aunt Martha? Do you get to see her much? I miss her terribly. Will you give her a big hug from me?

I will sign off dear Maggie, as I have to get to work shortly. I am working as a waitress, making good tips. I plan to go to school too so I can work in the fancy offices down-town. I think I would make a really good secretary. Don't you?

I wish good things for you, Maggie, and I think of you every day. When you say a prayer for Momma and our dear siblings, please say one for me.

Your loving sister,
Sarah

PS – please write back and tell me all your news!

I read the letter three times, gasping each time at the part where she said she was getting married. My heart leapt with joy. Sarah, a bride and Joanne, a new mother. Maybe I'll stand in her wedding? Be a godmother? What wonderful news and so much to be thank-ful for.

I wished I had someone to share it with. Someone who would be just as thrilled as I was.

I knew who I could share the news with, but Papa wouldn't be happy.

~

"My!" Aunt Martha exclaimed, "Isn't that wonderful? Wonder why she didn't tell me first? You check the post, Dan?" she hollered over her shoulder. "He must have proposed in writing, as we didn't hear about it in town or at church."

I shrugged.

"Doesn't matter," she said, her lips turned up, showcasing the lines around her eyes. "You must be so happy for her."

Aunt Martha passed me back the letter, which I folded and placed inside my pocket. "Well, you coming in or not?"

"Come in," Dan bellowed. "Let's get a look at you."

The hairs on the back of my neck stood on edge. It was his voice. "No, it's okay. I can't stay. I have to get back."

"But you just got here and we haven't seen you in ages, have we, Dan?"

I held opened the door but remained in the porch.

"But she'll get married here?" Martha pressed me to agree with her.

"Yes, I'm sure."

She blessed herself and kissed her fingertips.

"You're all in a tizzy," Dan said, "because Sarah left and she didn't have time to tell you in person. But we knew she wouldn't stay here. Not with her father the way he is. Backwards and all."

My cheeks got hot as Dan continued, "She had to go to get out from his clutches."

Everything he said made sense. I could see his hands as he held the newspaper taut between them. "You just want her around when she starts having kids."

Aunt Martha played with the crumbs on the table as he spoke. She scooped them into her palm, then piled them and poked at it with her finger.

"Not everyone wants to live on a farm," he said. "They have other ideas." He snapped the paper as he turned the page.

"Well, Sarah told me I was going to live with her when she got married and we'd have a farm."

Aunt Martha gave me a wide smile. "Really?" she sounded hopeful, clasping her hands together. "Well, you'll be around for a while, Maggie? Although I heard you've been staying at Art's."

I didn't realize anybody knew about my whereabouts. Or cared.

She grabbed my hand. "The nerve of your father. Sending you off like that. He did the same to Joanne."

The air went out of me. The rumour had travelled. Sweat pooled in my armpits and the room started to spin.

I rested against the door frame as Martha babbled. My mind drifted back to what Papa had said—that I was tarnished and no man would ever have me. That's why I was living with Art. It was my punishment. "I better get back," I said. "I have chores to do."

I left as quickly as I could, clutching the folded letter in my fingers, still feeling hopeful about my future with Sarah once she was married.

~

Not only had Sarah been sending money home to me, but odds and ends we couldn't get so easily here. An iron, for starters, and an ironing board. Art had to pick those items up at the post office in town.

Then along came a fancy alarm clock, even though Art had a rooster. We chuckled at that one.

She sent home all the modern conveniences she thought we rural folks needed in order to survive living in the country.

She sent new curtains home for our house. Papa didn't want them because he wanted to keep the ones Momma had hung on the window, even though they were worn and moth-eaten. She sent new shirts for Papa and sweet-smelling soap.

It was like Christmas whenever we got these items. We wondered how she was doing it, as she was supposed to be saving for her wedding.

Then, Art got a telephone, so Sarah was able to call me. It was expensive so we didn't stay on the line that long. But I loved hearing her voice.

Then she blindsided us.

She told me they weren't coming home to get married. Instead, they had booked their reception in a nice new hall there, and had rented a car for the ceremony. A black convertible, because they could never get that here. She made everything sound so glamorous.

And, finally, she told me they had found their forever home, she called it. In Windsor, Ontario, not far from where she lived now.

What happened to the family farm with cows and chickens like we had talked about? But how could I possibly ask when she was so excited about everything else? She was always so happy when I talked to her lately. And when she asked,

"What's new there?"

I had nothing to add.

I couldn't tell her about Joanne and her pregnancy because it wasn't my place. Joanne never answered the phone, anyhow, when Sarah called, skulking away to her bedroom. It seemed she couldn't bring herself to telling her and I wondered why.

Joanne always seemed angry. Was it because she thought she should have been the first to leave and the first to get married because she was the eldest? Was she jealous of Sarah getting out and away? Or for leaving her behind in her predicament?

Finally, when Sarah called home right before Christmas, I told her about Joanne. She was angry and I thought it was because I didn't tell her sooner. But there had never seemed to be a moment where I could bring it up. She was always telling me about what she did. About her wedding. About their house. About the city. How well she was doing. Her and Colin. Colin and her.

"I have to go," she said suddenly, and hung up.

I clung to the receiver. The phone line made funny sounds.

Just like that, she suddenly seemed so much farther away.

~

The labour started three days into the new year, an early Wednesday morning, and I vowed after hearing all that screaming I would never be in that predicament. It sounded like someone was ripping Joanne apart and there wasn't a thing I could do about it.

I tried getting cold water for her face and a dry cloth for the sweat.

The baby seemed to be stuck. I wasn't sure. I had never done this before.

I screamed to Art. He said he'd call the doctor, but Joanne begged him not to. She wouldn't hear of it because of Momma. Doctors weren't good for anything.

Art swore and left the house. Hours later he came back with a woman.

Mabel was her name. She was old but had a kind face. She helped with the baby and I told her, begged her not to say anything. For Joanne's sake.

She agreed.

Finally, the pain was over. Joanne had given birth to a tiny, five-pound boy.

Art waited until the coast was clear to come in and see him.

Papa didn't bother to come at all.

~

Darryl was deliciously pink and small, almost like a doll. His nose was no bigger than the edge of my thumb and his eyes were squeezed shut most of the time. His delicate lashes were so translucent, and he had fine wisps of soft, dark hair that stuck out over his small ears.

His fingers were balled into tight fists and he had a set of lungs that told you he was someone to be reckoned with.

"You can't be leaving him alone with me, Maggie. I haven't a clue what to do."

"You just hold him or pick him up."

Art waved his hand, dismissing me. "He's too small for starters."

He kept his distance as I scooped up the bawling, uncontrollable child.

Joanne couldn't console him, either. He cried first thing in the morning, after he ate, once he got changed, in his bath, late in the afternoon, before bedtime, and all through the night. He cried so much I swore his lungs were going to burst.

Joanne was worn out and ragged-looking. She hid in her room most of the time, avoiding us. She was so exhausted. The area under her eyes were dark grey. In contrast, her face was so pale and sickly looking.

I swore she aged two years in those first few weeks of being a new mother.

I tried to help. I made food Joanne would eat, washed diapers and blankets, hung them to dry by the wood stove. There was never an end to them because Darryl soiled through his clothes at least five to six times a day. I never thought a little person could be so much work.

Joanne got thinner and thinner. She survived on very little, fell asleep at the table with little Darryl in her arms.

One time I caught her sticking the soother in the clear liquid Art had at the house and popping that into Darryl's mouth. He latched on quick enough, but the second he had a taste, he recoiled and writhed like a snake, screaming louder than ever.

"Don't do that," I barked.

"Here, then," she snapped. "He likes nothing. Not even me."

I raised my arms to take him and she was only too happy to pass him along. She mumbled something incoherent and lay still for a few moments. She closed her eyes. A long snort escaped her lips which seemed to startle her.

"Go to bed, Joanne. I'll look after Darryl."

She barely nodded and picked up her limp frame, staggered away in case I changed my mind.

Old Art wasn't around a lot, either. Joanne said he must be sleeping in the barn with the animals because it was too noisy in here.

Poor Darryl didn't wish for this life, but here he was in all his unhappiness.

It seemed Joanne didn't much care for him either. She certainly didn't eat and drink the right food, for starters, was absent most of the time, and left me alone with the baby more than I should have been. All it seemed she wanted was less of Darryl and more of Art's spirits.

I placed my lips on Darryl's sweet, bawling face and whispered, "Who's the good boy? Who's the good boy?" all the while bouncing him.

He found temporary solace with my thumb. It reminded me of the calves when we used to stick our fingers in their mouths. His tiny hands held onto mine and slowly, slowly, his suction relaxed, as did the muscles in his face. His lower lip trembled a bit, looking like he was going to cry again and then, a smile found his way on his sweet face before it disappeared.

I so wanted Joanne to see this.

I sat down in the rocking chair that Art had managed to pick up somewhere and cradled that little boy. I whispered good thoughts, bounced and rocked him until he drifted off into a dreamless sleep.

Most days were the same. The baby screamed because of his sodden garments, because we couldn't settle him, because he was hungry. He belched and farted and had runny poops and it seemed there was nothing anyone could do but just pray and wish for him to stop.

I whisked him outdoors in the cold, winter air and talked to him about the crows that I was sure he had scared off—all to no avail. I begged Old Art to find something at the store for him: blackstrap molasses to add to the milk, cream for his bottom, anything that would make the little man sleep. We even tried to let him bawl it out, but that didn't work either.

Some days the little man worked himself up to a lather by the time I finally talked Joanne into letting me pick him up. I turned him upside down and then laid him on his stomach and patted his back but no, poor Darryl would not stop crying.

He had not gained any weight, either. Something he finally had in common with his mother.

"He's going to starve, Joanne, if we can't get him something to eat."

"Good," she said, defiant.

"Joanne!" I gasped, looking at my sister as she placed the squealing child in his basket.

She looked up at me, her eyes red rimmed, her face gaunt and tired, looking more of a mere shadow of the girl I once knew. Tears filled her eyes. "I can't do it anymore, Maggie. I'm cursed. He's cursed."

She looked down at the baby, her face full of anguish. "God is punishing me."

She then lay on the chair, curled her feet up so she was in a fetal position, and tucked her face into her knees. Her shoulders shook. "I'm just so tired, Maggie. I don't know what else to do," she cried.

"Can't you try feeding him yourself again?" I pleaded.

"I tried, Maggie. There's nothing there," she said between sobs. "Maybe God wants to take him, take him away to be with Momma and Mary."

"Stop!" I barked, "you're talking nonsense."

I was cranky, too, for lack of sleep, but at least I had some strength in me, and some stubbornness. I scooped up the crying Darryl and held him in my arms, gave him my thumb, which seemed to be the only thing that satisfied him for a few minutes.

"Just go," she said to me. "Take him. Take him out, away, anywhere but here so I can't hear him. I don't want to hear him anymore." She covered her ears.

Without a word, I left the room, not knowing where to go. I bundled him with a small blanket and took him outside, talking to him all the time.

I walked towards the barn, where Old Art may have been hiding, or avoiding us. He was out chopping wood when I came across him. The baby still whimpering.

"That babe still in misery?" he asked, and I nodded. I cradled the baby to my chest and patted him on the bum and lower back. "I think he's starving." My voice cracked.

Art stopped whacking the wood and poked his fat finger into the baby's cheek. The baby opened his mouth impulsively, looking to suck.

"Aye. If he wants this here," he said, eyeing his finger, "then he must be."

He cackled out loud. I moved about to get away from Art's dirty hand. "We don't know what to do, Art!" I said.

He scratched his wiry whiskers with his blackened fingers. His eyes twitched. "Leave it with me."

"The baby?" I held little Darryl even closer than before.

"Not that. I'll talk to Mabel. She mentioned if there were problems that the O'Donnells may have a nursing goat. Thought it was strange at the time."

He stroked his bearded chin, his daze drifting off in the distance. "I'll see if she can get some of that."

"Goat milk?"

"Well, we'll give 'er a try, eh? No harm in it. I'll go up after I finish here." He started chopping the wood again.

"No, Art! We've got to go now!"

9: I can do it

February, 1955

Joanne was suspicious of me. I felt her eyes on my back, her presence; even though when I turned, she wasn't there. Didn't she trust me? When I told her about the goat milk, she'd stare with those big, all-knowing eyes, like I was crazy.

Thank heavens, it worked. Darryl sucked that back like it was going out of style. It worked so well that Art bought one of the O'Donnell's goats so we could have the milk at his place.

Six weeks had passed and I was feeling stronger, but I was still not ready to go back to Papa's. There was an ache on my insides. It wasn't a sickness, just a void.

Joanne was absent most of the time so I watched the baby. I admit, I loved it. I loved the smell of him, how he cooed and smiled when I talked soft to him. The way he squealed and pumped his little fists in the water when I gave him a bath. The way he pulled my hair and suckled my neck when I held him close. The way his bottom lip quivered when he drifted off to sleep in my arms. Yes, I loved everything about him.

And Joanne? Well, I think she loved him, too. But mothers don't always have the time to nurture, sing songs, and play. No, not when there are a hundred other things to do.

I was only too glad to help her, yet sometimes, when I saw her looking at me when he'd laugh, I'd see resentment in her eyes. Or jealousy? She'd ask me to put him down, to go outside with him, or to leave her, and I would. Because she was my sister.

After I put the baby down for his afternoon nap, I asked if she would be going with me to Sarah's wedding.

She frowned and said, "I dunno." In the same breath, she asked,

"Shouldn't she be getting married here? Where she's from?" The heavy iron misted as she ran it over the stiff cotton fabric.

Over the coming months, Sarah's letters arrived and with them, a couple dollars here and a few coins there. I knew the little she was sending wouldn't be enough for the three of us to get to Ontario. I'd need to get a real job.

After I put Darryl down to bed and Joanne finished up her sewing, I asked Art if I could go with him to town.

"What about the lad?"

I thought for a moment. "Will you be long?"

"Half hour if you don't lollygag."

I smiled, eager to go.

"Yeah, you can hop in," he said. As quick as I could, I grabbed my scarf and hat, pulled on my coat and followed him outside.

He stopped the truck at the end of the driveway. My body swayed forward when he jerked the brakes. He looked back. "You sure you should be leaving him alone like that?"

"He's asleep, Art. And Joanne's there."

Art let out a lengthy sigh. "Go get him," he said. "We'll drop him off at Mabel's. She's on the way."

I didn't argue. I ran in and scooped up the sleeping Darryl and we sped off down the dirt road.

I didn't tell Art why I wanted to go to town with him. I didn't want to tell him because he'd probably want to keep me caged up, like Joanne. He didn't need to know all of my business.

I wasn't exactly sure where to look for work, but I had overheard Martha talking to Dan once about putting a notice in the store. He had needed some help around the barn. So that is where I'd start.

It was the first time I felt like I was making my own decisions, and I felt invigorated. A huge smile crept onto my face. This must be how Sarah felt. Independent. Confident. Mature.

Art dropped me off at the side of the road and I walked to the store from there. I couldn't stop thinking of Sarah. About her being alone in the large city by herself when she first left. How brave she was. I kept turning around, looking behind me as I walked, thinking someone was following me.

It must be so hard being on your own, I thought. At least I had Joanne and Darryl. Art, too, even Papa. But she did it solo. And if she could do it there, I could certainly here.

As I walked toward the general store, my confidence started to wane. Would they laugh at me when I entered? Chase me out because I was too young? Too inexperienced? Who did I think I was? My mouth dried and my heart pounded.

Despite the cold winter wind, my palms sweated. The bell tinkled as I pushed open the door.

The first thing I saw when I entered was a shiny mirror on a wooden vanity. It was so bright and new. I bent over studying my appearance. Was this really me? I reached out to touch the glass, feeling the cool reflection with my fingertips. My eyes looked tired and I had dark circles underneath. I thought I looked a lot like Joanne except for my hair colour.

I brushed a strand behind my ear and realized how long it had grown. Papa had hacked off several inches from Sarah and me the summer before last. He said we were using too much soap.

Eyes were suddenly upon me, staring, assessing. They spoke in whispers, glancing in my direction. I turned around, looked down at my wrist, pretending I had a watch. My face felt hot and clammy. I swallowed hard.

Instead of looking for job postings, I walked out, tried to catch my breath. I needed to feel calm and right now it eluded me, so I walked.

I kept in the direction of the post office because Sarah had sent so many items here. The post mistress' name was Ida. She was a petite woman with a thick mane of grey hair. She lived with her brother. I know she'd help me out if she could. She was always so friendly.

The door creaked as I opened it. A middle-aged woman turned and nodded to me. "Can I help you?" she asked, giving me her full attention. This wasn't Ida.

"Uh," I said, wondering where Ida was. "I'm, uh, looking for work —if you have it...any." I looked down at my feet, wishing I could look her in the eyes.

"I don't have anything just now, but I can take down your information." She reached for a slip of paper. "Can you tell me something about yourself?"

"I'm really good at math."

She smiled when I said this, nodded slightly.

As she wrote, I blurted, "I'm saving for my sister's wedding. She's getting married in Ontario."

"That's nice," she said. She asked me a couple of questions about my schooling and where I lived. If it would be difficult for me to get to work. I felt good about this woman. She seemed warm and approachable. Like I could tell her things.

"When I save enough money, I'll be leaving for Ontario. My sister Joanne might come, too. And the baby. Sarah said we would all live together, but now that's not going to happen. She wants to buy a house in the city so I'll probably end up living there. With her."

The post mistress's smile faded and she stared at me. She tapped the pen on the paper and looked at me in silence for a moment. "So, you only need a job until you save enough money?"

I nodded. "Just a few months. That's all I need."

"Well, thank you for coming in, Miss—"

"My name's Maggie. Maggie MacDonald."

"Maybe you should try looking at the postings at the general store."

I nodded, thanked her, and extended my hand because that's what men do.

I took two deep breaths before I walked back into the general store. If Sarah can do it, I said to myself, and tucked my clammy hands inside the pockets of my coat. Instead of looking for job postings, I waited in line.

The store clerk, Mr. Bouldry, stared at the empty counter where I stood, then at me. He looked me up and down. My mouth went dry when he asked in a sharp, clipped tone, "What are you wanting, miss?"

"I'm, uh, looking for work...if you have anything available. I'm a good worker and good in math and I think I'd be—"

He stopped me by holding out his raised palm. "Sorry, miss. We don't have anything. But there are a few postings at the back. You can take a look there."

I nodded and thanked him, although I don't think he heard me. I walked in the direction he had indicated.

The man behind me in the lineup, and not even in a whisper, said, "That John and Mary Louise's?"

"Think so."

"What's she doing here?"

"Looking for a job, by the looks of it."

My cheeks flushed so I buried my face in my scarf.

"It's a crying shame," the patron responded.

I calmed myself, ignored them as best I could, focused on reading the notice boards.

The doctor's office was looking for a stenographer and someone who could do shorthand. I couldn't do that. There were families looking for nannies or housekeepers for far away, like Boston, Detroit, Florida. I shook my head. I wanted to go to Ontario, not there. They were looking for farm hands to do heavy lifting, making hay and fixing a roof on a barn.

I was lifting my hand to take a look at another post when I heard my name.

"That you, Maggie?"

I looked up. It was James, James MacKellan, the boy who always picked on me at school. He had grown tall in the past year.

He walked towards me, smiling his sick, smug grin. I flinched. He grasped hold of a strand of my hair and twirled it around his fingers.

"How've you been? I haven't seen you since—"

I yanked my hair free and stepped back. His eyes widened. I turned to leave, knocked over the display of rubber boots.

"Don't you kids be fooling around here if you're not buying anything," Mr. Bouldry hollered.

The bell on the door chimed, catching James' attention for a split section. That gave me the distraction I needed and the momentum to move.

A mother pulled her two younger children by the hands into the store, leaving the door open. I hurtled myself out, and in doing so, I barrelled right into my father.

I nearly knocked him over. He wasn't paying any more attention to his surroundings than I was.

We stared at each other, stock-still. I had not seen him for months. He scratched his head and mumbled. And I remembered he had forbidden me to ever come here alone.

It only took him a minute to recall and, with his large hand, he grabbed me by the shoulder. I squinted, readying myself for his scolding.

Instead, we heard his name being called.

I turned toward the familiar voice. Papa loosened his grip as Art strode over, slapped his hand on my father's back.

"How've you been, John? Good? It's been a while." Art spoke Gaelic and Papa bowed his head and chuckled. Then Art steered Papa in the opposing direction.

With nothing left to do, I bundled up and started the long, cold walk home.

I didn't get far when Old Art pulled up behind me. The brakes squealed as he fishtailed to a stop.

I hopped in, thankful to be warm at least.

We drove for a minute as I tried to compose what I wanted to ask. Was I still in trouble? How was Papa going to punish me?

We were almost at my father's place when Art made the sharp turn and pulled into the driveway. We came to a sudden halt. "Don't worry about, John," he said, not looking in my direction. Instead, he stared at the barn that needed a lot of fixing. "I said you were doing stuff for me in town."

"Oh. Uh. Thank you, Art. Thank you," I said, stunned, wondering why Art would lie like that to my father. I had one hand on the opened truck door. "Why Art? Why did you do that?"

"Figured you needed a break, is all. Everyone needs one now and then. Even you."

I nodded.

"What were you wanting?"

"Huh?"

"In town. What were you wanting?" Art's face was heavily lined, his complexion both grey and scarlet. Most days you couldn't tell if he looked sick or sunburned. He had leaned over in his seat and I noticed deep burgundy veins wrapped around his thick, pudgy nose.

"A job."

"Why you needing that? Don't you have enough to do?"

"Yes, but I need money. I'm planning on going to Sarah's wedding." I trailed off.

Art looked thoughtful for a moment. "Mabel says the doctor's wife was looking for a housekeeper in the spring. Can you do that and still look after the babe?"

"Yes! Yes of course. I can do it, Art. Will you give them my name?"

"One thing."

"Sure, Art. Name it."

"You didn't hear what I have to say first."

He turned his attention toward the front windshield, paused, and ran his tongue over his dry lips. He tapped his fingers on the dash. It seemed he was reluctant to tell me. "Your father wants you back." He stared out in the distance, focusing his gaze on some unknown entity.

My smile faded but I thought for only a second. "Okay."

"You sure?"

I nodded.

"Here, then. Write your name on that." Art ripped off the top of his cigarette package and handed me a pen he had stashed in his shirt.

I wrote my name in neat printing along with my address. Art watched me, his arm resting on the back of the seat.

I handed him the paper and he tucked it in his breast pocket along with the pen. "I'll get Mabel with the babe and we'll bring back your things."

"All right, then. Will you miss us, Art?" I laughed.

"Just get your arse out of my way," he said gruffly.

I did as he asked. The tires screeched and spun in the snow as he backed out of our drive at full throttle and sped off down the hill.

10: Was that your first time?

August, 1955

Sarah's wedding was in two months, on Thanksgiving weekend. Aunt Martha wasn't happy about the date but there was nothing she could do about it. Sarah had booked the hall, bought the dress, sent out the invitations. Her fate was sealed.

And so was mine. I got the job at the doctor's house, one or two days a week.

In order to keep my end of the bargain while working at Dr. and Mrs. Murray's, I had to not only make sure the chores at Papa's were done and his supper ready by five, but I had to find time for Darryl and Joanne. Art said Mabel would have to help out in my absence. End of discussion.

If I couldn't ensure these promises, I'd have to quit. If I quit, I wouldn't have enough money to go to Sarah's wedding.

Everything hinged on this job. Everything hinged on me. And Joanne did everything to dissuade me.

I stashed the money I had saved in my bureau drawer, inside an envelope. In that drawer, I also kept Mary's brush. There were sprigs of her hair still attached that I sometimes found myself smelling or touching with my fingers.

There was also a small, wooden crucifix that had belonged to my mother. I wasn't sure where it came from. It may have been whittled by her father. Or perhaps by Papa. I dared not show him in case he confiscated it.

These were keepsakes to remind me of my family. The ones that I lost, but I kept together here, parts of them, in the drawer in my room. They were physical remnants of what was. When I put away my money, I'd tell them about daily life, about Joanne's baby and

Sarah's upcoming wedding.

Mrs. Murray had told me I 'shouldn't be late' or else. I didn't think I was. I had left extra early in case. I had even prepared myself by tearing up some of Momma's old aprons to use as cleaning cloths and dust rags. I suppose I had gotten carried away doing it but I wanted a part of her with me when I cleaned.

Mrs. Murray held the door opened a crack like she was scared I was taking the dust in with me. "You're late," she said, jutting her chin, and opened the door just enough for me to enter.

She asked me to remove my shoes, although hers clicked against the hardwood as she showed me around her home. She wore her hair tied back and it was silvery-grey, like her eyes. Her features were sharp: nose, cheekbones. Her lips small, her shoulders, bony. She looked like she weighed no more than a small girl herself.

She showed me everything that she wanted done. My eyes widened with each room, my voice getting smaller and smaller. *How would I do this in one day? Let alone two?*

"Sweep the floors first," she said, talking over her shoulder. She made a litany of demands. The quilts had to be washed and hung outside to line dry. The windows needed wiping and she had a silver tea set that needed polishing. "I want it gleaming," she said, "with no prints."

Once I had that finished, then I'd have regular maintenance of dishes and dusting and anything else she saw fit. I had to roll up all the rugs in every room and beat them with a stick before I could even get into that room to sweep and mop. And there were a lot of rooms. Five upstairs and that many down. The doctor's library needed dusting, so too did the dining room.

As she explained everything from top to bottom, my stomach made an unpleasant growl. I had forgotten to take myself a lunch.

"Today?" I asked, "you want all this done today?"

"You're competent, aren't you?"

She left me with my hungry belly.

The day, however, disappeared, and I was still washing the spindles of the staircase when her shrill voice scolded me for leaving the good area mats outside. "The dampness is setting in," she whined, her face gnarled up like her arthritic fingers.

I hadn't finished and already my limbs ached.

"I'm sorry," I said, feeling weak and nauseated, for I hadn't even had a drink of water since leaving my house this morning.

She shooed me away and told me I had to come back the next morning to finish because she couldn't 'have the rugs going back on dirty floors'. She rolled her eyes. "Oh, the dirt. The dirt. And the rocks will scratch the finish and if that happens, young lady, that's your fault and that will come off your pay!"

I left, feeling the stiffness enter my arms and back and felt I could have lain down upon the side of the road and curled up. I just needed a moment's rest, but I couldn't even do that as Papa had expected me hours ago for his supper and I doubt I could lift a finger to help Joanne with Darryl.

I tried to walk as fast as I could knowing I was already behind schedule, but my feet just wouldn't cooperate. Each step felt like my bones were ceasing. I was sure the muscles in my back would snap or splinter if I wasn't careful.

My palm shook as I unlatched the door. I hadn't the energy to even push it open properly.

Papa, as usual, was stretched out on his bed. He glared at me when I entered the kitchen. I removed my apron and shoes quickly, not saying anything, for what could I say at this point? My face must have said it all, though.

My weakness took hold of me then. I grabbed for the back of the chair and nearly fell down, feeling like a colt would on his first attempt at walking after coming out of his mother's belly.

Papa, for once, did not scold. Instead, he squirmed and turned his face to the wall.

I took a couple of breaths, went to the sink, poured myself a glass of water and gulped it down. I grabbed a biscuit I had made a couple of days ago and nibbled on that while I took myself up to my room. I just needed to close my eyes for a minute, just a minute, then I'd make my way to see Darryl.

~

I overslept. I felt it in my bones, heard it with my ears. The way the wind stirred the leaves on the trees after they lay quiet all night. It was at least six o'clock, maybe closer to six thirty.

And the sun shone on the side of the bed and spilled onto the floor. Another tell-tale sign.

I swore I heard Papa growling at me earlier, banging the edge of the post of the staircase, but I thought at the time it was a dream.

Everything ached—my fingers and arms, my head pounded inside my skull. My mouth was dry like sand and my throat hurt when I swallowed.

I pulled myself up and dressed quickly, buttoning my shirt as I tore down the stairs. Papa had to make his own breakfast and I knew this was a bad sign. The dishes were left from last night as well.

I panicked. Joanne would be angry with me because I didn't help with Darryl. Plus, I couldn't be late again at the doctor's. I had to make up my time. I'd have to make it up to everyone.

As quick as I could, I mixed up a pan of bonnach, threw flour and baking powder into a bowl although it seemed I spilled more on the floor. There was no time for cleaning. As I set the bonnach to cook, I started on Papa's supper. Tonight, he would be getting fish stew. I took the salt cod and peeled the skin off the cold potatoes. There were a few leftover carrots so I tossed them into the broth as well.

I washed all the dishes, wiped the counters, then scrounged for something for Papa's lunch.

There was a small piece of homemade cheese hidden behind a few canned items in the cupboard. I was saving it for myself, but figured Papa would need it more. With a small jar of strawberry jam I had made back in the early summer, his meal was complete. I hoped to make amends for my shortcomings but hope was an understatement.

This time, before I set out, I thought it smart to pack myself a small lunch. One of the day-old biscuits would have to suffice. I sliced it in half and scooped molasses on top. The sticky, black mess stuck to my fingers and I licked it off hungrily. I dug into the undercooked stew, spooning in several mouthfuls, and then I realized I had to go.

I grabbed my biscuits and tore out of the house, the stones and dirt crunching under my loafers. My sides started to spasm, so I slowed, catching my breath. At least the August weather was favourable today and I wasn't walking in a downpour. I was thankful for small miracles and appreciated the beauty of nature on my journey.

The morning air was fresh and the wild roses were all in bloom. Their fragrance was sweet and delicate. I would have liked to pick some for Mrs. Murray's table, but the stems were too tough and the thorns would cut my fingers.

Somehow, I made it to the doctor's house before nine, but when I knocked on the door this time, her small eyes assessed my attire and a heat came to my face. I should have dressed more appropriately perhaps, bathed and washed my hair but where would I find the time?

I smoothed out the wrinkles on my blouse with the palm of my hand and fussed with my hair as she let me in. I just wanted to get started and finish the floors from yesterday, but she already had a change of plans. She led me to her husband's library.

"I need this room cleaned immediately," she said. "Dust the books with a damp cloth. Not a wet one." She pointed a finger in the air. "That could spoil the pages. They'll stick together and then they'll be ruined. You understand?"

I nodded silently behind her.

"Can I trust you with this?" she asked, studying me.

I nodded again, and finally she left me alone. Her footsteps echoed on the hardwood floor.

My eyes went wide when I saw all the books. Never before had I seen so many. Not even at school. I went to them as if I was drawn by a magnet, pulled them out and stared at the titles.

Some dark leather texts felt smooth to my touch. Others were harder or had bumpy indentations. The first few titles read: *Volume Four Muscles, Bones, Joints, and Nervous Systems.* There were others that were *Volumes on the Diseases of Children (Defi-*

ciency Diseases, blood, infectious diseases), a solid red book called *The Practice of Medicine by A.A. Stevens, Illustrated*, and a whole slew of matching books from A to Z.

I was opening "B" to see what was inside when Mrs. Murray called my name. "Miss MacDonald? You get started in there yet? I didn't hear any water running."

I stuffed the book back onto the shelf as quickly as I could. "Uh-huh."

"Pardon me?"

"Sorry, ma'am. Yes, Mrs. Murray. I've started."

I filled up the bucket with hot sudsy water and retrieved my washcloths from the wood room where I had laid them to dry yesterday. They were stiff and hard. I plunged them into the water and began my day.

My armpits sweated, as did the back of my neck. I felt moisture on the top of my lip, too. But if I didn't stick to task, I'd be here another long day without finishing anything. Then I'd be in trouble.

I hummed while I worked and took out each book, wiped, dusted the shelf, and placed it back where it belonged. It was strangely soothing in a repetitive, hypnotic way.

Once I finished with the library, and the floors, a satisfied smirk crept across my face. I was making good time and the room smelled better. I hoped she would be pleased, if not with my appearance, then with my ability.

I took a quick break and sat outside on the back step. There was a nice breeze and the air felt good on my clammy skin. I gobbled down my biscuit and molasses, wishing I had taken more. This was harder work than at Papa's.

"Would you like a cup of tea?" Flora, Mrs. Murray's cook, had asked. Her arm was extended holding a steaming cup. She seemed pleasant. Wrinkles formed around her eyes when she smiled and a tendril of grey hair poked out of her kerchief when she bent down.

"Thank you," I said, accepting the kind gesture. "Can you join me? For a moment?"

She shook her head. She told me to wash the cup and put it away when I was finished.

"Of course," I said, and she disappeared back inside.

I was only supposed to be here twice a week if needed, but with so much to do, I would be here three days at least. That was fine with me. I needed the money.

My mind drifted off as I counted my earnings, chomping on the stale biscuit, washing it down with the good tea.

As I swallowed the last bite, I took in the Murray's property. She had married well. To a doctor, no less! The house was grand with all the wood floors and fine trim and mouldings. She had silver candlesticks and crystal glassware. There were large paintings on the walls and their own library stocked full of books. A beautiful home, but too swanky for me. Too much to clean, for starters.

I laughed at my gall. Like I, Maggie MacDonald of Port Hope would ever own such a thing.

"What are you laughing at?" The voice said.

At first, I thought I was imagining things. I craned my head and didn't see anyone. My heart thumped fast in my chest. Was I that tired I was now hearing voices?

Then I heard him the second time. It was his laugh I recognized. James. I stood at once and searched for him.

And there he was, looking how I remembered, albeit longer and now with whiskers on his face. He was sitting on the woodpile like a cricket, no more than ten feet from me. His knees were bent, his arm resting over the logs so casually.

"Wondered how long you were going to sit there and eat like a hungry horse. Thought you were ignoring me. You're stuck up now, are ya?"

He dug in his pocket and pulled out a cigarette. He lit it and brought it to his lips.

"What are you doing here?" I asked.

He smirked and stood up, walked towards me. There was something familiar about his voice I couldn't quite recall, but instinctively I took a step back.

"I suppose the same as you."

He stood at the base of the stairs and offered me his cigarette. He extended his hand, the white smoke circling around him like a cloud.

I didn't want to be near him, let alone touch his cigarette. He kept waving it, however, the tip turning to ash. *Why is he offering it? What does he want? Is he trying to get me in trouble?*

For a reason I couldn't explain, I took it. Pinched the rolled tube in my fingers and brought it to my mouth and inhaled. The smoke filled my lungs.

Immediately I coughed. I coughed and coughed and coughed. I threw the cigarette toward the wood pile and grabbed my teacup. As I gulped the remnants down, water ran from my eyes.

"That was your first time?" his eyebrows were raised and he chuckled, bemused. "I thought it was old hat for you."

I paused. "Why'd you think that?" I continued to cough and I wished I hadn't tried it. Moreso, I wished he hadn't offered it. I should have known better. Now I felt stupid. Idiotic.

He picked the butt off the ground and took two more quick drags before stubbing it out. "I just thought, because, well, you're at Art's, aren't you? And that night... at the dance."

My face went hot and I could no longer speak. Shame filled my body like a poison. I no longer heard his words. Shame. Shame for that night, for what happened. I swallowed as Papa's words screamed at me. 'You're tarnished.' They rang over and over inside my head.

People talked. Sarah told me so.

It all became so clear. I finally understood everything. It was why I couldn't get a job in town, why the doctor's wife didn't like me, why I will always be alone. It was why Sarah moved away.

I blinked back tears. Without another word, I picked up my cup and rushed inside. I needed to get away and be alone, I needed to wash the stink off my fingers and get the taste out of my mouth.

His words repeated over and over inside my brain for the rest of the afternoon. I wanted to hide forever.

But I needed this job. I needed the money. The only way to get out of here was to work hard and save.

Then I thought for a moment. I needed a plan. I'd turn the tables. I would try and be nicer to James. Maybe then he'd leave me alone.

11: James

It had been almost two weeks, two weeks of trying to be kind, when I realized that it had backfired. I only wanted him to leave me alone, that we would come to respect one another because we worked at the same house. I answered his questions and once, God forbid, I shared my lunch, a meagre piece of bread and homemade cheese. But instead, he followed me around like a mangy old cat.

Today, when I snuck out after work to walk home, the echo in my footsteps meant I had unexpected company.

I hoped it was a joke. I thought he would catch up, say something rude and leave me be.

I bent down, pretended there was a rock in my shoe, waited for him to pass me by. A stupid move. I curled my loose strands behind my ear, and he bent over and looked at me. His sickening smile slathered across his silly face.

"You don't have to stop," I said rudely. "I'm just getting this rock out of my shoe."

He stood waiting, scratched his head, shifted his weight to his other foot.

I took off the other shoe.

"Forget which foot has the rock?" His impish grin remained on his repugnant face.

"Go!" I yelled.

"Now, Miss Magpie. There's no need to yell. I'm right here. I can hear you loud and clear. Why don't you let me help you?"

I threw my shoe at him. It hit him on the shoulder. It didn't hurt. That wasn't the point.

He grabbed my shoe, shook it, turned it upside down, even peered inside it. He stuck in a finger, then made a face. "Nothing there. Imagine that."

He threw the shoe back. "Get it on now and let's go. Your old man will be wondering where you're at."

"No, he won't," I snorted, folded my arms, and took a seat on the road. I didn't want to go anywhere with James MacKellan.

He took a deep intake of breath and crossed his arms. "I'm not leaving you here alone. What if something happens?"

I looked up and down the deserted road. There was nobody there except the two of us and the chirping crickets. Why was he so annoying and paranoid?

"Can you just go away, please and leave me alone?" I wasn't going to budge.

Without warning, he swiped the shoe off my lap and, as quick as a fox, forced it onto my foot. He grabbed my arm, hauled me upright and looped his arm in mine. He began to drag me along. *Drag.* I was mortified.

I tried to stop him, even bent my legs in a crouching position, but he was too strong. I was sure he'd keep dragging me even if I fell. I imagined my face and knees scratched and skinned and bloody. What would Mrs. Murray think then?

Finally, he stopped trying to make conversation because he caught on that I was angry. Tired and so very angry.

As we speed walked in silence, I thought about the Murrays and how I thought I had a good thing going with them. But now, I wasn't so sure. This was simply too much. Him. It. All of it. I'd finish off the rest of my week and then I'd give my notice.

The job was too hard, anyway. Every limb and bone ached from all the scouring. From washing and waxing hardwood floors and stairs. From wiping windows and cleaning cupboards, and for what? So, I could be harassed by this man?

That was it. The decision was made. I was going to quit. Quit, quit, quit! I sighed so deep James thought I was winded.

"What?" He asked with a quizzical look.

I couldn't answer because deep down I knew I couldn't quit. I needed the money. Every red nickel counted. How could I get to Sarah's wedding otherwise? How I wished she were getting married here, at home. I could do so much to help if it were here.

And I had to go because Papa wasn't. Couldn't. For spite or because he didn't have the money? Or for other reasons? Why wouldn't he want to go to his daughter's wedding? Sarah said he had to look after the animals and to prepare the gardens for winter. Pffft. That's as believable as saying Art was good looking.

But he said he wasn't going and that was that. You couldn't argue with him.

I had been lost in my thoughts thinking of Sarah as James pulled me by the hand, almost forgetting he had me in a tight grasp. Surely, if anyone had seen us, they would have thought we were a couple because we were walking so closely and in unison. Thankfully, there wasn't.

When the roof of my house came into view, I told James, "I'm home now. You can let go of me."

 He turned and faced me and said, "How 'bout you give me a kiss first?" He puckered his lips in a mocking gesture and closed his eyes.

With one good strike, I slapped him. Open palm against soft cheek. I heard the *thwack* and my hand burned because of it. I hadn't meant to hit him so hard, but it stunned him enough to let go of me.

But this didn't deter him, he laughed out loud and planted his his lips on mine.

For an instant, I froze, feeling the softness of his mouth but I wiggled free as the heat reached my cheeks. Without saying anything, he grabbed my hand again and continued walking toward my house.

With my free hand, I brushed my lips with my fingertips, felt the roughness of his whiskers on my skin and I shuddered.

He walked me right up to my door and knocked on it hard and rough. "Let go," I said forcefully, trying to unleash him, but his grip tightened. Papa would be asleep on the daybed right now, and cross if awoken. I wanted to run away but his hand still held me tight. He banged again a second time, but instead of waiting for Papa to answer it, he pushed his way in.

Papa met him halfway. I tried to keep my head down, to avoid Papa's eye contact and scolding but it was hard to look away. Like a mouse scurrying from the hawk, I had to know how to brace myself. Papa towered over James and stared down like a great vulture. His dominant presence filling the space around the porch entrance. He glared at me, at our connected limbs.

I experienced an unfathomable hotness in my body and felt as if I would collapse right in front of these two men. If James was intimidated, he didn't acknowledge it. He nodded to my father, finally releasing me and extending that outstretched hand as if he were a gentleman. "Hello, sir. I'd like to introduce myself. I'm James MacKellan. I'd like permission to date your daughter."

My hand flew to my mouth and I coughed.

I strode over to the sink, and poured myself a glass of water. I kept my back to them and bowed my head to say a small prayer. I passed the minutes as I waited for the exchange. Braced for it. In Papa's agitation, he would surely send James packing, and no telling what he'd do to me. But nothing was said.

I turned around to see Papa had sat back on his daybed with only a look of annoyance on his face.

James, however, had made himself comfortable. He had sat down, stretched his arm over the back of a chair, and looked at me like he was gloating.

I wanted to wipe that off his face with my glass.

With a broken glass.

When I realized Papa had no interest in conversation, I mouthed to James to leave and pointed to the door. When he didn't budge, I grabbed him by the shirt and steered him toward the porch.

"You're crazy." I said, I didn't wait for his reply.

He gave me a goofy grin and I pushed him out, locking the door behind.

Despite the disturbance, Papa simply stared at me like he was in a drunken stupor. I wanted him to say something. To at least ask, so I could set him straight.

But Papa didn't ask anything. He didn't care enough, it seemed. He closed his eyes, stretched his legs and drifted off like he always did.

I couldn't believe it. I didn't understand his lack of interest. Anything ever out of the ordinary with me and my sisters warranted some sort of discourse. But with James? Nothing. I wanted to scream at the top of my lungs, or pound my fists. Instead, I grabbed a plate and raised it high in the air. I imagined the noise when it shattered. Would that rouse him? *Speak to me! Say something.* For the love of God!

But he didn't look at me. He just lay there, motionless, like the statue of St. Anthony.

I placed the plate on the counter and curled my fingers into tight fists.

I tossed the washcloth in the basin and stomped to my room, threw myself on top of my bed. I did all I could not to scream for if I started, I would not stop. I stuffed the pillow in my mouth and writhed back and forth, willing my anger to go away.

And James! What game was he playing? Was he trying in his own way to humiliate me? Does he hate me that much? What have I ever done to him? To anyone?

As I lay there thinking, Sarah's face crossed my mind, the way a cloud drifts across the sky.

Sitting up, I stared at the drawer where I kept my savings. I realized what I had to do. "I have be like Sarah," I said, feeling justified. "And leave."

There was nothing for me here. No one would miss me.

And Darryl? Could I leave him behind? Should I? I held my head between my hands as I thought about it all.

My mind spun around thinking of countless scenarios. *Could I stay with Sarah? Could she get me a job in the city?*

I focused on my room. The one I had shared with Mary. There wasn't even a picture to indicate that she even lived here with us. She disappeared like all the others, faded out of our minds like the colours on Momma's quilt. And I'd be no different.

So, I'll go. Yes, that's what I'll do. The matter was decided.

My muscles suddenly relaxed as I tossed the covers over me and lay down. I was still dressed in my work clothes. It didn't matter.

Nothing mattered anymore. Sleep came easily and I drifted off.

I awoke early. I had too much time to think. I thought all night and in my dreams.

I dreamt of the train with Darryl on my lap. He was laughing. Joanne was there too. She wore a pale, blue dress. I don't recall what I wore in the dream but I was happy. I knew then I was doing the right thing.

I needed to discuss with Joanne how she could get money to help pay for her train fare. I was sure Art could lend her some. She didn't work outside the house, but she always had money for cigarettes. I'd tell her the fare was more important than her smokes.

When I entered the kitchen, I stared at the man who had probably said no more than a dozen words to me since my mother died, and maybe a dozen more while she was living. I wanted to tell him that very minute my decision but I clammed up when he looked at me. Instead, I stared at his pink scars he never spoke about. His protruding nose, his long whiskers. His hands. They still had that look of power. Large and calloused and hardened from time.

He grunted when he finished his breakfast and stood up. Pulled his suspenders over his shoulders, one at a time. I watched him preparing to leave and wondered what he looked like long ago. When he and Momma first met and married. Was he happy then? What did she see in him? How could she love this man, this man that barely spoke and grumbled all day? Who kept to himself and only occupied himself with his thoughts and chores?

I wanted to say so much but I said nothing. As I busied myself by clearing away his dishes, I found the words and blurted, "I'm going to Art's today," my tone heavy.

He glanced my way for a second, went to the porch and paused. No, 'good morning' or, 'thank you for breakfast'. No small talk or conversation. He simply grabbed his hat and walked out, closing the door behind him.

I turned, placed the dishes in the sink and it all came out. I screamed till my throat scratched and I lost my breath. My heart beat fast and wild. I thought for sure he would come rushing back but he didn't. My hands trembled and my lip quivered but I dare not cry. I finished the washing, wiped down the table and the counter and walked out, more determined than ever, slamming the door behind me.

12: It was all arranged

September, 1955

"Where've you been?" Joanne asked, irritated. She had deep, dark circles under her eyes, her hair was a mess about her head, and her face and arms: thin and angular.

She lifted Darryl out of the crib and passed him to me. I kissed the top of his head. His sweet, dark hair tickled my lips. I hummed to him the song that I used to hear Momma sing and he snuggled into my arms and drifted off.

"Well, that's not fair," she hissed, looking at the peaceful child. "He tormented me and Mabel the last two nights. I didn't catch a wink. Not even a moment to myself. And there you are." She grimaced in jealousy.

To appease her, I said, "I remember Aunt Martha once saying they like a different pair of arms."

"Let me cut yours off then," she snapped, her lips pressed in a straight line. It was supposed to be funny but I think deep down she meant it.

She went to the cupboard and opened it, poured a liquid into her tea that was definitely not milk. She didn't seem to care if I was looking. She placed the bottle back up high on the shelf and closed the door. She grabbed her pack of cigarettes and lit one, sat down beside me.

Only then, it seemed, did she relax.

That's when I told her about James. She puffed on her cigarette like she wasn't really listening. She studied the smoke as it came out of her mouth, like she was in a trance.

"You should be so lucky," she finally stated. "I would kill for a man to treat me that way."

I tucked my neck in, shook my head. "You're not hearing me. I don't like him! He was mean at school and now he's playing me for some stupid reason. You remember him?" I paused. "I just need to get out of here and away. Away from it all."

Her eyes focused on me like the sun had suddenly shone some light in the room. Like she finally understood me. "How?" She flicked her wrist and inhaled again, sat up closer, like she trying to hear more intensely.

"I have some money," I said. "I've been saving."

"Saving?" she asked, her face as steady as stone.

"Do you have any? I mean, does Art pay you for anything? Maybe if you didn't smoke so much, you could use that money for—"

"Sure. Yes, yes," she said. Then she whispered, "when will we leave?"

"Soon. Sarah's wedding is only a few weeks away. I could write her and tell her we'll be coming early."

"No!" Joanne shouted a bit forcefully. She lowered her voice and her demeanour. "We shouldn't tell her...in case she lets it slip. It should be a surprise."

"Ahh. We just a need a little more," I said.

She winked at me. A smile spread across my face and I felt warm all over. I wanted to jump up and down and kiss her. I wanted to swing Darryl around in my arms, but I just stood there, feeling satisfied, sated. Everything I had worked so hard for would pay off.

"I'll go to the station and get the tickets. It's the only way without drawing attention to ourselves," Joanne said.

"Will we tell anyone? Art? Aunt Martha?"

Joanne shook her head. "Art will tell Papa and no sense telling Aunt Martha anything. She'll sell your soul as quick as you look at her—the old tramp."

My brows furrowed. I hadn't heard any of my sisters talk so ill of our aunt before. The aunt who always did what she could for us.

"Why do you say that, Joanne?"

I placed Darryl in his bed as my arm was getting tired. I put him down on his blankets as slowly and as delicately as I could so as not to wake him, and I covered him.

I asked Joanne again in a dull whisper.

She turned her head, looked out the window. A sneer crossed her face and she hooded her eyes. "Aunt Martha has ulterior motives."

"Like what?" I asked, still not understanding what my sister meant.

"Can we drop this line of questioning? I need to lie down now, I'm exhausted."

And before she left, she said, "I'll get the tickets the next time Art is going to town."

I nodded and let her be, feeling excited as I knew when we'd be leaving. One week from Thursday.

~

It was all arranged. I'd work another week and get more money from the doctor's. I hoped that, by the end of the week, Sarah would send another letter and we'd have enough for everyone.

I felt both excitement and nervousness all at the same time. Half the time I couldn't even think, let alone concentrate. I must have checked the mail ten times one day. I was sure Art began to wonder about me.

And Papa knew when Sarah's wedding was but he wasn't going —too far, too expensive, too...he'd mumbled something I couldn't understand.

Art said Papa had never left Port Hope before. How could anyone stay in one place without seeing what's beyond it?

I hummed while I cleaned Dr. Murray's, probably too enthusiastically.

Mrs. Murray asked, "What's with you today?"

"It's just such a beautiful day, isn't it?" Today was also my last day there, but I would tell her at the end of my shift.

"Oh?" she laughed, "James told me he was your sweetheart. I thought that was why you were in such a happy mood."

I stopped dusting, shook my head. Acted as if I didn't hear her.

No, that wasn't going to stir me up. I could just about ignore everything today, including James.

I went about my chores. He worked at one end of the house and I at the other. He banged outside and I cleaned in. And when Mrs. Murray snapped at me to do the front windows over again because 'Dear God, they're streaky', I just nodded and washed them again. Nothing, and I meant nothing was going to spoil my mood today.

While I took a few moments to eat my lunch, James had the audacity to search me out and sat beside me. I glimpsed at him from the corner of my eyes. He still looked like the mean kid I remembered from school. His hair was long, his eyes dark.

He always made me shudder when I was younger but something about him had changed. Or was it me? I wasn't as frightened as I had been when I was a girl in school. Even my anger towards him had subsided somehow.

"What happened to your forehead?" I asked, noticing the white scar that ran across the middle of his head at an irregular angle. His hands, too, were puckered with white scars and his fingers looked crooked.

He pointed to his temple. "This here is from the wood pile."

"The woodpile?" My eyes searched his face and then back to his cut high on his forehead. "That doesn't make sense. You slip or something?"

"Kind of. More like my father took a piece of wood and swung it at me. I fell on the woodpile. You should have seen the lump on the back of my head. This here is nothing."

I nibbled at my bread, wondering what else to say. "Why did he hit you with the wood?"

"Dunno, really. I think I was cutting it too thick for the stove."

"Did it hurt?"

"Like a bugger, but I didn't cry."

My eyes got big and then small. Papa slapped us a few times, but he didn't beat us.

"Do you get along better now? Now that you're older?"

"Ohh, yeah," he said as if it was a joke. "He's dead now. We get along real good."

"Oh my gosh. I'm sorry. What happened?"

James held his hands to his heart and stuck his tongue out the side of his mouth. "Went down the top of the stairs. We thought he tripped. Everyone held their breath wondering what he was going to do or who he was going to blame. But he never got up."

He made a face. "It's just me and my mother now and my two sisters and three brothers. They're still at home. I'm the man of the house now so I work."

He pulled the cigarette package out of his pocket and lit one up, inhaled. "You're no different than me except it was your mum that died." He winked at me and grimaced. "Your father does barn work and stuff. No money in that. He used to work in the mines, I heard."

"Yeah, but then Momma got sick and he had to stay behind to look after us."

"Look after you?" James shook his head then. "You had older sisters. They could have watched the house and all of you. Like I'm doing."

I sat in silence, having finished my bread and my tea, thinking about James' words. "Well, I better get back to work, else Mrs. Murray won't pay me."

"Yeah, alright, alright."

He hopped up, stubbed out his cigarette, "I'll walk you home later." He said this more of a statement than a question, "Maybe then I can get a proper kiss."

"I don't think so," I said, standing up.

"What? The walk or the kiss?"

"Both." His cheeks turned pink and I laughed.

"How else am I going to court you? How 'bout if we go to the dance on Saturday? I can make plans to pick you up. It would be a real date."

I smiled, but not at James and the prospect of a real date. I smiled because I'd be long gone by then.

I opened the door to the doctor's house and let myself in. Sometimes it was good to leave them wondering.

~

"You want to go to the store today?" Art asked Papa.

But that simple request meant a conflict. If Papa was with Art, there'd be no time to get the tickets. I blinked and my mouth hung open.

"What's wrong with you?" Art asked, his face studying mine.

"Nothing."

I scooped Darryl up and bounced him in my arms. "Papa doesn't need to go," I stated. "He should rest. He looks tired." Art looked at me funny but Joanne grinned. The two men regarded one another.

"Alright then," Art said and left.

Joanne followed, whispered, "Back soon."

I rocked back and forth as they left. I heard the door slam and Old Art's car start up. The sound of the engine faded away as he drove down the road.

Papa sat back down on his bed, but this time he didn't lay back or close his eyes. He sat with his hands resting on his knees watching me, or rather, watching Darryl. It was, as far as I knew, the first time he had seen the lad.

Darryl was getting big, holding his head up, cooing and squealing. For a split second, I swore I could see a sparkle in Papa's eye and maybe even a hint of a smile.

I wasn't sure exactly what came over me just then, but instead of asking him if he'd like to hold his grandson, I walked over and dropped him on his lap.

"Whoa, whoa," he said. "Hold on, hold on."

But he didn't push him away. He held him awkwardly at first, his elbows held high in the air while his two large hands wrapped almost fully around the tyke's waist. Immediately, Darryl's hands reached for Papa's nose and he squeezed it tight.

I was well aware of Darryl's grip and he could make a grown man cry if he grabbed you the wrong way with those sharp little finger nails. I lunged for the baby, thinking Papa was going to holler or drop him, but he did no such thing.

Instead, Papa placed his lips on Darryl's cheek and blew, making a strange sound, almost like a fart. Darryl's face lit up and he squealed in a fit of giggles. Papa did it again and the baby went into hysterics.

I couldn't help but find it funny myself, and watched in amazement how Papa handled this little boy.

When he finished blowing on his face, he stared at him and talked to him in Gaelic, drawing his finger along his face, feeling his skin, tickling him.

"Tha thu math gille? Far an do òrdagan?" Papa squeezed each of Darryl's toes, counting them softly.

They gazed at one another like the two could understand each other's language. Either that or they were having a staring contest.

After a bit, Darryl's eyes grew heavy. I offered to take him, to put him asleep on the couch, but Papa shook his head. He tucked him in the crook of his arm and lay back on the day bed. The two of them drifted off to a tranquil slumber.

To say I was in awe was an understatement. I couldn't believe what had just happened. The two were absolutely enamoured with each other.

I couldn't explain it. It was as if there was an invisible bond between grandson and grandfather. A connection so powerful that went beyond anything that could be logically explained. Something spirtual.

I sat and watched the two sleep in their dreamy, magical state.

The afternoon ticked on. To keep myself busy, I repacked my bags, double-checking for everything. When I finished, I picked up the broom and swept the floors.

I'd catch myself, standing in the same position staring at the two of them, my mind lost in thought. How fitting, as Joanne and I were leaving. Why couldn't Papa have always been like this?

I let them be for a few moments to go to my room and check around one more time, to make sure I didn't leave anything worthwhile behind.

I thought of leaving Papa a note, but decided against it. I'd call him once I got settled. I couldn't imagine him wondering where I was anyway. Old Art's and the doctor's house were my usual hangouts and I had been coming in at all hours. Papa would be bound to think I was simply at one place or the other. Sadly, I realized Papa's thoughts were not with the living.

I rooted around Sarah's room looking for a skirt. There was nothing there. Instead, I rummaged through Joanne's old things that had been packed up years ago.

I found an article of her clothing and held it up. It was grey tweed skirt and it used to belong to Momma. I couldn't believe my luck—it was still lovely. Long and straight. I hoped it would fit. I had a soft pink blouse that would go well with it. I longed to put the clothes on now, so I could look as fitting as Joanne.

I folded them neatly and took them down in my arms, hiding them in my bag. As I tucked them away, I heard my father's snores. I looked at the clock. The afternoon had flown by and the baby began to stir.

Papa shuffled in his seat and cleared his throat, passed me the baby. "He's warm."

"What?"

"Means he's getting sick."

13: Leave him where he's at

Darryl's hair curled with the dampness and he wouldn't settle. He became cranky and agitated, something like his grandfather.

"You better not be like him," I said rather sharply.

My tone must have caught Darryl by surprise because he stopped for a moment and looked at me. Then he wrinkled up his face, opened his mouth and wailed loudly.

I hoped Papa wasn't right about him getting sick, because travelling with an ill child just wouldn't be wise.

I tried to feed him some water but he pushed it away. Instead, he let out a large sour burp and drifted off in my arms. I lay him on Papa's daybed and watched him sleep.

He was a handsome lad. Anyone could surely see it. He had fine, dark hair that curled in the heat, a well-proportioned head and round cheeks, big beautiful eyes with delicate, long, lashes and perfectly-pink pouty lips. His tiny fists rested beside his face and his bum stuck up in the air, arched gracefully, with his small feet tucked under himself.

If I could draw, I would have sketched him. But instead, I stared to remember how in awe I was of him. How happy that he came into the world, although I was sure Joanne felt differently most days. This was not exactly how she planned things: she was young, unwed, and living at Old Art's. But things could always be worse.

I hummed as I watched the baby sleep soundly and glanced at the clock. Papa would be looking for his supper soon. I hadn't really thought of preparing his meal as my mind was so full of thoughts of our leaving. About work once I'd get there. And a place to stay. And who would look after Darryl if both Joanne and I were lucky to find employment at the same time?

In Sarah's last letter, she said there were lots of girls our age who went to Boston to work as nannies and maids. I thought that might be a place I'd like to go, because they said the money was good. She said our lodging would be looked after, too.

As I stared at the sleeping child I wondered how could I possibly leave him? If Joanne stayed in the city with Sarah and I had to be elsewhere.

I sighed and erased the thought right out of my head. There would be no such talk about any of this until we had the tickets in our hands and were seated on the train. Joanne and I could talk and make plans then. All I knew was that we had a couple of weeks till Sarah's wedding and that would keep us busy enough.

I had put on potatoes, and checked on them; they would need a few minutes more. They were the new ones from the garden and would be delicious with our salt cod. We also had fresh turnips and carrots. I loved a producing garden.

Turning toward the clock again, I started to get nervous. What was taking Joanne? She should have been back by now. Darryl would be hungry and she only sent one bottle.

But Old Art liked to talk and he usually had a million things to do. Plus, a million things to get at the general store for his moonshine that everyone knew he made and sold.

My body shook as I thought of that noxious substance. Whatever it was I drank when I went to the dance with Sarah, the taste forced its way back into my memories and a wave of nausea penetrated through me.

My memories of that night weren't all negative. I remembered standing in the hall, watching the MacMaster sisters dance. Everyone had been fascinated with their steps that their mother and father had taught to them. They danced in front of the stage looking so graceful, their legs flashing and feet tapping in perfect synchronization, as light as air. It was mesmerizing, magical.

Everyone clapped but the dancers didn't stop. They kept on as the fiddler played. It was almost like a contest to see who would quit first.

But they came to the end together, and the sisters stopped, as if on cue, and turned to the fiddler and bowed, paying homage.

The fiddler played again and others got up to dance, to show off their talents and their skill. Even I got up brazenly, and attempted a few steps that Momma had showed me, but I was no match for what the MacMasters did, or the other dancers.

The fire in my veins had made me feel grandiose and unstoppable, yet shame filled me now.

At the time, my sister had stared from the doorframe, her eyes wide, her hand covering her mouth, "What are you doing?" she mouthed, clearly mortified.

She disappeared behind the crowd and I skipped off to follow her only to stumble, flinging my shoe across the dance floor. They laughed and I did too as I looked around for the missing shoe.

He had balanced it on his index finger and stared at me with his lopsided grin, his bangs curled into his eyes.

James.

I had not remembered this event until now. I couldn't recall if we had spoken or if I had simply removed my shoe from his hand. All I remembered was his smirk and his laugh.

James.

I drained the potatoes and finished preparing our meal. We would have curds, too, because there was some left.

I removed one of the potatoes from the pot and hoped by eating, it would help settle my nervous stomach. All the waiting was making me anxious.

The new potatoes peeled so easy, you could do it with your fingers. I placed them on the plate to cool and would mash them down to mush for Darryl.

Supper was ready but Darryl was still dozing. I walked towards him to get him up but Papa raised his hand in the air.

"*Chan eil.* Leave him where he's at. He'll need to sleep."

Papa took his seat at the table and rested his long arm against the counter. He took off his cap, placed it beside him and ran his fingers through his grey hair. He rested both his feet on the chair opposite him, something I'd never seen him do before, and I let out a laugh.

"What?" he asked.

"You look funny sitting like that."

I gathered his food and placed it in front of him. He jutted out his chin, toward the direction of Darryl. "What am I supposed to do? He's lying there."

He turned towards his supper, picked up his fork and started shovelling it in. I picked up my plate and sat down opposite him. I found I had no appetite, though, and picked at my meal.

It was now after five and Art had left before lunch.

"Art's late," I stated, wondering if he knew why they were running so behind without having to ask it directly.

"Hmph," he said. It was a bad time to be asking, Papa like to eat in silence.

When he finished, I took his plate and gave him his usual: a biscuit and molasses and a scalding cup of tea. It could be one hundred degrees out and Papa still needed to have his tea.

Darryl stirred and I knew that meant he was hungry. I warmed his bottle and waited for him.

He squealed and complained and made a small ruckus, causing Papa to chuckle at first.

But then Darryl wouldn't eat. He forced out every spoonful of food and every ounce of milk He grabbed the spoon with his hands and pulled at his ears. Darryl went from calm and happy to upset and agitated. I sat and huffed as he continued with his squealing.

To help calm him, I filled the sink and stripped him naked and sat him in it. The water seemed to soothe him temporarily. After the bath, I offered him room-temperature water which he drank little of. His cheeks were flushed and his eyes, glossy.

I stared at the boy, then back at the clock. "Of all the days!" I spat. "What's taking Art? Papa?" I was becoming unnerved.

Papa didn't answer but took his place on the daybed and closed his eyes. It was as if Darryl and I were no longer there. Perhaps he only liked agreeable babies.

I realized if Art wasn't coming here, I'd have to walk to his place. I lay Darryl down and packed up my things.

Papa said nothing when I wrapped up the fussing baby and

scooped him in my arms. He did not say anything, either, when I went to the door and opened it, when the hinges creaked, signifying I was leaving. I wanted to leave it ajar just for spite so the mosquitoes and lazy house flies would get in and torment him. The way he liked to torment me.

But I didn't. I closed it tight and strode off. I looked back several times to see if was in the living room window watching us, imagining and wishing he'd say, 'Wait! Don't go. Don't leave me alone.'

I looked for his image in the upstairs windows, too. I even stopped walking a few times in case he called out and I hadn't heard him. But nothing.

I realized he didn't care if I left. He dozed off on his daybed as the sound of the ticking clock lulled him to a deep slumber. There would be silence again within his house. He'd have all the quiet he wished for.

But where were Art and Joanne?

I focused on the scenery around me to take my mind off things. At least the weather had stayed warm and balmy this mid-September. The sky was soft blue and I heard the summer crickets clicking away in the fields, enjoying the last days of their summer parties. I envied them, always seemingly happy and singing together. Why couldn't I have been a cricket?

I clung to Darryl tightly, felt his warmth against mine. Maybe Papa was right. Darryl was getting sick. He complained when I had to reposition him because the muscles in my arms ached

After rounding the turn, when I could no longer see the roof of my house, the walk became silent and lonely. I hummed an old tune to pass the time. It vibrated between my lips and, as the sun set, it became the Gaelic song our mother sang to us when she did chores or put us to bed. I hadn't realized I knew the words and yet they came out as if I was hearing her sing.

By the time I finished the song, my arms throbbed, yet Darryl's eyes remained shut. I kissed him softly on his forehead and took in his scent. How did we ever survive without him?

I kissed him again and looked up, my feet carrying me the whole way as if the fairies lulled me themselves.

Finally, I turned into Old Art's drive, thankful the long walk was over. I let out a sigh of relief: Art was home.

I walked past the vehicle and stood on the porch step and raised my hand to knock, but stopped myself. I had been coming here so often with Joanne, I felt I shouldn't have to knock anymore. I pushed open the door and walked in.

I wanted to scream at Joanne and Art for taking so long. I placed Darryl in the makeshift crib in the downstairs kitchen and yelled in anger.

"Art! What's going on? Where you've been all day?"

He flinched and looked over his shoulder. "For Jesus' sake, woman. What are you doing here? I thought you were going to stay with your father from now on."

"You didn't pick me up."

"Didn't know I was supposed to."

My mouth fell open. I watched as he went to the cupboard and poured himself a drink. "Joanne said—"

He stopped suddenly and bent his head. He turned around, rested his back against the counter. "What exactly did Joanne say?"

I couldn't tell him what Joanne had said. It was our secret. I squirmed as he waited for me to answer. The silence lingered like stale air between us.

I swallowed this time and the spit in my mouth went down as hard clay. "Where is she?" I demanded.

Art eyed me skeptically, while taking a sip. He wiped his mouth with the sleeve of his shirt. "Maggie. You know she's gone."

He clunked the glass down on the table a bit too forcefully. He didn't take his eyes off me. He sat down and lit himself a cigarette. He held it tight in his blackened fingers.

"Art! She wouldn't...just...." I jumped up and ran to the back room.

"Easy there, lassie."

My head did circles. "You're lying to me!" I hollered and ran up the stairs as fast as I could.

I flung open the door to her room. "Come out, Joanne. This isn't funny." I pictured her hiding behind the door, sniggering, her eyes squinted.

But she wasn't there. Her bed wasn't even made. I tossed the bedclothes, looking for an invisible body. I opened her closet. My heart pounded when I saw some of her things still hung there. There! Her stuff was here.

I went through her bureau, but it was empty. There were no shoes under her bed, either. I checked for her bag. Her suitcase was missing.

I opened every dresser drawer: all her undergarments were gone. I pulled open the curtains and forced open the window. I hollered her name, but she did not answer.

I sat on the unmade bed. The room was stifling hot. The humidity of the upstairs caused my armpits to moisten and the nape of my neck slickened with sweat, yet I shivered. I felt cold and empty. As empty as Joanne's room.

I checked the rest of the upstairs rooms. All had unmade beds, empty closets, musty blankets, yellowed pillows.

I walked slowly downstairs, holding onto the railing, my shoes clicking on the hardwood. When I landed on the main floor, I checked the rest of the rooms in the house: the living room, the kitchen, even the wood room. I walked back to where I had left Art sitting and a numbness fell over me—shock, despair.

By now, he had poured himself a second shot and had butted out his cigarette, leaving a stream of smoke amongst the ash.

"When, Art?" I asked, quiet in my voice.

He looked at me but didn't answer at first. Finally, he said, "You already know the answer to that."

I thought of the money that I had saved and worked so hard for. I scratched my fingernails on the table. There were cigarette burns and water stains and knife slashes, whether from cutting or carving. Joanne's name etched amongst it.

The air had gone out of me. I sat there, unable to process what had just happened and why. Why? Why had my sister left me? She knew how much this meant to me? To us? She knew how long it took me to save. We would have a better life and we would all be together, the four of us.

"Did she say when she was coming back?" I asked, feeling hopeful. Maybe there was a misunderstanding? Maybe that's it. My heart raced, thinking of the possibility till Art opened his mouth.

"Why don't you go lie down?"

He didn't look hopeful. He looked glum.

That's when I picked myself up, bowed my head. My shoulders stooped as I walked out to the porch. Without saying anything, I pushed opened the door.

The air had cooled as night settled in. The sky was now a deep azure with little pin pricks in the night sky. Oranges and soft marigold settled over the tree tops, signifying the sun's last rays, as it, too, put itself to bed.

I shivered, perhaps from the heat of the house and then the night's cooling air, but also from my sister's deception. I placed one foot in front of the other, my steps leading me to a place I did not know. Back to Papa's? Back to my home where the silence was as cruel and distressing as my sister's betrayal?

Maybe I'd just walk until I no longer could. Until I lay down upon the earth and let the good Lord take me.

The door creaked and his words startled me.

"Maggie?"

I turned around.

"Where you going?"

I couldn't answer. There was nothing I could have said that would tell Art the answer to his question.

My eyes blinked. I turned again and kept walking.

"Maggie! The babe is waking up."

14: A low buzzing sound

October, 1955

Joanne left behind her baby. Her sweet, innocent, little boy. Was it because she thought he may have been stricken with something so awful, she simply couldn't handle it? Like consumption or small pox or something far worse? That the only thing that she thought best was to leave? In case of the evitable? But, if she just knew that it was something so insignificant. That all babies get sick no matter what we do to prevent it. I wished I could have told her that. That it wasn't anything she'd done.

But her actions said otherwise.

I could still see her staring at me when she came in that day holding Darryl, her face expressionless. She held him as if he were no more than a bag of flour in her arms, and she handed him over easily. Perhaps the detachment started then? She didn't say good-bye or kiss his cheek, give him one last squeeze or even cry. She did none of that. Maybe she just felt so incredibly guilty that she just couldn't be around him at all? Or me? Or was it all a ruse?

I had understood time was of the essence that day. Art had things to do, and places to be. She didn't want to appear nervous or anxious. Things had to run smooth. Flawless.

But for her to simply leave without saying anything. And, with all my hard-earned money? All of it?

I shook my head. Did you leave me to be with Sarah because you missed her so very much? I prayed that you arrived safely.

And when I thought of Sarah's wedding, the tears stung my eyes. I told myself not to, because weddings were about joy and happiness. But how could I not feel sadness when I would be absent from my sister's happiest day? I bent my head.

Shame.

I knelt on the floor in my room, palms pressed together. I had taken in the shock of Joanne's betrayal. It had been four days since she had left and I had not heard from either sister. I prayed that Joanne had arrived and they were both together.

But what if Joanne had no plans to see Sarah? Nor go to the wedding?

I chewed on my fingernails. I decided it was best not to contact Sarah. I looked down at my nail beds. I had nothing left to pick.

On day five of Joanne's disappearance, I decided to write to Sarah after all. I started the letter three times and each time, I jumbled it up and threw it away. What could I say? How do I say it?

> Your sister, the thief, has run off. She left behind the baby –
> if you see her, can you tell her to contact me?

Never have I felt so alone in all my life, even though Darryl filled the void in so many ways.

Yet I remained empty somehow. Papa maintained how he always was, quiet, uncommunicative, unresponsive. At times, he'd interact with Darryl. When the baby babbled a blue streak, Papa would stand behind me, stroke his toes and the soft pads of his feet. He'd speak to him softly in his mother tongue and the boy would simply stop and stare as if he were hypnotized. Their eyes locked together in an enduring trance.

And while that was happening, my mind kept playing back to Joanne. To the day I first told her about my savings. Her face had remained cool but her eyes, I recalled now, had opened just a bit bigger. She must have planned on leaving then.

My heart ached. It ached for what I was supposed to be doing. Was I supposed to be on that train? Why was I still here? Why was I being punished?

Darryl stirred in his sleep.

I rummaged through all his stuff Joanne had dropped off that day, looking for something, a letter, a note. But no, there was nothing.

It was now seven o'clock and it had rained heavy all day. The grounds and fields were so saturated with water we surely thought we'd sink to our chests if we ventured out in them. We were cooped up inside, with Papa lazing most of his day in his usual spot. Or growling looking for something to have with his tea.

Even Darryl was unnaturally fussy today, Papa's unhappy mood making him tense.

The night had finally settled in and there came a low buzzing sound at the window.

I got up to see what it was. I rolled up a piece of paper into a tube to kill the fat housefly. They get sticky and noisy this time of year. Buzzing at intermittent intervals just to irritate you.

But it wasn't a fly. It was a bee.

I wasn't sure how it got in the house or, more specifically, up into this room. He was small, not the usually plump ones you see in the summer clinging to dandelions and wild roses, filling their faces with pollen. It was slow moving, too, like it had been stuck up here all day, tired and weary like the rest of us.

I wondered if he was calling for his family, shouting the way bees do. But no one heard him, no one knew he was here. They were all tucked away in their hives, I supposed, feeding on their thick, sweet, honey they had been busy preparing all summer.

I studied him for a moment, listening to his sad, pathetic sound.

I opened the window and watched him fly off and vanish into the darkness, feeling a sudden tinge of jealousy.

15: The spit of his father

I was sixteen now, a few years older than Joanne was when she first looked after all of us, when Momma got sick and had to stay in hospital. I was looking after my sister's baby and I wondered which was easier: Three girls under ten? Or one ten-month-old boy?

To say I loved Darryl was an understatement, but I found mothering very hard. He constantly needed my attention, thus the reason why Joanne looked so worn out. I was not exactly sure when we were supposed to get sleep.

It didn't help when Papa banged on the ceiling with the broom stick because Darryl woke in the middle of the night, when the gas pains hit, or the teething pain, or from his sore red chafed bum.

Through my countless sleepless nights, I awoke to Papa standing over me, his face, two inches from mine, cussing in Gaelic. He'd fire the blankets off me and point to a screaming child whom I had not heard, thinking instead it was horses whinnying in some sleep deprived dream.

I didn't recall the baby waking so often with Joanne in his first few days of life, although I remembered Old Art taking shelter in the barn.

But whatever Darryl was going through now only agitated me more, because I truly and deeply felt he was missing his mother. It was as simple as that. Yes, the teething could be responsible and the sore bottom, but the scent of his mother's skin or a touch of her hand or even her voice would be something that could have helped soothe him. There was nothing I could do to appease that loss. I was only his aunt, with no more ability to look after and care for a new baby than a stray dog.

I knew not how to care for a child other than to love him and do odd bits an auntie can do. I didn't even help care for my own siblings, as I was a mere child myself. Yet, oddly, I had always felt like I was the youngest because I was so shy and nervous. Mary could run circles around me. She even talked long before I did. So, I was not the fittest person to be caring for this child, but who would that leave? Papa? And as bad I was, he would be worse.

There were times when I thought I would lose my mind if he made another whimper in the middle of the night. Or when he was getting ready to wake and his lungs were preparing to belt out that painful screech he had perfected. Yes, I admit, on those dark nights in the thrust of mid-fall, when night came early and frost covered everything with its shimmery blanket, I wished for him to stop—for me not to be his caretaker. I wished for his mother or some other person to take him.

But I never actually meant it.

~

Sarah's wedding had happened and I longed for a picture. I was happy to hear it all went well.

Sarah told me what she wore, what they ate, and the many gifts and telegrams they received. I hadn't even thought to send one.

I sighed, feeling ashamed, and closed my eyes, imagining the day and the festivities. Imagining she was happier without me in it.

But it appeared no one questioned Joanne's attendance, or lack of, or why I wasn't there. It was assumed, I supposed, that I was too young, that it was too far, that I had no money and since my father was not going, that I shouldn't go also. But it was a disgrace that Papa didn't attend.

And I longed to tell Sarah about her sister's transgressions, but how could I? I couldn't disclose the degree of our sister's dishonesty on the happiest of Sarah's days. No, I simply couldn't.

She was disappointed I couldn't go and told me so. She asked about Darryl, though, and said she'd try and come home the following summer to meet him.

"Oh, I'm so happy for you, Sarah. I wished we were there."

I felt a sudden sadness, an ache in my chest for what could have been. Why couldn't all of us been together that day? Not just myself, but Momma and dear Mary, too.

"Oh, thank you, Maggie. I wished you did, too." She began talking, then, to someone in the background.

"Are you talking to Joanne?" I asked.

She fell silent for a moment, then responded, "We're going to—"

At that moment, I bounced Darryl a bit too hard and cracked his head on the phone, prompting a loud wail. I patted the back of his head, which only made him cry harder. He was mortified that that was my best attempt at solace.

"I better go," Sarah said. "Your hands are full. We'll talk again, okay, Maggie?"

"But...but when is Jo"—the phone clicked—"coming back?"

But I already knew the answer. I had felt it in my heart the day she left and took the money.

Joanne wasn't coming back. Ever.

~

It was strange, now, to be in the house at the age of sixteen when I should be out in the world. Although I knew every nook and cranny here—the fourth stair that creaked, where to put the bucket when the heavy rains come—it still seemed foreign. I felt trapped, or maybe deserted, and so my longing to leave was all the more urgent.

I needed to remember the people who once were. To see them, to smell them. But I had no photographs to remind me of their faces and my memory of them was fading like the yellow embroidery on Momma's curtains.

It was almost three weeks since Joanne left. I hadn't seen anyone in that time except for Old Art. I had not ventured into town, either, as I had had no need nor desire to go.

I had told Dr. and Mrs. Murray I no longer required employment, that I was leaving Port Hope for good, and for them to pass along the information to James. I wished that I hadn't, as I was again without employment and no employment meant no money. How could I ever get to Ontario without money? The thought of begging for my job back with a baby attached was simply illogical.

I retreated further into myself.

The depths of despair I felt then were overwhelming. There were days when I thought I was losing my mind. I didn't want to get up, or eat, or play with Darryl. All I wanted to do was sleep.

I spoke to Momma and Mary, asked for guidance, but they never answered. Deep down I knew if I wanted to survive, I needed to get out. Anywhere. I just needed to get out of the house.

The day was clear and cloudless, a warm autumn morn. The landscape was peppered with brilliant colours: tangerine, mustard, crimson, and deep forest greens. The day lured me to take Darryl out.

I wasn't even sure exactly where I was headed. I just walked. After some time, I saw the house, and Aunt Martha's blank expression as I walked up the lane.

I had Darryl cradled in my arms. She had her face pressed to the window, mouth twisted, eyes narrowed into tiny slits, trying to identify me by my walk. Or by my hair, but that was pulled back and tied with a kerchief.

I could tell she didn't know me until I stood on her porch door; then I saw that look of recognition. Her mouth dropped and her eyes rounded. She kept glancing at me and then at Darryl, and looked at him with utter amazement. Like he just dropped from the heavens.

She scooped him from my arms instantly, tucked him into the nape of her neck despite his squeals and protests, and bounced him in her arms. I could see hints of Momma in her eyes and mouth when she smiled. Her hair, though, was mostly white, and she kept it swept high off her face and tied back in a tight bun.

She had been making bread and had just finished kneading the dough and putting it to rise in its bowl. The house smelled pungently of sweet yeast.

"Why weren't you at your sister's wedding?" she demanded,

looking at the baby. "It was beautiful," she cooed in baby talk.

"I-I couldn't make it," I said mournfully.

Aunt Martha stared at me for a moment. She looked at me like I was lying. "The first niece to be married on my side, and your sister. You should have been there. No excuses. Shame on you. Your father, on the other hand..." She shook her head.

Then her tone changed. "But you know, if she had gotten married here, where she should have in the first place, then it would have been a proper affair."

She nodded at me. That was her way of telling me she didn't agree how Sarah got married; wondering too, I supposed, if she had a bun already in the oven, as most young girls do when they go away to get married.

"It wasn't like that," I said, but Aunt Martha didn't pay attention to me. She had her mind already made up.

She didn't mention Joanne, either, and I was glad about that. I didn't want the questions, the interrogation, or having to say anything that would make her look bad in any light. I was sure Joanne had her reasons for doing what she did. At least, I hoped so.

"No, I didn't get to go..." I trailed off, wondering what to say next.

By now Aunt Martha had the baby sprawled on the table. She had stripped him out of his blankets and looked over every inch of him as if she was studying the embroidery on a fine quilt.

Then an expression formed on her face as one of surprise, if that's the best word. Confusion, maybe. Her eyes shifted from side to side, then her mouth turned down at the corners.

She studied Darryl, her hands under his armpits, her face a mere inch from his. "He's a dead ringer for Jarod."

She got quiet then, and I saw water fill her eyes. It streaked down her face in fine beads.

Jarod was her only son, who was killed during the war. He was older than Joanne by about three years and had passed away before Momma got sick. There had been an explosion. He happened to be near and he didn't stand a chance.

It was something Martha had had a hard time accepting at first, checking the mail daily for any letters he may have sent, thinking they had him confused for someone else, that there had been some dreadful mix-up and it was sure to get straightened out. She had believed that for years. Seeing little Darryl didn't help her.

"Doesn't he?" she stared into his dark eyes and at his tuft of hair. When he started to cry, she pressed him against her chest and hurried out of the kitchen into her living room.

I heard the sound of drawers being pulled open while she said, "Where is it?" She dashed about from room to room looking for the mysterious something.

She brushed past me and into her room, rifling again, then came out and passed me the baby, still in a daze, mumbling, "Hold on a moment," and went back to her room.

She shuffled around this and that, with boxes being pulled out from under beds and bureau drawers squeaked open 'til, at last, she hollered, "Here it is!"

She came out holding a piece of paper, only it wasn't. She held it up for me then placed it down on the table so I could get a better look. It was a black and white photo, an old one, of a baby—dark tuft of hair and rich, chocolate eyes. The face was a bit elongated compared to Darryl's, but had the same sort of chin and nose. I was looking at Darryl's twin, if he had one.

"That's bizarre," I said, studying the picture and the uncanny resemblance of the cousins.

"Mmmm hmmmm," Martha said, looking more at Darryl. "Is this your baby, Maggie?"

"Well, no." I blushed, feeling suddenly embarrassed for some reason I couldn't explain, even though I shouldn't have felt that way at all. I felt like I was being charged with something. Or accused. It was Martha's tone that made me nervous. "I don't understand, Martha. Why all the fuss about the picture? We just came down to see you. I was feeling a bit off, lone—"

Martha snatched Darryl from my arms and placed him on the far corner of the kitchen floor with a clean rag to chew on. She tapped him on the nose and smiled and talked softly before turning toward me, with her brows furrowed and a change of voice.

"Did you come here to throw this in my face?"

"What?" I asked, confused.

"Get out, Maggie. I want you out of my house!"

She pointed her index finger to the door. When I didn't get up right away, she lifted me by the arm, pulled me up off the chair and pushed me toward the door. The sudden aggression and tone upset the baby, but this didn't stop her.

She had me by the back of my shirt and pushed with such force. With all my might I struggled, but there was nothing I could do. With her free hand she turned the knob.

She almost had me outside, but I managed to grab hold of the door frame. "Aunt Martha? What are you doing?" I was frantic and confused, my heart beat so fast. "The baby! Aunt Martha. He's crying."

We stumbled. "What's wrong?" I asked again and when she didn't respond except with her physical strength, I shouted, "All right, then! Just give me the baby and I'll go."

"Oh, no, I won't, young lady. He's staying with me."

She shoved me with all her might to release my grip. I'm sure we must have sounded like lunatics, the three of us, crying, and grunting and shouting.

"Aunt Martha!" "Why are you doing this?" I gasped for air.

"Get out!" she screamed. "Get off my property, you lying bitch!!"

"I can't leave the baby! He belongs with me"

She stopped suddenly and became as calm as a millpond. Her dark eyes stared back at me like something had snapped inside. It was eerie. The baby stopped screeching, too, taking a sudden reprieve from the noise.

This strange quiet that came over the three of us caused me to relax in that moment. I panted still, but released my grip from the door. Standing opposite her on her porch, I asked, "Martha. I'll leave, okay? I'm s-sorry if I did something to hurt you or said something to insult you. I didn't mean anything. I-I just, wanted to come see you is all. Honest."

But Martha said nothing. And I didn't have the guts to make a move. Every ounce of my body was frozen till Darryl's sudden squawk shook us out of our stupor.

"He's the spit of his father," she said coldly, "so that makes him mine. It was our agreement."

She slammed the door and turned the deadbolt.

I banged on the door with both fists, screaming for her to let me in. My knuckles turned red from flesh hitting wood.

I ran around the house and checked all the windows but they were locked tight. I ran back to the front door and kicked it with my foot.

My voice cracked as I called out to her, begged her. But my calls fell on deaf ears.

I placed my ear to the door and listened, really listened. I heard her soft murmurings, talking so sweetly to Darryl to try to calm him.

I cupped my hands around my eyes and peered in her window, watching her as she held the baby in her arms, kissing him, and then they disappeared into the other room.

With nothing left to lose, and nowhere else to go, I ran home to tell Papa. I ran. Even though every part of my body dripped with sweat. I ran. Even though my tongue stuck to the roof of my mouth. I ran hard. With each spasm, I kept running with everything I had.

It was the sound I heard first, Art's horn. *A whooo ah*—his signal for me to get off the middle of the dirt road.

But I didn't. I turned around and waved my hands in the air, frantic. I shook them so high and so fast, like an airplane's propellers.

His brakes squeaked and the car skidded to a halt. I limped to him, threw my hands on the roof and ranted incoherently.

"What are you saying?" Art asked.

I opened the door and crawled inside.

"*Dè tha thu ag iarraidh?*" Nothing came out but a mixture of ramblings and screaming.

I pointed towards Martha's house.

He slapped my hands and mumbled to himself as he made a U-turn. We were driving in the opposite direction.

"To Papa's!" I yelled.

"Jesus, girl. Okay! Alright."

I hung onto the dash of the car as he braked suddenly. His toothless mouth opened wide and he cussed as the car slid making the manoeuvre.

"Hurry!"

Art did as I instructed and we rocketed toward Papa's at an ungodly speed. "Jesus, Maggie. You were jumping around like a screaming banshee in the middle of the road. What's gotten into ya?"

He parted his long bangs to the side of his head to help him see before tossing his cigarette out the window

We finally rounded into the drive with our heads hitting the roof of the cab. Our bodies jerked and swayed with the motion of the car.

When it came to a stop, I flung open the door and ran out as fast as my feet would take me. I ran to the house searching for Papa. I called to him, but he wasn't on his daybed, or in his room.

I ran to the living room and started up the stairs before I caught myself and rushed back outside.

Art was just getting to the porch when I told him Papa wasn't inside. By now, I must have spooked Old Art because he was rushing after me down the hill toward the barn.

I didn't bother to open the gate, instead leapt over and cleared it by a mile. The cows chewed their cud with timed precision. Their soft eyes paying me no heed.

Around the back of the barn that's where I found him. He was holding a pitchfork, scattering the old hay and manure. His eyes met mine. "*Dè?*"

Breathless, I said, "It's the baby! Martha took him."

By the time Art had caught up to me he was out of breath, too. He bent over, heaving and rasping and spitting on the ground.

Papa's eyes got as big as wagon wheels and he stuck the pitchfork in the ground with such force I thought he was going to plant it.

He walked toward me with one great stride with those long legs. "*Can sin a-rithist?*"

So I told him. I told him about me going there because...because...I couldn't tell him why. I couldn't explain it. But it didn't mean anything. I told him that. *But then she thought the baby looked like Jarod.*

Papa looked at Art, who had his back tilted at an odd angle. It looked as if he had given himself a massive kink from the running. Papa grabbed Art by the forearm and muttered in Gaelic.

"She went crazy," I said, "and then she th-threw me out...and I did-didn't know what to do."

My body gave way and I collapsed onto myself, but Papa caught me and held me. He cupped his hands under my armpits, like the way he held Darryl when he sat on his lap.

His hands were strong and, as I found my strength, he released his grip. He placed his hand on my shoulder and squeezed it before setting off toward the house.

I tried to race after him, but Art grabbed me by the shirt and held me there. "Let him go on his own. This is something he has to deal with. Something he has put off for a very long time."

16: What your mother used on all of you

I tried to shake off Art's grip, but he was too strong. By now, Papa was out of sight. His long legs walked with purpose and he surged along like a creature of the forest, disappearing before I had a chance to catch up to him.

"Come 'mere," Art said to me, holding me by the shoulder and steering me towards the house. "You can make me a cup of tea."

Without warning, he swatted me in the rump with the back of his hand, so sharp and hard that I let out a yelp. "You should know better."

I ran my palm over where he hit. *I should have.*

Art took his place at the table, the seat closest to the porch. His hands were stretched out and I noticed his fingers and nails were black with soot. "She'll get what's coming," he said, his voice deep and hoarse from smoking.

"What do you mean?" I asked. "Papa wouldn't hurt her, would he?"

He waved his hand in front of him like he was swatting a fly. "You have an overactive imagination."

"You just said—"

"I said," he pointed a finger at me, "he'd do what he had to. Now, get going with my tea. I'm starving."

Art didn't open his mouth till he finished his first cup of tea and had inhaled the biscuit and molasses. He then took out his cigarettes from his pocket and lit up. He flicked his ashes on his plate as I watched the clock.

I turned to him. "Now?"

"Do you have anything stronger in the house?"

I sighed. "Papa doesn't keep anything in the house, Art."

He laughed and I felt self-conscious and stupid. He knew more about the man I had lived with for the past sixteen years than I did.

He walked to the high cupboard at the farthest end of the wall and reached up. "Here, pass me that chair. Your father is a lot taller than I am."

The chair scraped across the floor as I dragged it over to him. He stood on it, rummaged around, and brought out a small jar full with liquid. He opened it and inhaled. "Ah."

He stepped off the chair and took a quick glug. It splashed onto his cheek and he wiped it off.

Then he leaned forward, rested his forearms on his thighs. "Your father couldn't speak a word of English. Did you know that?"

I shook my head. "What does that have to do with the baby?"

He stopped, grimaced, like I had insulted him. "Will you give me a God-damn minute to talk without interrupting? Where do you get those manners?"

My face heated and I bowed my head. I tried to collect his plate to put it in the sink, but he said, "Now, sit down, sit down. You're like a mouse in the attic, scurrying about shittin' and smellin'. Pass me a small glass."

"But you just told me to—"

"Give me a glass," he barked.

I did as he ordered and he poured a wee drip into the glass and passed it back to me. "Now, drink that...slowly, just a nip now. And shut up while I tell ya. It's not your first, I know. So don't go all silly and foolish on me like a young girl."

As he said 'young girl', he made mockery by holding his hands together, sticking out his tongue, wiggling his shoulders and crossing his eyes. I guess that was what he thought of us girls.

I held the jar to my nose, shuddered, and took a sip like he instructed. It tasted like fire.

"Now...where were we? Ah. Your father. Yes. He couldn't speak a word of English. You know why?"

I shook my head.

"Because he lost all of his family in a fire. Before this house, there was another. They lived not far from here. Your father was only a boy, you see, and his father spoke the Gaelic to him. He only knew a handful of words of English, taught to him by his mother."

"I don't get it."

He closed his eyes for a minute processing my interruption but continued. "He was out helping with the horses or the cows, I'm not sure which, probably both, and it was just coming spring but cold as a hatter. So cold it froze the tip of your nose and the toes in your boots, if you were lucky to have them. The missus, was, we think, throwing wood in the fire and it caught on her apron. Your father heard the screams, so he ran. He could run like a deer but, even so, he was too late. The clothes had been hung to dry by the fire, sheets and night shirts, and they would have gone up in flames like that."

He snapped his fingers.

"And the girls, well, they were a lot younger than John and they hid upstairs, I suppose, after watching their Momma burn to the ground. That's where they found their bodies. The kitchen was in flames by the time he got there and he couldn't get in. Something blocked the door and the water was frozen in the well so he couldn't put it out. He burnt all his hands and most of his upper body trying to get those poor souls out. By the time his father, your grandfather, came home, the rest of the house had caught and there was nothing and nobody left."

I gasped, appalled. "Where was his father?"

"He was at your other grandfather's place. But not your grandfather at the time, you see? The place where Martha lives now belonged to her parents, Duncan and Belle. Their children, your mother, Mary Louise; Martha; her sisters; and brothers lived there, too."

He winked. "Your father was only a boy then, remember, but your grandfather, Red John, was doing some work there, fixing the roof. Your mother and Martha were just young then, too, so they shared a history going way back."

Art looked up to the ceiling. "But when it was time to rebuild this house, "Duncan the Traitor," he spat on the plate, "wouldn't lend a hand, nor offer to help, not send a biscuit or even a few coins for lumber. And if your grandfather hadn't been there that day, well, none of this would have happened."

"Duncan the Traitor?"

"That was his handle. He was known to be sort of dirty, you know." He made a face. "And your Aunt Martha ain't no different, from what I'm seeing."

He took another snap of his drink. "That's why, when it was time to rebuild, your grandfather wanted the stone. Thought it would be safer, you see? He became a stone-mason and a very good one. He built a few of the houses around here—The MacAskills down in Glengarry, and the MacLeans on Chisholm's Brook."

I found myself caught up in the story, but when he stopped and sipped, I wondered if he was telling me all of this just to pass the time, or to shut me up. He seemed to like to talk, unlike Papa, who maybe had reasons not to.

"So, now you're wondering what this got to do with your aunt?"

I took a sip, my eyes glued to his. "How did Papa end up with Duncan the Traitor's daughter then, if he spurned his family?"

"Ah, you're smarter than you look. Well then, your father had terrible burns on his face and hands, he was pretty grotesque, let's say that much. Part of his face looked like melted wax and he didn't talk for a very long time. Your grandfather, sadly, died a few years later. It was his heart, I reckon, or the bottle, and so your Pa was alone again. He was no more than twelve, thirteen maybe, and that's where I come in. We lived where we do now and so he came to stay with us. I was like his big brother, you could say. He learned the English from my mother all the while he finished his own place, where you live now."

He planted a firm finger on the table. "He always planned on living alone because he knew no one would have him, you know, because of his ugliness."

I thought about Papa's face. Maybe that's why he always had whiskers—to cover up the burns. They'd dissolved over time to a soft pink, then grey, the same as the embers from a long-ago fire.

"So now, more time had passed and Duncan the Traitor's daughter found herself in a pickle. Well," he laughed, "knocked up the stump and, back in those days, as blasphemous as Satan himself. What could they do but marry her off?"

"What happened to the man who—?"

"He went off to the war. And anyway, she hadn't even realized she was pregnant when he left. And not soon after he went off, they heard he'd died. That's when she found out she was with child. She didn't know what to do."

I was stunned. I had no idea my parents had had such tragedy in their lives. "That's so sad, that he died."

"So there she was, pregnant and unwed with no prospects of marryin' the father, or so she thought. So, her family, they took advantage of your father. With his burns, he couldn't fight in the war, and he was the only bachelor living nearby. He had his own house, too, and he was working on the stones at the church, respectable-like. And maybe your mother's mother felt badly, you know, that they hadn't done more for him. So, she gave him someone to take care of him and cook and clean for him."

"You mean..." My mouth hung open and he slowly nodded. I reached for my glass and took another drink.

"Your mother married your father to keep her integrity. She would raise the baby as John's."

My eyes swam in my head. My sister was not my father's daughter! "Are we—?" I choked.

Old Art nearly pissed himself laughing. He slapped his leg hard with his hand and he rubbed his eyes. He chuckled when he lit his cigarette, but then he coughed and spewed, taking a fit as he hacked. He drank the last of the liquid from the jar, which seemed to somewhat suppress his coughing.

"Well, yes, as far as I know, your parents are your parents. But not Joanne. And what do you know, like mother like daughter. She too got herself knocked up."

Poor Joanne. "Art?"

"Mmm hmm."

"Did Jo know that Papa wasn't her father?"

"As far as I know, no, but she certainly looked different than the rest of you."

"I always thought she looked like Momma."

"Aye. She did. Now remember, your aunt has the same dirty streak as her father. Martha couldn't have any more children for whatever the reason. The Lord"—he pointed to the ceiling—"thought one was enough, I'm guessing, and with your mother not well and in and out of hospital, ample opportunity for Martha to get Joanne's child and raise her as her own."

"But Joanne was sent to live with you! Papa wanted her out."

"Yes," he pointed a finger in the air, "but not for the reasons you think. Who do you think sired Joanne's bastard?"

I shook my head. "I thought it was you."

Art's eyes bulged and he remained silent for a minute before laughing out loud and slamming his hand on the table. "Me?" He shook his head. "I've no use for women in my bed."

He jutted his chin to see what I had left in my cup and then reached out and took it from me and finished it off. "Joanne came with me so I could keep an eye on her. To protect her."

"Protect her from whom?"

Art grimaced. "From them people. Your aunt and uncle."

"But why?"

"Your Uncle Dan was the father of her baby. I think your Aunt Martha talked Joanne into that bizarre arrangement, but I don't think she understood the depths of it. Your mother wasn't around to explain these things and your father certainly didn't know, till her belly gave her away. But the deal was, your Aunt Martha would raise the baby as hers. Who would know the difference?"

He shook his head. "They tried to have all this arranged before your mother came home."

"And you know this to be true?"

Art nodded slowly, "Sure as shit stinks."

I gasped.

"Martha would've sold her soul for that baby. Any baby. She was always jealous of your mother having all of you and she couldn't.

But when your mother came home, Joanne had confessed and changed her mind. So, Martha was going to tell Joanne she wasn't her father's child. That she was illegitimate. The dirty cunt."

"Oh." I couldn't think of anything else to say.

He wagged his finger. "She's manipulative, and her sticking her nose in and creating situations, well, that's probably why your mother died. The stresses were too much for her delicate heart."

Art emptied the jar, cleared his throat and bowed his head. "Things never went according to plan. They seldom do." He clinked the glass on the table several times. "That why your father had to go there today. He'd never see that boy raised in the arms of that deceitful, manipulative bitch."

He paused, licked his upper lip, his eyes staring off ahead.

We heard a commotion and both turned to the direction of a wailing baby. Papa was home. He held him under his arm like a parcel tied up with string.

"Papa!" I shouted. "You're not holding him right."

Darryl's face turned scarlet as his body shuddered and he pumped his small legs. I held out my arms and Papa passed him to me. The little thing convulsed in short even gasps. I shushed him and held him close.

Papa sat on his bed for a moment before getting up again, agitated. I wasn't sure if it was from the baby crying or from what had just happened between him and my aunt.

Art didn't stay and ask questions either but said goodbye in Gaelic and then left.

I tried to console Darryl, but he was too upset despite my shushing and humming. I swung him in my arms and tucked my nose into his belly. He smelled of urine and sour milk and feces.

This wouldn't help him to calm, so I stretched him out on the table and stripped him off. I heated the water, all the while, holding naked Darryl while singing and hushing. His head bobbed up and down over my face.

Papa stood beside me when I placed Darryl in the washbasin. I carefully submerged him and this soothed him dramatically. Papa watched as I soaped him down. I cupped the water in my palm and rinsed his small chest.

He spoke to him in a soft voice, "You're a strong boy. *Thu làidir gille*. Shhhh."

The lad looked up at him, dark eyes staring into darker ones.

Papa took his forefinger and ran it across his cheek. "He's hungry," he said.

I was mesmerized. I knew they shared a bond, some affinity with which I could not describe nor understand. Maybe because he was a boy? Or maybe reminded him of his younger siblings that passed away all those years ago?

Then I thought of Joanne. Had he felt the same way about her, too? The fact he helped raise her from birth? Or maybe he simply enjoyed Darryl because he had time now. He realized how fast they grow up.

I hesitated to spoil the moment we all shared. It felt like we were finally a family. We connected, maybe because I understood just a little bit more what my father went through as a young person. About his losses. We were both about the same age when we lost our mothers.

I looked up at him and he smiled at Darryl soaking. I waited a moment longer, knowing the special time we shared would end, then I lifted Darryl as quick as I could out of the water. He did not deserve any more suffering today.

When Papa saw his red, chafed bottom, he reached up high in the cupboard, where Art got the jar of liquid, and pulled down a tin.

"What's that?" I asked.

"Talcum. It's what your mother used on all of you."

He opened it and handed it to me. I looked at it. It looked like flour. I smelled it but it had no scent.

I coated his sore bum with the white powder. I fed him then and burped him and he started to drift off in my arms while I hummed one of Momma's songs. My voice trailed off when I heard another voice, my father's, singing the same tune in Gaelic.

As the baby drifted off with the sweet lullaby and from his exhausting day, I thought about asking Papa what happened between

him and Aunt Martha. I opened my mouth, then shut it.
    I decided it was best not to say anything.

17: Art was right

February, 1956

My relationship with my father had grown into a somewhat respectful, working, albeit nonsensical arrangement. I had this baby to raise. I was not the mother, and he was not the grandfather, but he provided the food, shelter, amenities, and I did my part by cleaning, cooking, and ensuring a quiet and subdued atmosphere —although that proved difficult with a very verbal, busy, little boy.

There were times when Papa near lost his mind and grumbled and complained when Darryl woke in the middle of the night due to teething or sickness. But he adjusted somehow, and the three of us, learning to adapt to one another, although some days more successfully than others.

I often wondered how Papa coped when we were all babies, but I was told that he was away at the mines for most of it, and Momma raised us by herself. I couldn't fathom what it must have been like raising so many children, when I could barely manage one.

The winter months trudged on like a person walking in waist-high snow. Slow, painful, exhausting. The weather prevented the possibility of any visitors, too. Not that we received many, but even Art's face would have been a welcome sight on those grey, dreary days.

Papa reserved his vocabulary for himself, mumbling or saying his prayers in private as if one utterance would cost him a penny. The only company I had was Darryl, and even my days with him passed deliriously slowly...yet the calendar months turned over.

I awoke one morning and found the cradle empty. I leapt to my feet, called out, shouting excitedly. I ran down the stairs, taking two at a time and nearly collasped at the landing when I heard them. A great big rolling, belly laugh.

I stopped midstep, peeked in and watched. Papa had Darryl on his lap, his large hands cupped under his arms, empty bottle on the counter and, in his Gaelic, speaking with the boy. Papa opened his legs and let Darryl fall through, the wind thrusting his hair sideways with the dip. When Papa returned Darryl to his closed lap, Darryl laughed and laughed. Papa did this over and over while Darryl put his finger in his mouth and chewed on it waiting for the next fall, his cheeks as red as winter apples.

Papa caught me out of the corner of his eye and then said something so low I couldn't hear. He pressed the baby close to his mouth and signalled for me to take him. I walked across the floor and reached for him. The baby turned instantly and opened his arms back to him.

"Thank you," I said. "For letting me sleep in. Sounds like you were having fun."

Papa shuffled in his seat, then got up and said he had to go to the barn.

That's when Darryl said his first word. Not "no"or "mama" or "dog." He said it as clear as you or I would.

"Papa."

~

There was no other way.

It was wrong. Everything. All of it. The state of our lives. Nothing made sense, and if I remained, everything would just get more complicated. The only reasonable thing I could do, should do, was leave with the baby and find his mother. I contemplated this over and over in my mind till my head hurt.

I explained to Art that the baby had said his first word and what it was.

"He should be saying 'momma'," I told him, concern in my voice. "He should be with his real mother."

"There's no way of knowing what his first word could have been if someone else had raised him," Art said. "It could have been cunt."

"Art!" I yelled, shielding Darryl's ears.

"Ah, he don't know what that means."

He bent forward and tickled Darryl's chin, and then he started saying curse words. "God-damn-it, arsehole, f—"

"Art! Stop it! That's enough!"

But all I heard was his wheezy laugh. When he calmed, I asked, "So you think Papa will be alright then...on his own? He won't care if we leave?"

Art waved his hand, dismissing me. "He'll be alright. He's been on his own before, remember? He'll probably be glad to be rid of you."

I felt insulted, but Art wasn't one for sugar-coating. He told the truth, matter-of-fact. After supper, I'd tell Papa we were leaving.

~

Art was right.

Papa didn't say much, really didn't even acknowledge what I had said.

I asked him a second time if he understood me, if he heard me right. He nodded, finished eating, drank his tea and lay down.

I wondered if he had done the same ritual when Momma was alive and we were small. Where would we be at suppertime? Here? At the table? I imagined Momma trying to keep us quiet while feeding us, all our mouths opened wide like little birds, and her shovelling in mashed potatoes and carrots, like what I did now for Darryl.

He was fourteen months and getting plump. His cheeks were round and his hair had sprouted out on his once-bald head. But he needed to be with his mother. I knew that. It wasn't right this little boy should be saying his grandfather's name first—no, it was wrong. Dead wrong, and my insides boiled when I thought of it.

Joanne had left her flesh and blood because why? Because of Uncle Dan and Aunt Martha? They wanted Darryl and would do anything to get him. It had proven too much for her to handle.

I tried to quell my negative thoughts as I packed the last of our belongings and placed them in the suitcase. It was Momma's from long ago. I recalled her having it, and Papa hauling it in the last time she came home from the hospital. I was happy to see it then. Although I didn't understand it would be the last time she would use it.

I pressed my hand over the top of it. It was a smooth, rubbery fabric, light blue, almost faded to white. I remember thinking it was quite fashionable and imagined where Momma got it, and where she went with it.

I had always hoped there would be something inside it, like jewels or toys, maybe a special dress. But there was nothing when I opened it. It was as empty as my memories of her, now fading with time.

I had left word by letter with Sarah that I was coming. She called me when she received it and said she was thrilled and excited to meet Darryl. When I asked her if she had any contact with Joanne, she huffed. She had not seen hide nor hair from her, and she promptly changed the subject. She said she had some special news to share but I pressed her to tell me now.

"We're expecting," she said, excitement in her voice.

Our conversation was interrupted. "How long are you two going to be on the phone line?" It was Mrs. MacNeil, her voice harsh and rough. "I need to make a call."

"Mrs. MacNeil, I'll be off in a minute. I'm speaking to my sister Sarah, long distance."

"You better not stay on long, then. It'll cost you. And you've got no money." The phone clicked suddenly.

"Who was that?" Sarah asked.

"Penny's grandmother. She's on Art's party line here."

"When's Papa going to get a phone?"

"I doubt he will. He doesn't drive yet, either, you know. And Art is older than him and has his own pickup."

"Is he taking you to the train station?"

"Yes."

"Okay. Well, I'll see you when you get here. Take care. Don't forget to bring some food for the trip. You'll get hungry. And I'll have dinner waiting for you when you arrive."

My mouth watered at the thought of Sarah's meals. I hadn't eaten that good since she left. She was, after all, the main cook in the family. Martha said one time that Sarah took after her mother, my grandmother, for being so good to throw a meal together.

Martha always complimented Sarah and made comparisons to her side of the family. She told me I was like Papa.

Finally, I knew it was time to go because I heard the vehicle pull up. Art's truck door squeaked open and groaned shut. His loud voice carried up the stairs.

I clicked shut the suitcase, grabbed it with two hands and lifted it off the bed. I walked awkwardly down the stairs and into the kitchen and dropped it before Art's feet. Then I ran back and bundled up Darryl.

When I got back down stairs, Art was already out in the truck and Papa sat on his daybed, head bowed, tapping his fingers together.

"Well," I said. "I guess it's time."

I looked at Darryl, who seemed to sense the tone. I was so nervous, going away for the first time, being on a train, wondering how Darryl would fare out—what if the noise and sway of the locomotive would upset him? Would he miss these surroundings?

I took a moment with him, pointing to the stove and the sink, talked softly while catching my breath. "Say good bye to Papa." I took his hand and waved it for him.

Papa looked up but his mouth remained downcast. He stared at Darryl. He stood up and rushed to us, "I'll—" he said, but then silence.

He touched Darryl's hand and spoke so low in Gaelic. I had no idea what he said, but Darryl seemed to know. He placed his small fingers in his mouth and then on Papa's chest, right over his heart.

"Papa," he said.

The horn honked.

I looked towards the door. "I have to go," I said again and pulled away, turning around to see him take his seat back down on the daybed. "I'm not sure when we'll be back."

He waved his hand at me, dismissing me, and when I went to the door and looked back the third time, the house took on a whole new dynamic. It suddenly looked old, and cold, and neglected. Like no one lived here, just an old man who wanted to be by himself.

Before I shut the door tight, I took one last glance at my father. He had buried his face in his hands.

18: She's not what?

Ontario, March, 1956

"Really? Like real tears?" She sounded like she didn't believe me.

"Yeah, Sarah. Really. Oh, I don't know." I sighed. "It looked like he was. Maybe he was thankful we were leaving."

"I never saw Papa cry. Ever. Even when Momma passed."

"I'm just telling you what I saw. I'm not lying. My God, this is delicious. What is this again?"

Sarah beamed with pleasure. "Lasagna."

"Never heard of it."

"No, you wouldn't back home because there are no Italians. My neighbour showed me how to make it. I thought you'd like it."

I grinned back at my sister, thankful to see her so happy and doing well. She had cut her hair after the wedding. It was short now, a sleek coif that looked sweet on her, and when I watched her buzz around her kitchen, she looked like she had always lived here, belonged in this city.

Her house was so warm and cozy. The walls were a soft, creamy yellow. She had pictures displayed of her and Colin over their fireplace. The brick house was small, but had three bedrooms on the second floor. The main floor contained the living room, kitchen, washroom, and porch.

"You don't burn wood," I said, noticing the absence of logs.

"Electric," she said. "So easy. Just turn up the dial." She pointed to the small rectangular box on the wall.

"All the latest technologies, I see. I think we live in another century back home."

We both laughed.

"Yeah, I was really taken aback when I first arrived here. I thought I was from Hicksville. But you'll adapt pretty quick once I show you the ropes and your way around. You can stay with us as long as you like. You know this." Sarah grinned.

I recalled a time when all I wanted was to was live with my big sister on a farm, somewhere close to home. Everything was so different here from what I was used to. The streets were paved, for starters, and the stores were massive. Some even had restaurants in them. Long countertops with stools serving malt shakes and hamburgers.

Sarah's neighbourhood was busy and loud. Everyone had cars and you could hear the kids playing on the street. Something we never heard at home. We only heard the whoosh of the wind and sound of the rain as it hit the windows. I wondered if I could ever get used to the noise, living here.

I got up to help Sarah. She was just getting over her morning sickness and didn't have so much as a bump to tell she was pregnant.

She saw me staring at her belly and intuitively patted it in a circular motion. "We're just so excited." Her eyes sparkled. "My only wish would be that Momma could be here. Or even Aunt Martha. I have so many questions."

"Why ask Aunt Martha? Joanne would know about delivering a baby. Ask her?" My eyes narrowed. "Or, do you mean, you won't ask Joanne?"

Sarah placed the cutlery on top of the dishes with a clang and started clearing off the table. I helped her by putting the plates in the sink and turned on the water. She squirted in the soap from a bottle and it instantly created a frothy, bubbly, sweet-smelling lather. She didn't respond to me all the while but after she dried her hands on the towel, led me to the table and asked me to sit down again. She stared into my eyes. Her expression was serious and I flinched when she squeezed my fingers in her own. They felt soft and strong, like Momma's.

I let out an uncomfortable laugh. "Sarah?"

"I should have had this conversation with you ages ago...but really," she said awkwardly, "I wasn't sure if you would've come. You bailed on me the last time."

"I didn't bail, Sar—"

Sarah closed her eyes and held up her hand. She breathed deep. "Okay, Maggie," she said in a very quiet voice.

I searched her eyes. They were full of concern. Her lined forehead and furrowed brows told me something bothered her. She squeezed my hands tight again.

"Ow, Sarah. You're hurting me."

She released her grip. "Joanne is..." She looked away, like she was searching for a word. "...is...not. Joanne is not."

"What's wrong with Joanne? She's not what?" My voice raised. I tried to rush it out of her. "Not what, Sarah? Tell me."

She sighed. "I'm trying to be delicate here. I love Joanne. I loved her. She was my first best friend. Jesus, you're not making this easy."

My heart raced. I remembered when they shared a room together and told each other secrets. I remembered feeling jealous of their friendship because I hadn't shared it with Mary.

"Joanne is not here anymore." She sat back in the chair. It groaned as she moved. "She's gone, Maggie. She's gone." Sarah shook her head and placed her hand on her tummy again, patting it gently. "She's—"

"I know, Sarah," I interrupted. "I know what you mean. She had a baby and changed. She changed so much."

Sarah shook her head.

"She drank a lot of Old Art's shine and she smokes a lot, too. I didn't want to tell you, Sarah, because I know how close you two were."

I bit my lip, swallowed. "She stole from me, Sarah. I'm sorry. She took all my money I saved and ran off. She left me behind. That's why I didn't come to your wedding. I would have come. I would have."

Sarah's mouth hung open in disbelief. I had told her the worst thing she could possibly hear.

I bowed my head. "I'm sorry, Sarah. I didn't want to tell you. I'm so sorry."

Sarah placed her hand on my head and stroked my hair, shushing me, telling me it was okay. I lifted my head and stared into her dark eyes. Her face smiled but her eyes looked sad. She didn't say anything for a long while.

"Well, Maggie," she opened her mouth but nothing came out. Her eyes scanned the room and she took a deep breath. "If Joanne's...a thief... then I can't have her here. Period."

"What? That's a bit harsh, isn't it?" This wasn't the way I wanted things to pan out.

"She stole from me, too, Maggie. She stole whatever she could take and whatever would fit in her purse."

I gasped out loud.

"She stole the pearls Aunt Martha gave me as a wedding present, for starters."

"Aunt Martha gave you pearls?"

Sarah got up and walked to the living room, reached for her wedding picture and admired the pose of her and her husband before setting it on the table in front of me. There, around her neck, was an elegant strand of white pearls. "All the MacPhee women wore them on their wedding day. They were passed on from our grandmother Belle, and from her mother and then given to their girls. Martha wore them and Momma did too and then all of us would. But Martha wanted me to have them as she knew I'd be the only girl left to get married in our family."

I felt shame but I knew this to be true. I was tarnished and no man would ever have me.

"Anyhow, Joanne helped herself to those."

"Oh, Sarah. That's just awful. I'm so sorry."

"I know. But she also stole money from our wedding cards. She stole my clothes. My shoes. And you should have seen her at the wedding. She held it together for the service but she got loaded drunk and then went all pie-eyed with the groomsmen at the reception. Uncle Dan had to escort her home."

"Uncle Dan?" I started coughing.

"What's wrong? Here. Drink some water."

I gulped the water down, trying to suppress my cough.

"So, I don't want to see Joanne around here. She's not welcome. The girl is troubled. You understand that, Maggie? Imagine! Stealing from your own sisters. We were never raised that way. I really don't know what to do for her. Dan had to take her home the night of the wedding. I can't stay in touch with her now that I'm pregnant."

She patted her stomach again. "It will be too hard on me and the baby. Putting up with that nonsense. Okay? No more word of Joanne." She nodded like I had agreed with her.

"But Dan took her home?"

"Yes. Always had a soft spot for her. But everyone loves Uncle Dan and Aunt Martha."

I choked. "Not everyone."

Sarah seemed like she didn't hear me. She yawned, stretched out her arms. "Maggie. You'll wash up those dishes. I think I'm in need of a nap. All that food and discussion made me tired."

"Of course. Of course." Before she went into the other room, I hollered, "Where is Uncle Dan, by the way? He's not still up here, is he?"

"Yes. He's here. He comes for dinner on Sundays. He's working, not quite sure where. I told him you were coming, so he decided to stay around. You'll get to see him tomorrow. He's rather excited to see you both. Darryl especially."

My expression must have alarmed Sarah because she took one look at me and said, "What? What's the matter, Maggie? What on God's green earth is wrong now?"

By the time I had finished explaining to Sarah, Darryl had woken up and he was cranky. He cried for most of the afternoon, fussing, not sure what he was wanting. Maybe it was the new surroundings.

Sarah was pale and exhausted-looking. I knew pregnancy was hard on her. Maybe it was all these new revelations about our family, or the fact that she couldn't get any solace with a crying nephew.

"Here, let me try holding him for a while," she said. "Sometimes fresh arms help."

I handed him over to her.

"Hard to believe I'm going to have one soon." She cupped her left hand around his head and pressed him to her chest. She walked around the room with him, singing and talking softly. When he wailed, she'd bounce him again. She must have done this for a good ten or so minutes before handing him back to me.

He finally settled when I wrapped my finger in a clean dish rag and let him chew on it. "He must be cutting teeth," I said.

"Gosh, all these things we have to know. How are you doing it?"

I shrugged my shoulders. "I'm winging it, I guess. Isn't that what everyone does?"

"Not sure. How did Momma do it when she was alone?"

"I don't know," I sighed. Poor Momma. How *did* she do it? "I wonder if Aunt Martha was any help in the early days."

"She would have to be. Gosh, her only sister living so close to her. The rest of them moved away. One of them died young."

"Like Momma?"

"Yes. Something to do with the heart. She was twenty-two. A year older than I am now," Sarah said, shuddering. "I hope that doesn't happen to us."

She thought for a moment. "You know, when I think of it now, Momma and Joanne always shared a special bond."

"How so?" I switched arms to hold Darryl, who was getting so heavy now. The muscles in my arm started to ache.

"They talked a lot, you know, whispering in the kitchen. And laughed about things. I just thought it was because she was the oldest and had more responsibility. I remember being jealous. But now it all makes sense, doesn't it? Joanne was her first, and her sweetheart's daughter. She must have seen his face in hers all the time."

"Like it brought her comfort?"

"Maybe. I just couldn't imagine planning on marrying someone, getting pregnant and then they died! Imagine how awful that would be? It would be devastating," Sarah said.

"Don't be thinking such sad stories. You could be upsetting the baby."

I placed Darryl down and gave him a toy. He started to chew on it and then slapped it on the floor. He only stayed satisfied for a few moments, however. His mouth turned down and he crawled over to me.

I gave him the rest of his milk and he drank it, running his little fingers through my hair as he sucked.

Sarah watched in awe. "You're a natural."

I bowed my head and smirked, embarrassed at the compliment. I wasn't sure why.

"You'll be great to help me out when I have my little bambino."

"I'll do what I can but I really think I should take Darryl to see Joanne and—"

"Oh Maggie. Didn't we just have this conversation?"

"I have to, Sarah. For him." I nodded in Darryl's direction.

"And what, Maggie?"

"But she's his mother," I cried out.

"Maggie. You're his mother."

I didn't say anything but felt my face getting hot.

"Let's just see what Uncle Dan says tomorrow when he comes?"

I shook my head fervently. "No, Sarah. I don't want to see him."

Sarah turned her head sideways, like our old dog used to when he didn't understand a command. Her eyebrows furrowed, "He already knows you're here and he really wants to see you and Darryl."

I sighed out loud and felt my hands tighten while my insides churned. I cradled Darryl into my chest. "Then I can't stay."

"Maggie! You're being foolish." She opened her mouth in disbelief. "Where will you go?"

"It doesn't matter. I'll—"

"You don't even know your way around. And you have no money."

Sarah grabbed my arm and spoke in a strong but steady voice. "Uncle Dan and Aunt Martha have been nothing but good to me, Maggie. To us. If you really believe all these...these allegations, then

I'll get to the bottom of this."

I shook my head. "I don't want you to, Sarah. Please."

"Why?"

"Because Art said he was not to be trusted. Among other things."

"Art said that?" She made a face and laughed. "Art. He's nothing but a—"

"Art was good to Joanne and me! And Darryl. And Papa and Momma, for that matter. He has never asked for anything in return. Ever. He was there for Papa when he was younger, when he lost his family. I'd believe Art over Uncle Dan any day."

"Well, Maggie. Uncle Dan said that Art was not an honourable man, nor Papa either, and the only ones that kept us well and fed *was* Uncle Dan and Martha. So, it looks like we are at a crossroads."

I agreed, but what was I to do? I had to find Joanne and ask myself what was going on. "Just tell me how to get there, Sarah. Please?"

Sarah groaned. She looked more tired than ever. "Very well," she said in a cool, defiant tone. "But you won't find anything and the person with all the answers will be here. For the record, Uncle Dan is the sweetest, kindest, most generous man. You'd understand if you spent some quality time with him. Honestly," she laughed a little too exuberantly. "And when you find Joanne, you can ask her herself who the father of that baby is."

19: Why'd you come?

I left shortly before noon on Sunday. The snow clumped in spots on the walkways and the air had a sharp bite to it. I tucked Darryl's scarf taut around his face. He didn't say anything as I held him in my arms, wishing I had a stroller to push him, like the other mother I saw earlier. I held Darryl tight and hoped spring wouldn't take long to come here. I was sick of winter.

Darryl had plumped up and filled out in the past few months. I wondered if Joanne would recognize him.

I sighed. *Am I doing the right thing by bringing him here?*

Doubts constantly swam inside my head. Sometimes I thought I should have stayed home with my father. I could have raised Darryl there in the country, the way we had been. I would have done my best to take care of him and school him, and I was sure Papa would have done his part in his own way, too.

I stopped walking and gave my head a shake. The cold was making me stupid.

The apartment was on the corner of Lancaster and Wilson. Sarah had written the address on a piece of paper that lay folded in my pocket. I reached in and touched the corners, felt the smooth paper, reminding myself it was still there even though I had it memorized.

I jerked to a full stop when I saw it: her building. It was a three-story brick complex with large windows and a walkway leading up the centre. Never had I seen a place so modern-looking.

The street was relatively quiet despite the fact there was a garage directly across the street and a corner store beside it. I also passed by a barber shop. as well as a grocery store. Joanne was lucky to be living in such a close proximity to everything.

I pushed open the heavy glass door and looked for her name, but it wasn't there. I pushed a button beside her apartment number. It made a terrible buzzing sound and Darryl whimpered.

I pushed another number and the door made another sound. It clicked and I was able to open it and go through.

Sarah had said the apartment was on the third floor.

My arms vibrated carrying Darryl up the three flights of stairs and I was happy I could soon put him down. Standing in front of door three-zero-five, I knocked. When there was no answer, I waited for a few minutes before rapping again, louder this time. My knuckles reddened with the force.

Still, nothing. Sarah had told me where the spare key was hidden, and when I pulled back the mat, there it was. I stuck it in the lock and the door gave way.

"Hold on," she said from the other side.

"Let me in, Joanne. We're tired." She opened the door a crack and I could see her long hair and the corner of her face peeking back at us. She had a cigarette in her fingers and its smoke billowed up to the ceiling.

I took the key out of the lock and offered it back. She seemed embarrassed as she signalled for us to come in. It looked like she had lost more weight.

The room was dark and littered with bottles, and ashtrays a mile high with cigarette butts. There were unwashed pots on the counter in the small kitchen and dirty plates on the table. She walked to the living room and opened the curtains to let in the afternoon brightness. She moved a few articles of clothing out of the way and pointed for us to sit.

I sat with Darryl on my lap, looking around. I unzipped his coat and took off his hat.

"Aren't you going to say something?" I asked, patting down Darryl's wild hair.

Joanne sat opposite me in one of the dining room chairs. She lifted her leg up, brought it close to her and rested her forearm on her knee. "How's he doing?" She pointed, staring at him.

"He's good. Don't you think?" I looked down at him, smiled, and adjusted him on my lap. "Do you want to hold him?"

She shook her head. "Not just yet. He might get scared or something."

She stubbed her cigarette, stood up and walked toward the kitchen. I always knew she was slender but this was the thinnest I'd ever seen her. "Want some tea or something?" she asked.

She clanged around until she found the kettle, and filled it with water.

"Sure." I wasn't sure what else to say to her, even though I had come all this way. She stayed out in the kitchen until the kettle whistled. I heard the stove click and water gurgled as she filled up the teapot.

"Did it take you long to get used to that?" I hollered.

She didn't answer. Cups and bottles were moved around. Obviously, she was looking for something clean. After a few minutes, she came out holding two cups, one steaming, and the other really not doing anything. She wasn't having tea.

"Why'd you come?" she asked, taking a slurp.

"You mean to the city? Or here, to see you?"

She turned her head sideways, popped another cigarette into her puckered lips, struck a match and inhaled. Smoke came out her mouth and she sat back, opened her arms. It looked like she relaxed a bit. "Both."

"Well, I came here to find work and make some money. There was nothing back home. You can attest to that. And I came here to see you because I miss you, but more specifically I wanted you to see your baby."

She waved a dismissive hand in front of her face.

"Why'd you leave him? Leave us the way you did. Don't I deserve an explanation?"

This was when she smiled and I could see her teeth were as rotten as Art's. I tried not to stare but she caught me and cupped her hand in front of her mouth.

She didn't answer the question; instead, she replied, "I borrowed that money so I could get these fixed. They wanted to pull them out back home but I didn't want to do that. Sarah said they have good dentists up here. So, I thought"—she shrugged—"I'd do that."

"You took my money without asking to get your teeth fixed up here? Why didn't you just tell me?"

"I didn't think you'd let me."

"Oh, Joanne."

"What?" she snapped, looking at me like I had insulted her.

"I'm not here to fight, okay?" I said in a soft voice. "We...just wanted to see you."

"Well, you've seen me so you can go now."

"Joanne!" I felt my eyes brimming with tears.

I stood up with Darryl and walked towards her with him. She raised her foot to keep her distance.

Darryl recoiled, and whimpered and squealed when I tried to put him down. I turned him around and cuddled him while looking at her. She butted her cigarette and finished off the drink she had in her cup.

We didn't say anything to each other for a few long minutes. I just bounced Darryl while she stared into space, then studied her nails.

Finally, I placed him on the floor. "It was just so terribly lonely home with no one. It was just so hard, Joanne. And then you left me."

My tears started then and I didn't want her to see me. "Here," I said, sniffing. "Watch him and I'll clean up."

I forced the two together and walked into the kitchen to stop the sadness before it started and to find the soap and a clean dishcloth.

What has happened to my sister? She was no longer the person I remembered. Not only physically, but her demeanour and attitude were unlike the girl I once knew. Was my memory failing? She used to be so patient and kind, and caring. She did everything to make us feel loved while Momma was in hospital. Even before then. She cooked and cleaned, braided our hair, told us stories.

I could still picture the four of us in her and Sarah's bed, tucked under the covers on really cold nights, our feet meeting in the middle and Joanne making up these grand stories. 'Once upon a time', 'a long time ago', 'In the dark, dark night.' Sarah and I would bunch the quilt up to our lips with only our noses sticking out.

I recalled when she'd get a piece of candy and she would all let us take a nibble, just so we could have a taste—so it wasn't just her, the eldest, who got to see, and sample, and do. She wanted us to experience all the joys she had, as little as they were. She, however, being the oldest, got to experience all of it, the best of our mother, but possibly, the worst of our father. She was both envied and revered by the three of us.

My heart felt heavy. I longed for the sister that I once knew.

I peeked around the door frame and watched her with Darryl. She looked down at him as he held his bottle. His little pinky finger stuck straight in the air, and she stroked it with her long, skinny fingers, like she did when he was first born. Then she brushed her hands through his hair.

I tore myself away to allow her some alone time with him. I soaked the pots and wiped the counters with hot, sudsy water. What luxuries to have, and yet not to appreciate them.

There was so much mess, I wondered what she did all day besides drink. At least at Old Art's, she was responsible for keeping the place in order. There was food to be made and she had to cook it. Here, even the fridge contained very little.

What did she eat? There was orange paste in a glass jar, a bottle of milk that looked thick as cream, red broth in a bowl, eggs. There were a couple of bruised apples. The freezer had mostly frost and a thin cardboard box housing an aluminum tray that said *TV dinner*.

I wondered what that was as my stomach made noises. While the hunger pangs groaned, I daydreamed about Sarah's roast beef dinner with gravy and mashed potatoes.

Again, I peered around the corner. Darryl had gotten pretty comfortable dragging himself around the apartment, squealing. Joanne even smiled.

I came back and we sat in silence for a while, watching Darryl playing on his own. This seemed to give Joanne some solace. She waved to him, played peek-a-boo behind her hands. I wanted to comment how wonderful this was but kept quiet. I didn't want to spoil the mood, the moment.

There was so much I wanted to say. So much I wanted to ask but I didn't feel it my place to do either.

I didn't believe Joanne's story, but she did leave me. Maybe she had a valid reason. Maybe I would never understand it. Maybe she didn't either, but seeing her look at him made me think that maybe everything would be alright. She could be a great mother if she was anything like the way she had been with us.

I recalled those times, the happy sadness we always felt. The longing for a mother who was more absent than present. The father who was present but always absent and bitter. All I wanted to do right then and there was hug my sister and tell her it was going to be okay and that everything would work out. I'd help her in whatever way she needed. How many times had she been there for us?

It was nearing two thirty and I knew I should be getting back. The two of us, however, had said little, too lost in our thoughts, or too scared to say anything at all.

When I looked at her, she looked in the other direction, avoiding my eyes. I glanced at the clock again and sighed. It was time to go.

As I was putting Darryl's hands back in his jacket, the door rattled and the handle turned. Joanne and I looked at each other.

"Are you expecting someone?" I asked.

Uncle Dan walked in as if he owned the place. He paused briefly, gazed at Joanne and then looked at me, seemingly startled. But he caught himself. "Well, isn't this fine? Getting to see you, Maggie. Sarah said you were coming by. I just thought it would be when I was here. And what happened here?" he laughed out loud. "Some magician came in and poof, snapped his fingers and cleaned this place up?"

Joanne chuckled like it was funny.

I nodded hello and tried to get Darryl's arms in the jacket, but my hands fumbled.

"Oh!" Dan said in his gruff voice. "Who's this?" He smiled and my guts rolled.

He removed his hat and peered down at Darryl. Joanne remained quiet and aloof but when I saw Dan touch Darryl's face, bile crept into my throat.

"Let's get a good look at you."

Before I could say anything, Dan pulled the baby out of my lap, scooped him into his arms and held him high. "My! He's a looker."

Then Joanne stood beside Dan and the two of them looked like they were suddenly playing the part of a perfect family. They cooed and laughed, admired the handsome boy they had created, while I stared in stunned disbelief.

I reached up and grabbed Darryl right out of Dan's arms, the same way he snatched the baby from me. I gathered what I could and ran for the door, rushing down the stairs, leaving Darryl's bottle, and his hat and scarf, too. I didn't know what else to do but run. That's what my brain told me.

I ran hard. The wind picked up and tousled my hair. It bit my ears and nose but I couldn't stop until I was clear of that building. Clear of Joanne, and clear of Dan.

I heard them holler for me to stop. Joanne called my name, then there was nothing. All I heard was the slap of my feet on the pavement, the sound of my breath and the pounding in my ears. The baby was heavy in my arms but that didn't stop me either.

I ran until I couldn't and finally, when I did slow, I took deep gulps of air and panted. I had run a marathon. I felt exhausted, and hot, confused and dazed, and when I looked around, I didn't have a clue where I was.

~

"My God, Maggie, where've you been? Do you know what time it is? Uncle Dan's been calling. He said you just bolted out of his place. He thought you were insane. You really have us worried. Enough is enough. Okay?"

Sarah looked at me, concern in her face. She held open the door as I walked in with a very stinky, tired child. I turned and waved to the woman who gave me a ride.

Sarah closed the door. "Who's that?"

"The lady who gave me a lift here."

Sarah followed me to the bathroom and I signalled for her to run the water as I stripped Darryl out of his dirty clothes. The stink permeated the room and Sarah started to gag.

"You'll be doing this soon enough, Sarah. Get used to it," I snapped. I was tired and cranky, too.

"Oh my God. I can't."

I heard her gagging outside the bathroom. then her footsteps faded away.

I wiped Darryl down as best I could and plopped him in the warm water. I took the bar of soap and lathered him up till he looked like a pile of bubbles, then rinsed him off with a cup.

"Can you get me some clean clothes for him? And a diaper?" I hollered.

Within a few minutes, she entered with his things, yet she still gagged when she came into the room.

"I'll watch him if you get rid of *that*." She pointed to the soiled diaper still sitting on the counter. I'm not washing it," she said in disgust.

When I came back from disposing of the soiled diaper, Darryl was cooing and babbling. I crouched down to lift him out and get him towelled off.

"So, who was that," Sarah asked again, "and where were you?"

"I-I got lost, okay."

"You got lost? Why didn't you call me?"

"I forgot your number. I just forgot." I lay my head back on the couch. "I managed to get to a restaurant where Marion worked before the rain came. She said she would drive me home. Thank God."

"Thank God is right. So, what happened at Uncle Dan's? He was going to give you a lift back, by the way. Why did you run out?"

"I think he wants Darryl," I said, tears ran down my cheeks. I wiped them away but it felt like someone had punched me in the face. Sarah remained silent for a few minutes.

"Oh, Maggie. What are we going to do?" She said it like she didn't want anyone to hear her.

I shrugged and the tears continued. "I have no choice." My voice raised higher than it should be. "He's not mine. He belongs with... you should have seen them." I sniffed and wiped my face with my fingers.

"Maggie. What are you doing to yourself?" Sarah looked distraught.

I held Darryl close and breathed in his sweet, familiar scent. I felt the weight of him in my arms, the curve of his back. "I just don't know what to do, Sarah."

"We'll figure it out, Maggie. You've been through so much."

She leaned into me and started to braid my hair just like when we were kids.

Part III – Maggie

20: My first real friend

Boston, 1958

"Maggie! Maggie!" Byron squealed, delighted that he found me squatted, hiding behind a chair. He erupted into a belly full of giggles and I led him around the living room in search of his sister, Lucy.

"Now," I said looking down at him, "where do you think she is?"

I peered around, pretending I didn't see her small body lying there stretched out on the sofa, a blanket tossed on top.

Byron shook his head. "I don't know."

"Let's look again."

We walked silently on tiptoes, forefingers to our mouths 'till he saw her. He ran at full force, throwing himself on top of her.

She sat up, brushed her long hair out of her face, a smile as grand as the piano showcased small, white, evenly-spaced teeth.

"Again, Maggie. Again."

"One more time. Quick—"

"Ahem." Elsie cleared her throat as she walked into the room. "Miss Maggie. You were hired to cook and clean, not keep the young ones up past their bedtimes. That's enough, children. Now, off you go."

They walked off, shoulders drooping, doing their 'awwww's and 'one more time's as they were shuttled out of the room.

As far as I was concerned, Nanny Elsie was a harsh, mean-spirited, old woman who had more wrinkles and sag lines on her face than the O'Learys' pug.

She looked at me over her shoulder and said, "You're going to turn them into hooligans with those silly games. If you want to play so badly, why didn't you have your own children and be done with it?"

My face flushed as bright as the Cana lilies the O'Learys had planted in their front garden. It wasn't the first time Elsie had lectured me about playing wildly with the children, but I just couldn't help myself. I didn't think I was doing anything wrong. I simply played with them and it filled a void.

Deep in my heart, I wished I had Elsie's job. I thought I was better suited for it, in some ways, but she did teach them important things I couldn't, like music and manners. And because she had her driver's license, she could take them to their parties and family functions. What was wrong with playing a few games? I didn't get to do it much, anyway, as I was too busy cleaning their enormous house and preparing breakfasts and lunches.

The house seemed empty now that they were led off to their rooms. I fluffed up the pillows on the sofa and refolded the blanket Lucy had used as a disguise. I caught myself laughing, thinking of her obvious hiding place. Wouldn't it be something if I could just take them out on a picnic? Or for a walk to the park?

When I thought the living room looked respectable, I made my way back to my room.

It was small, with a single bed, a closet and a bureau. Big enough for me. Bigger than my room in Port Hope, but the smallest room in this house. Even Lucy and Byron's rooms were bigger than mine. So were their beds.

My room was comfy and warm, though, and I had the use of the bath just down the hall. All the meals were included with my employment here, and I even had a couple of evenings to myself.

Carol, a woman who worked next door, and I would sometimes get together and go out. We would go shopping, or catch a movie, or visit a nightclub. We'd dress up in skirts and blouses, and wear make-up. I had cut my hair to my shoulders and Carol showed me how to style it with rollers.

Carol's dream was to work at a salon one day. She was here in Boston, like me, to make and save money. Her plan was to go to hair-dressing school and get her ticket, but in the meantime, she practised on me and her boss lady, Mrs. Gertrues.

"That's pretty much what I do every day. I style her hair and she falls asleep in the chair. If she doesn't fall asleep, she makes me drive her around in her car, showing herself off to her old lady friends." Carol laughed.

I loved her smile. She had a wide gap between her front teeth and her eyes always twinkled. She had rich, chocolate hair I envied, and her eyes were dark like mine. "It's great practice for you," I told her.

She ran her fingers through my hair and puckered her lips as she held the pins between them. I passed her the next roller. "I'd kill for your colour. Trade you."

I looked at her like she had three heads.

"Seriously. But stop moving. This will look amazing when I'm finished."

And she was right. When she took the rollers out, I had big, soft, bouncy, hair that swooped up on one side. I beamed.

"Wow. That's a good look for you," she said as I blushed scarlet. "And don't be getting embarrassed every time I give you a compliment. Your face turns the same colour as your hair."

She snorted when she laughed which made me laugh even more. I liked this Carol. My first real friend.

~

That night, we were going to a local dance. I had butterflies that felt more and more like knots tightening. I didn't really like going out, hanging around, meeting fellas, but Carol did and she was my friend. I went along to appease her. Plus, she had her eye on someone.

We agreed to meet at the curb at eight-thirty because my employers didn't like me consorting with strangers, even though Mrs. Gertrues lived next door to them for most of her life and Carol had been there for almost two and a half years.

Carol said Mrs. Gertrues wanted her to stay with her 'til she dies, but that might be in ten years, or even twenty. "She's old, but as bright as a copper penny. She's still up on the latest news, the latest gossip, the latest trends."

Mrs. Gertrues said hanging around with the young people kept her mind sharp, but Carol thought it was because she was rich and had the best of everything growing up. She never had to work or worry. Worrying was the killer of the older generation.

Sarah said she was worried about me and that was why she had asked me to leave. That was why I ended up here. She had said I needed some time and she'd look after Darryl until I got myself sorted. I agreed because Sarah knew better. She was both older and wiser.

After I left Sarah's, I had moved right across the bridge to Detroit. It wasn't far, but Sarah didn't need me hanging around as she adjusted to married life and to motherhood. I had visited her as often as I could, especially after she had her baby.

She named him Carl Angus. A tiny, little thing with a red face and hair like mine. I had laughed about it, although Sarah hadn't seemed impressed at the time.

"He'll get teased," she'd said when I saw him for the first time.

I dismissed her comment and told her he couldn't be more beautiful or perfect. That had seemed to make her happy and she'd stopped commenting after that. His hair had dulled anyhow to a mousy brown then as dark as coal, so she told me.

I'd stay with her a couple of days to help, even though she'd said she didn't need me. Her neighbour, the nice Italian lady, had helped quite a bit, sending over food, looking after Darryl when Joanne couldn't. I'd tried to help, too, doing what I could, making meals, tidying up, doing the wash, regular menial chores. Just so I'd get to spend some precious time with Darryl, and Carl too, of course.

Sarah had told me Uncle Dan kept his apartment because he'd wanted his own place in the city. He'd worked in the auto plant when the farm got slow. Aunt Martha had lived home on her own before and hadn't seemed to mind him being away.

When I asked Sarah about his supposed relationship with Joanne, she huffed and changed the subject. Then I called Art.

"Aye," he said. "You still going on about that? There was word, yes, that Dan and Martha weren't together, but the rumour got squashed when they both showed up to Sunday mass, sitting in the first pew, front and centre. So, who knows, Maggie? How's things with you?"

Sarah kept telling me to leave it well enough alone and that I seemed happier now that I was on my own and out of Port Hope.

Darryl grew like a weed. At the age of three, he had starting losing his baby fat because he was walking and running. Most times I did all I could to keep up with him when I visited. He was as wild as Joanne, I could see.

Then Sarah got pregnant again, almost six weeks after Carl, so I was back and forth. I ended up staying with her for a few weeks after Brian was born. He was identical to his older brother, plumper perhaps, but with the same colour cheeks: full and red, dark eyes, same hair.

It was hard on Sarah looking after a newborn and two other little boys especially with Colin working so much. Plus, Brian was fussy. He was up most nights, behaving like an owl, and when he started squawking, it woke the whole house. Most of us didn't get too much sleep those first days.

Initially, Sarah needed me, and in her own way, Joanne needed me too. But then Sarah said I was getting too difficult to be around again, so after Brian's first month home, she told me I had to leave.

"It's for the best," she said. "You'll see."

It was sad. I cried. We all did, but Sarah needed to do things her way, she said, without my influence, and I needed to get out on my own and make some money. I would never have a man to provide for me, so I'd better start doing it myself.

This time she thought it best I went farther away. I took a job in Boston, working first as a waitress and that's when I met Carol.

She happened to be in the restaurant one day. She said she noticed my hair and said she wanted to get her fingers into it and tie it up.

It was Carol who told me about the O'Learys, Mrs. Gertrues's neighbours. They were looking for a maid as their former one had left.

So, I filled out an application, which Carol helped me with. A meeting was arranged and I got the job.

The money was decent, but the days were long and hard. They expected quality and perfection. One time, I had folded the sheets and Mrs. O'Leary happened to walk by the linen closest. She called to me and asked if I was rushing, or if the children had helped me fold.

I wasn't sure what to say.

She took all the sheets out and tossed them on the floor and then said I had to refold them the right way. As she watched my haphazard attempt, she tapped her leather-soled moccasin against the hardwood.

"Wrong," she said, and immediately called for one of the other maids to show me the 'correct way.' I was so embarrassed.

We were never taught how to fold sheets at home. We never even had them. We had handmade quilts on our beds and used every one of them.

So, everything had to be taught to me. How to make a bed, to fold a napkin, to iron tablecloths and dress shirts. I had to be shown how to correctly carve a grapefruit, which she requested at breakfast each morning. Every segment had to be meticulously carved with no pith or membrane so she could scoop out the fruit without it attaching and flinging back, squirting juice, or dropping on the table. Heaven forbid! And the centre of the grapefruit had to have either a maraschino cherry, a strawberry, or a blueberry, depending on what was in season.

I was a nervous wreck in the beginning. But I was good with the children, something she seemed pleased with. Her children were the moon and the stars to her, and I think she tolerated everything else I did because of my ability to make her children smile, something Nanny Elsie did not.

I sat in my room, waiting for the time to pass to meet Carol. The grandfather clock chimed eight bells and I still had a half hour to wait.

I hadn't a clue what to wear as I didn't have much. I sent any money I could to Papa for things he needed: clothes, chewing tobacco, household items. I even sent home an arm chair. I figured

Papa would like it as his daybed was worn out and lumpy. I sent Art some things too. Real booze, for starters. I sent Sarah's boys and Darryl little things, and I always sent a note. I hoped Sarah read it to them out loud. I didn't want them to forgot about me.

I decided to wear my pleated skirt and a long-sleeved blouse. Carol had showed me how to wear my hair. She was always after me to keep up my appearance in order to catch the eye of a young fellow. Something I was not interested in at the moment.

When we met on the street, she smiled with her big gap and I saw lipstick on her front teeth. I told her as such and she stuck her index finger in her mouth and slid it back and forth like a tooth-brush.

"There? Better?"

"Yes," I said and she looped her hand in my arm and we walked like that in unison until we came upon the dance hall.

We waited a few minutes outside, making small, nervous talk. Then she spotted Walter, her potential new suitor. He was parking his mint-green Plymouth sedan, a cigarette hanging off his lip. It balanced there like a teeter totter.

Carol went weak in the knees. She squeezed my arm tight and smiled the biggest smile.

We walked up to the car and he got out. He was as skinny as a piece of kindling and his cologne nearly bowled me over. I wasn't sure how Carol could stand it, but she seemed oblivious to the scent, having gone all googly and chatty.

The two regarded each other, she more than he. He seemed more focused on his car. He had straight, reddish-blond hair and red-rimmed eyes, and he reminded me of a crane, like he had been staring at the sea too long waiting for fish. Ironically, he too had big gaps in his mouth, similar to Carol's.

I wasn't sure why I had come, already feeling like the third wheel.

"Walter: This is my friend, Maggie."

He looked at me stone-faced, blank.

"She's the finest girl you'll ever meet."

"What am I doing with you, then?" he said with a laugh.

I rolled my eyes, suddenly wishing I hadn't come.

Walter threw his cigarette on the ground and Carol detached her arm from mine and latched onto Walter's. I followed behind like a little dog.

If there was one thing agreeable about the Dedham Square down-east dances, it was the music. The fiddler and the piano player were outstanding.

I watched Carol and Walter. They danced up a storm during a set, their bodies on fire, perspiration glistening on their faces, strands of her hair stuck to her forehead. They danced three in a row while I sat and watched the crowd.

I was really out of practice anyway and too shy to get up. I should have asked Carol for help beforehand. She assumed I knew how to dance.

I wasn't drinking either, as I didn't want a repeat performance of my last time at a square set.

I was asked to round dance, although I am sure the man who asked me regretted it later. I stood on his toes more than the floor. My hands felt sticky and gross in his and, to top it all off, I banged him in the nose with the back of my head. I felt so bad. Humiliated really.

I tried having a drink then. Carol said it would help me relax but everything tasted horrible.

I sat and watched those around me gabbing and dancing, and as the night went on, their words began to slur and the room got louder. Movements became clumsy and wild and the awkwardness I felt at being there, grew.

Walter kept guzzling his beer and drinking shots and smoked a hundred cigarettes. The room became heavy and thick with smoke, like a dense fog. I tried a cigarette just to fit in a little, but all it did was make me dizzy and sick to my stomach.

Then the fights broke out and the screaming started. One guy picked up a chair and threw it across the dance floor, narrowly missing Carol. It hit the stage and ricocheted off the piano with a thunk. Another fellow had blood all down his shirt, while the man opposite him had his shirt off all together. They snapped at each other like boxers in a ring.

Carol pulled me by my sleeve and hollered, "Let's get out of here."

I was only too happy to go and followed her out, not even bothering to look for Walter. He was already in the car, half asleep. I closed my eyes, just wanting to get home, vowing never to go with Carol again.

When Carol got into the front seat, she kept chuckling, slapping at Walter's hands. I wasn't even sure if he *could* drive. He started up the engine and we lurched forward while he turned up the radio and lit a cigarette.

One thing I noticed was that we weren't going home, but heading in the opposite direction.

"Hey? Where you going?"

They didn't answer me.

"Carol!" I shouted, frantic.

"To a party," she said with a giggle.

I slumped back, but the stale smell of booze and cigarettes caught me in the throat. I couldn't breathe. I opened my mouth and gasped for air and tapped Carol over and over on the shoulder.

"What, Maggie?"

"Stop." I yelled and then Carol hollered for Walter to pull over.

"I think she's getting sick." she shouted.

Walter instantly pulled the car to the curb and we jolted to a sudden halt. I practically somersaulted into the front seat with them. Reaching for the handle, I forced it open, and fell onto the ground. Rocks and gravel pressed into my stockings.

"Maggie! Are you okay? How much did you drink?" Carol searched my face.

I didn't answer her. I just splayed open my arms then marched off toward home.

"Maggie? Come back here!"

"I don't want to go to a party, Carol," I hollered back.

There was a collective groan from inside the car. I knew we weren't that far from the dance hall and it wasn't that far after that to the O'Learys'. It was late, too, and I shouldn't be walking alone, but anything was better than being in the car with the two of them 'going to town.'

I continued my walk, happy for the fresh air but the headlights, were blinding.

It was then I felt someone grab my arm. I screamed.

"Maggie. It's just me."

"Sorry, Carol. But I don't want to go, okay?"

"I'm sorry. I should have asked you first."

"Girls!" Walter barked. "What's the deal? Are we going or not?"

You could tell he was getting irked. He had turned his car around on the street and was following us slowly, the orange blinker ticking on and off.

"Come on, Maggie. Just for a little while. Walter has a friend—" She grabbed my elbow and tried steering me back toward the car.

"No! I don't want to."

She released her grip. "You're as green as the day is long, aren't you?"

I crossed my arms.

"I'm leaving," Walter hollered, revving the engine. Carol told me to a wait a minute and she ran across the road toward Walter and stuck her head in the driver's window. Cars honked when they passed them by. After a minute, she went around the passenger's side door and waved me over. "C'mon, Maggie. We'll take you home now."

When we arrived on my street, I told them not to pull up because the headlights would shine in the windows. "It might wake up the O'Learys, or disturb the children," I said.

Walter stared straight ahead.

Before Carol could so much as say good night, I rushed out and up the back steps, thankful to see Walter's tail lights as he pulled away.

21: Blood on the backseats

"I think Walter likes you," Carol stated while stirring her tea.

I rolled my eyes. *You've got to be kidding me*, I thought. *We barely said boo to each other*. I took a quick inhale of Carol's cigarette, then stuck out my tongue and made a face. "God, that's awful. Why does anyone smoke?" and washed the taste down with a gulp from my cup.

"We look sophisticated." Carol said as she flipped her head to the side and thrust her hand in her hair.

While we talked and laughed and ate freshly made sugar cookies, I tried not to take things for granted. It was the abundance of everything that still utterly amazed me. Not only the fine bone china that Momma would have died for, but even the simpler things like having a fully stocked pantry. Items we rarely had back home,

I savoured every single crumb that landed on my plate.

"Let's go on a double date," Carol said, that big gap-toothed smile staring back at me.

"No, I don't think so."

"Oh, come on, Maggie," she whined. "Let me introduce you to one of Walter's friends."

I closed my eyes.

"He has a friend named Johnny. Or maybe it's Joey. Anyhow, he's actually more handsome than my Walter but, oh, Walter, he's so charming," she gushed. Her cheeks turned a pretty shade of pink. "I'll get it all arranged. We'll go to dinner at a nice restaurant."

"No, Carol. I don't want to."

"It will be fun, Maggie, and it's high time you meet someone. Come on. Please? For me?" She had me almost convinced with her big pleading eyes.

I hemmed and hawed. *How can I say no to my best friend?* I wanted her to be happy and if that meant going on a date, so be it. It couldn't be that bad.

I had finished serving the O'Learys their supper and was cleaning up the dishes when Leo, the butler, stopped by. He was a kindly man with a dark complexion and dark eyes. Streaks of silver-grey ran through his thick mane just slightly above his ears. He never called me by name, only Miss, with a deep accent that I found soothing. He had told me he was married for over twenty-five years and had three teenaged sons and that his wife did the same kind of work as me. "Cleaning and stuff. And tends the children just like Nanny Elsie."

"There's a package for you, on the back table in the kitchen. Came this mornin'." He smiled, his teeth gleaming white.

I was thrilled. I never received packages. My imagination soared.

But as I stood looking at the parcel with my handwriting and *Return to Sender* stamped across the top, I was confused. Joanne's gift —returned.

I picked it up and flipped it over. The wrapping was torn in places although the twine still held. *No such person at this address.*

My heart got heavy. *Poor Joanne. Where is she now?*

I tried calling Joanne's phone number so many times I lost count. The phone just rang and rang. I thought for sure that it was just my sorry luck she'd always be out when I called. Maybe she had found a better job or was working crazy hours. Maybe she had moved in with Sarah full-time?

I was sure the package having been returned was a mistake, like the postman couldn't make out my handwriting, that I had not put enough postage on it, or that someone was new delivering and got the houses mixed up. The simplest solution would be to send it to Sarah and she could deliver it for me.

~

Carol had our date set up. I would go with Walter's friend, Joey. We were going to Steuben's restaurant on Boylston Street.

When Walter picked us up, Carol hadn't changed a bit. She was still all gooey and giggly around him. This time, however, he got out and opened the door for her. At least he was attempting to be a gentleman that is until I saw him reach his hand around her backside and give it a squeeze.

Joey, my date, sat in the backseat, looking preoccupied with his feet. I felt like I should do the same.

We drove without the radio on as Carol said we should all try and get to know one another better. "You can't talk with the music blaring," she laughed.

She controlled the conversation, however, and told Walter everything. About her day, about Mrs. Gertrues, about her house and the money she had, even what she ate for lunch.

"Caviar," she laughed, turning around in the seat to see if we were paying attention. She stuck out her tongue. "Imagine? Yuck."

Carol 's voice raised when she got excited and it seemed being with Walter made her excited all the time.

Joey and I barely acknowledged one another. I hadn't much to say. I didn't know him for starters and it didn't help he didn't seem to want to engage in conversation either. Maybe he was shy? He kept his focus on the window, tapping his foot and smoking. He had three cigarettes on the drive over. One right after the other and the smoke made my head fuzzy.

When we arrived at the restaurant, Carol took Walter's arm and they strode in together. Joey and I followed behind.

We sat at a table for four and the pretty waitress brought over our menus. I skimmed it but there was nothing that really interested me. I ordered a grilled cheese with Canadian bacon, because it reminded me of home. Carol ordered the fried chicken, Walter, the roast beef dinner, and Joey, beer.

As we sipped on our drinks, waiting for our food, Carol kept the conversation going. She talked about living and working in Boston and mentioned her desire to open her own hair salon. You could tell she was rather proud, the way she spoke about it, how she was saving money to take a beautician course.

"And where exactly would you open this here salon?" Walter said.

Carol laughed; her voice sounding higher than normal. "I haven't worked out all the details yet." Everything above her neck went pink.

"Well, you must have some idea." He tapped a finger on the table. "Sounds kind of foolish though."

Carol's colour did not change. "Um," she said, trying to get off the subject, "the waitress forgot my drink, Walter."

Walter raised his arm in the air snapping his fingers, looking around and calling, 'Waitress'. When she arrived, Walter asked about Carol's drink and ordered another for himself and Joey.

It was obvious Joey felt attracted to the waitress. He sat forward, placed his elbows on the table and looked up at her, longingly. She had a round face with blondish hair pulled back, and a large bosom. Joey grabbed the strings on her apron and played with them with his fingers.

She told him she'd be right back with the drinks so he released his hands, grinning from ear to ear.

After our dinner had been served, we ate in relative silence and it appeared Carol had lost her appetite all together. She picked at her meal and took small bites.

"Eat up there, Carol. I'm not spending money on this here food so you can waste it."

"Oh, Walter," she said through her mouthful, raising her fingers to her lips. "I'm so full. You want some? You finished all yours."

Walter shook his head and lit a cigarette. "Go on now." He pushed the plate closer to her.

"Maggie? You didn't eat all of yours, either. Would you like to try some of mine?"

I could tell she looked a bit uncomfortable so I offered my plate.

Walter barked. "I didn't buy the food for you to give it away either." The plate landed with a thunk and Carol tried eating again.

"So, tell me about this here plan of yours?"

"It's just a dream, Walter. I like styling hair and I thought... it would be fun to have my own place. You know? The way you have your business doing building." She smiled at him and lightly touched his hand.

When the waitress came back to check if the food was okay, Joey became completely fixated on her. It was actually embarrassing. He complimented her eyes and her delicate hands and what she did to keep them so soft. She didn't know what to say. She was trying to be polite and said she had other tables to get back to.

Carol and Walter didn't notice Joey's infatuation because they were engaged in their own drama. She kept saying, "It's not a big deal." Over and over.

Joey now held the waitress's hand.

"How 'bout you and I go out some time?" He looked pathetic.

"I don't think your girlfriend would like that too much," she nodded in my direction.

"Well, the woman's place is the house. None of that bull crap you're talking about. My mother knew her place, as did my grandmother, my sisters, and no woman of mine is gonna be out at all hours when there's supper to be made."

Carol's face went all misty. "Does that mean, Walter, you want me to be your steady?"

"Nn-no, no, no," he stammered, shaking his head. "You're taking this out of context. I didn't say that at all. Now you get that idea out of your head right this very minute."

The drive home was as uncomfortable as the drive in. Walter looked cross and barely spoke as Carol tried to talk to him, stroking his face and neck. He kept pushing her hands away.

Joey seemed rather smug. His smirk never left his face, even while he hiccoughed.

"Take a deep breath," I said to him.

And just like that, it's like he noticed me for the very first time, the lone female occupant in the backseat.

He leaned in. And that's when I knew he was bombed. His eyes swam around inside his head and the smell of booze nearly knocked me over.

"Did she give you her number?" I sniggered. "You practically forced it out of her." I wasn't sure why I said what I did or why I spoke to him like that, given his current state, but my comment seemed to amuse him.

He opened his mouth and his head fell back laughing. Then his hand went to my knee. I slapped it away.

"You're jealous," he said, gloating. "That I was talking to the waitress."

"Of course not," I snapped. I scooted over to the window, to get as far away from him as I could.

This move on my part also seemed counterproductive. Instead of discouraging his advances, it actually encouraged them. Joey slid across the seat and whispered in my ear "Don't go pretending now, Mary. I know you want me."

"It's Maggie." I prayed we'd be home soon.

"Don't be like that." he said calmly, but slurring, running his hand through my hair, down my neckline.

"Are we near home, Walter?" I asked.

Walter didn't answer, and now Carol turned on the radio.

I hoped Joey would just get bored and move on, or pass out. I curled myself into a ball.

He grabbed my hand then and started kissing my palm. I froze. When his eyes met mine, he had an ungodly grin pasted across his face and, in one quick swoop, slid his hand down the front of my shirt.

"You tell me you don't want it, but your body says otherwise," he whispered.

Shivers ran up and down my back. I wanted to scream but my voice stuck in my throat.

His greasy lips slid up and down my neck till his mouth was on mine. I bit down, hard, catching his lip.

He let out a yelp.

The car swayed as Joey's sudden outburst startled Walter's focus.

Carol turned around just in time to see what happened next.

Joey's fist came across not once, not twice but with three aggressive thwacks. My head ricocheted off the side window while he yelled at me.

As I lay stunned and silent he crawled on top, ripping open my blouse.

His rough hands were all over me all the while Carol screeched in the front seat, "Walter! Do something!"

"What the hell's going on back there?" he demanded.

Carol grabbed Joey's shoulders, trying to hold him back, but he was too strong.

Walter finally pulled over and hauled Joey out of the car. And off me. "What have you done? She's bleeding!"

"That stupid bitch asked for it."

Warm fluid spilled down my chin and dropped on my chest. My nose felt numb and my eyes started to puff. I swallowed and tasted metal.

Carol brushed my hair back out of my face and she grabbed a tissue from her purse to dab my mouth and nose.

"Ow, ow."

"Is it broken?" Carol asked Walter. When he didn't answer, she held my head to her chest. "You're an animal, Joey! A filthy pig!" she screamed so loud she hurt my ears.

"Take us home, Walter. Now!"

Walter hopped back in the car and barked at Joey to get in the front. As we pulled back out on the road, Walter looked in his rear view. "There better not be blood on my backseats."

They drove Joey home first. Carol had a few choice words for him as he got out. She must have hit a nerve because he slammed the door. And this pissed off Walter.

He got out and chased after him. "I paid good money for this, you asshole. Have some respect."

Carol searched the seat where I lay for blood. She spit on tissue and scrubbed some suspicious spots. "It's all right, Maggie. You hear me? You're fine. You'll be just fine."

Her eyes were wide and her tongue kept slipping in and out of her mouth as she concentrated on wiping the seats. Her beautifully-coiffed hair had fallen around her face. It looked like she was out in a windstorm. A bobby pin dangled low on her forehead. I wanted to pin it back.

As I closed my eyes, I heard her say to Walter, "It's okay." I wasn't sure if she meant Walter's car, or me.

Finally the trip was over. "You might want to put some ice on that," Walter said as Carol helped me out of the car. She grunted when I held onto her for support.

"Can you walk a little, Maggie?"

We stumbled to the O'Learys' back door, where Nanny Elsie greeted us.

"Dear God in heavens. What happened here?" Her palms were raised to her cheeks and her mouth hung open.

"Shush now," Carol scolded. "Let's just get her to her room to lie down."

"I won't be party to this." She shook her head.

That's when Leo appeared. He scooped me up in his arms and said to Carol, "Show me the way, miss."

But Elsie caused a stink. "No, no! She can't stay here looking like that. The O'Learys won't stand for it."

"You mean *you* won't stand for it," Carol barked.

"The children!" Elsie raised her voice and wagged her finger in my direction. "They cannot see her like this. No, Leo. Get her out."

Leo clutched me tighter and I felt his breath on my cheek. He took me to my room anyway.

In a weird way, I felt like I was on display, a spectacle, a sideshow disaster. Everyone stared and no one knew what to do.

Leo finally motioned for Diane to get some clean clothes and some water. He told Carol to wash my face.

But all I wanted was for everyone to leave me alone. I closed my eyes and imagined them like birds, chattering, and for a briefest moment I *was* home, near the woods with the chickadees and the starlings as they flitted back and forth between branches. Those images soothed me to sleep.

Before I awoke, I imagined myself sitting near the stove at Papa's, cooking soup of all things, and making tea. I was as hot as a crackling fire. I had no idea what time it was, but knew it must be late.

Teetering over to the door, I opened it, tiptoeing as best as I could to the washroom. It took every ounce of energy. It felt like I had spun around the room one hundred times.

When I caught my reflection, I gasped, horrified. My skin was swollen, and stretched. A ghoulish mask stared back. It had already started turning different colours around my eyes. I bent over to take a sip from the tap, and couldn't—my jaw throbbed in pain.

As quietly as I could, I disappeared into my room to change out of last night's clothes, and then sat on the bed, waiting. I wasn't sure what to do. I was too scared to leave. I didn't want anyone to see me. It hurt to move, to yawn, to lick.

There was a soft tap upon the door, and the voices of Carol and Diane, another of the O'Learys' housemaids.

"I'm so sorry, Maggie," Diane said mournfully.

I grunted for her to come in but kept my face covered as best I could.

That's when she told me Elsie had blabbed and I had to leave. By tomorrow.

"Tomorrow?" I asked, startled. "But what did I do?" My heart beat so fast.

She tried to hug me then, but I pushed her away and went to my bureau to pack. *Where would I go? What would I do?*

Carol asked if she could help but I shook my head.

Before she closed the door, she whispered, "You can stay with me."

As soon as they left, I packed everything up. Everything I owned. I'd leave no trace behind. I stayed in the room until it was dark and I knew no one would see me.

When I tapped on the Gertrues' back door, Carol was there, waiting. She wrapped her arm around my shoulders and took my bag. She kept her finger to her lips as she led me quietly up the back stairs.

22: The nicest thing

March, 1958

The world was a dark place.

I lay in Carol's bed, staring into the blackness. She had thrown on an extra blanket, thinking I'd be cold, but the wool scratched my neck, reminding me of back home. I couldn't bear to think of home right now.

Carol helped me to sit up. She fixed me a broth because I couldn't chew anything. She had cut the vegetables into tiny pieces, so small it resembled a bowl of porridge. My jaw hurt to close yet I couldn't open my mouth wide enough to chew.

The soup helped. It was warm and smelled good and my belly growled as I ate.

"What did the old bat say to you anyway?" Carol sat on the edge of the bed and squeezed my foot with her hand. My foot twitched. She scooted up and lay down beside me, using her arm as a pillow. She faced me and brushed my hair out of my eyes.

"Doesn't matter," I told her.

"Sure, it does." She poked my shoulder. "Tell me what she said."

I stared at the ceiling.

"Maggie?" she pleaded.

"Why Carol? Why do you want to know?"

"'Cause when I leave here, I'm gonna go over there and give her a piece of my mind. And I need to know what you said, so I don't get things mixed up."

She smiled in a fake sort of way. I didn't reply. I hoped she would just let it go. But she didn't. She incessantly nagged and asked, questioned and poked. All I wanted was some peace and it looked like I couldn't get it here either.

Finally, I answered her. "Okay Carol. She said..." I paused, "It was just so degrading and horrible. She wouldn't even look at me. It was like I had the plague. She belaboured me with questions about who I was hanging out with and what sort of girl I was."

I caught my reflection in the mirror. My skin was now soft green and yellow in spots. My fat lip had subsided and I could finally see out of my eyes again. It didn't hurt so much when I blinked or applied pressure on my cheek.

"Go on."

I hated thinking about it. I just wanted to ball it up like a piece of paper and throw it in the trash so it would never be spoken of again.

"Go on, finish it."

I couldn't look at Carol. The shame and guilt of the meeting embarrassed me. I twisted the ribbon on my night dress around my finger. "She said she was ashamed that she had hired me. That I was not fit to be an employee and that I was fired, having disgraced her house." My voice went to a hush. "That she didn't owe me any money because I left her high and dry without proper warning, and that I shouldn't see the children as I would scare...not scare, *traumatize* them."

I took a deep intake of breath. "That part hurt the most."

"Well, that's sort of true. You would have."

"Yeah, I would have." The thought made me sad and sick to my stomach. "I loved those kids!"

Tears formed in my eyes. "Sometimes I think I loved them more than she did, and when I couldn't see them to say good-bye, it broke my heart, Carol." I bowed my head and felt myself weakening.

Carol touched my arm. Her warmth radiated on my skin. "There, there," she whispered.

I held her hand. "I loved them kids, Carol."

"I know you did. Like your very own."

I nodded, swallowed.

"But, Maggie. Don't get all sad in the face about them. You can have your own someday. We'll have our own children and they can play together. Be best friends. You watch. You'll see."

But Carol was wrong. *I'll never be married; therefore, I'd never have children. I am damaged, tarnished, cursed.* "Yeah," I whispered, pulling away from her and turning over.

"She had no right"—Carol kept on—"to just fire you. To let you go. Your work was good." she paused for a bit. "What if I ask Mrs. Gertrues for a position for you? She might have something?"

"No," I said too sharply.

"I could at least ask. She won't mind me asking. She doesn't even know you're here. No one does. You're as quiet as a mouse. Quieter. I'm not even sure you're here myself till I see your lump in my bed."

I stared at her, smoothing my hand on the sheets, then said in a softer tone, "No, but thank you, Carol. I don't want charity or pity. I'll stay here until I look decent enough to leave. I'll go back to Sarah's for a while, maybe I'll..." I wondered where else I could go. "Maybe Joanne will need me, or I can get work in a factory near her, or maybe waitress again."

"Maggie. You're my dearest friend. And no matter what happens, or where we both end up, let's always stay in touch."

A sudden wave of warmth washed over me, right from my toes right up to the top of my head. I stared up at Carol. "That's the nicest thing anyone has said to me."

"What did I say?" she laughed.

"Just that I'm your friend. Thank you, Carol. As long as I'm living, I'll always be here for you. Maybe not in person, but here," I pointed to her heart.

Her big lips spread apart, showcasing that space between her teeth, and somehow, that made me feel all the better.

23: Pearls in the dust

It was mid-morning. Carol got up at her usual time and kissed me good-bye. Simple and sweet. Nothing too corny. She said it was better that I just slip away and write to her or call her when I got to my sister's place.

When things were quiet, I got up and dressed and grabbed my bag. Today I was leaving.

I tiptoed down the back stairs, holding my shoes in my hand. I looked left and right, hoping not to run into anyone. I made it to the landing without being seen, and noticed how bright the sun shone. I hadn't noticed it all week because I had kept the drapes shut tight, locking out the world around me. It was blinding and I squinted, cupping my palm to my eyebrows, feeling foolish in a way.

That's when I noticed the house. I hadn't paid attention to it before. It was a grand home with its elaborate and ornate mouldings, rich wallpaper in jewelled tones, thick draperies and large-scale paintings.

The dining room caught my eye in more ways than one. A silver tea set sat upon the largest table I had ever seen, flanked by two floral arrangements of roses, orchids, and some opulent purple flower I didn't recall ever seeing before. A magnificent crystal chandelier hung from the centre of the ceiling, reflecting beautiful hints of blue, red, and gold against the walls. My eyes danced about, wondering what Mrs. Gertrues did for a living that allowed her such luxuries and grandeur.

Then I focused on the thick layer of dust that had accumulated on the dining table. It looked like a woollen blanket. The O'Learys were always after us to stay on top of this particular chore, but you simply couldn't fight sunshine and dust particles, no matter how much you wiped.

I ran my finger on the table, drawing a line through the dust. Without thinking, I used the sleeve of my shirt as a dust rag, tiptoed to the far end of the table and, with the arm of my sweater, wiped away the dust in one clear motion. I knew I wouldn't want to get in trouble for not having done my work, and it was the least I could do, really.

I wasn't even sure who exactly did what in Mrs. Gertrues' home. It seemed Carol did mostly hair and small chores, ran to the grocery store, kept the old woman occupied and entertained. She had a cook, like the O'Learys, and Carol said the food was really good.

That's when I noticed a strand of pearls, draped around the sugar bowl. It didn't look like it belonged there. I didn't think it was part of the flower arrangement, but who's to know? I lifted it and moved the centrepiece, dusted around the tray set and put it back.

In my periphery, I thought I saw movement, but I dismissed it. It had looked like a child's toy, like a porcelain doll with large glass eyes, perched in the corner of the room.

When I finally looked over, I took a deep intake of breath.

Her lips turned up in the corners as she narrowed her wrinkly eyes at me. "You're blinder than I am."

"I'm sorry, ma'am. I didn't see you. I mean..." I stood at attention, keeping my feet together, looking down at the floor.

"I see that," she said in a sharp, authoritative tongue. "You stealing my pearls?"

I glanced over at them to be sure they were still there, then focused my attention back on her. She looked no bigger than a doll, still and petite. I stared at the floor again. "No ma'am."

"They're just costume." She chuckled, "but I leave them out from time to time for the staff. To see if I have any thieves in my midst."

My eyes widened and I stared into her dark, blue orbs. They glinted like black sapphires.

She cackled out loud, threw her head back like she had said something funny. "You don't think anyone's a thief—you don't know what you're missing till they've left."

I nodded. My hands felt clammy. "I'm sorry. I should go now," I offered, mortified, wishing I had just left when I said I would.

"No, you won't, young lady. You come here and let me get a good look at you. Who are you, anyway and what are you doing in my house? As far as I know, I didn't hire anyone new, but this old brain gets forgetful."

I swallowed hard. I couldn't say I was staying with Carol because I didn't want to get her in trouble. "I—" I stammered. I went completely blank.

"Now, don't go on losing your tongue or lying. Only thing I hate more than liars is thieves, and if you lie, well then, you're no better than a thief."

I swallowed again. The spit in my mouth had evaporated and every ounce of my body felt slick with sweat. "My name's Maggie and I—"

"Come here now. Bend down. Let me look at you."

What could be even more uncomfortable and embarrassing than an old woman staring at my bruises and swellings, even if I looked a hell of a lot better now than I did a week ago? My face was still a bit tinged with green, making me look sick in an odd kind of way.

I was kneeling at her feet and so she had the upper hand. I looked up into her face.

She was wrinkled like a dried apple, her lips a brilliant pink and her saggy eyelids were covered in teal eyeshadow. All in all, she looked garish, but her hair was elegantly swept off her face and she wore pearls in her ears. Upon her bony frame she wore a satin blouse and a dark, pleated skirt. Her fingers were gnarled around each other at an odd angle, like they were broken at the knuckles, and her hands were peppered with age spots. Her shoulders hunched so it looked like she had no neck, just a head on her curved frame, and she smelled like powder and flowery perfume, but something else, too.

She had a china cup beside her with what looked like cold tea and a glass or crystal ashtray with a cigarette barely smoked. Her bright lipstick encircled the butt and matched the rim around her teacup.

"What do I smell like?" she asked as I remained kneeling before her. My leg had started to cramp.

"Pardon?" I asked, confused. Was this a game? Was she mad?

"I asked you a question. Now answer it honestly." She had a powerful, commanding voice and she scared me.

"Powder and, and..."

"Say it!" she demanded. I blushed. I wasn't sure what she wanted me to say. "And speak up, for God's sake. I'm old, so don't go jammering on like a scared little bird. So? Powder and what?"

I shrugged my shoulders and leaned in, twitching my nose, trying to pick up on the scent that she was obviously masking. I shook my head in quick, jerky movements.

"Piss. I smell like piss."

"No! No, you don't." I sounded defensive. "Honestly." I leaned back on my knees. "It's not that."

She turned her head and looked at me from the corner of her eye, and her lips turned up again at the corners. She picked up her cigarette and took a puff. Her teeth looked yellow like the embroidery in Momma's favourite curtains.

"I'm a good judge of character, my dear. Lucky for you."

She blew out the smoke out the side of her wrinkly mouth. "So, now that we got our introductions out of the way, go get me a cup of hot tea and then you can tell me why you were skulking around my house."

I did as she instructed; however, I felt embarrassed, nervous, and scared. I wished for Carol to come home, or anyone, but it seemed no one was around.

The teapot sat on the back of the stove on low, so someone must have made it for her. I know there were others who worked here, but where were they now?

The kitchen was clear and clean, there was nothing on the counter, nothing cooking in the oven, and the main floor appeared empty. I dumped out her cold tea and poured her a fresh cup.

"Get yourself one too, if you like," she hollered. I stopped, furrowed my eyes. I didn't know where this was going and had never seen the like, but I did it just to appease the old woman. I rattled around the cupboards till I found the teacups and poured myself one.

I walked out holding the two cups and placed hers where I had picked it up, on the table beside her. She told me to pull up a chair and to sit down in front of her. She stared at me for a few moments before she said anything.

"You're Carol's friend. The maid next door." Her watery eyes didn't blink. She wasn't asking.

I nodded slowly.

She picked up another cigarette and leaned forward for me to light it. "Ex-maid."

"How?" I struck the match and she lit up.

She put the cigarette in the tray and picked up her teacup and took a sip, then pointed to her temple with her index finger. "I listen and ask questions and sometimes play dumb or deaf depending on the circumstances. People talk. Especially the O'Learys' staff. They're no-TOR-ious!"

She rolled her eyes in disgust. "I'd never have that with my staff. What happens here should stay in here." She pointed a finger. "You think no one has had troubles or a made a mistake? My God, woman, look around."

Which I did, but there was still no one here.

"Those O'Learys, and especially that one that watches the children, they have secrets." She waggled her crooked finger at me. "They have more skeletons in their closets than the cemetery down at St. Vincent's."

I kept my cup to my lips and sipped as she spoke.

"So, you've been staying here"—I stopped sipping my tea and placed it on the table—"Since your unfortunate accident?"

"I'm sorry, ma'am. I will gladly pay for any room and board you wish to charge—"

She raised a hand to stop me from talking. "You're jammering."

I fell silent.

"If I didn't see you today, I would have forgotten you were here. But now, since you are here, and on my property, you owe me. You must tell me exactly what happened. You didn't get in an automobile accident?"

I shook my head.

"Well, speak up."

I stalled. "It was, ah..." I wasn't sure what to say. "A fella wanted to—"

"What? Kiss you or get down your pants?"

I couldn't believe this little old lady was so feisty and raw and my face must have said as much because her mouth opened up in almost a sinister smile, exposing her yellowed teeth.

She pointed a finger at me. "Don't you think I've been through all that before? It's a man's world, darlin', and they think they are the rulers of all our kingdoms." She crossed her legs. "But don't you go taking it. Look around you."

Which I did, again.

"You think my husband did this alone?"

I found myself following her every movement.

"Yes, he was a smart cookie, but if it weren't for me, he'd have pissed it away long ago. He was the man, but I wore the pants. Every woman should. We're good for it."

"What'd he do?" correcting myself, "You do?"

"That's more like it." She butted out her cigarette. "Those are bad habits, but at my age, who cares?"

I stayed perched on my chair and picked up the cup, held it in front of my face with my fingertips, sipping the minutest amount at a time, not wanting to make any noise. I was mesmerized by this woman.

"We started with a corner store, selling goods right from our own pantry, and as we earned money, I'd buy things like sugar and flour, and then I sold baked goods, bread, pies, pastries, tarts. I was an excellent baker, you know. Then we took over a restaurant. I was the cook there, too, until we hired a fellow and then got another restaurant, and then, of course, the building, and then another building here, a house there. It just kept adding up. We had children then too, five of them, three boys and two girls. The girls are spoiled but they married well. One to a doctor, the other to a lawyer. The oldest, Stan, he's in mining. The second oldest boy, he took over the real estate and restaurants, although we sold them back years ago for a pretty penny. The other boy," she rolled her eyes, "he likes a wealthy lifestyle but didn't want to work for it like the others, so he found his own approach to a career. He's looked after, at times"—she closed her eyes and held her gnarly hand to her chest—"by women of my stature and age, although I hope not as old as myself."

She opened her blue, saggy eyes and stared at me. "He'd be what you would call"—she thought for a moment—"a gigolo." She waited for my reaction but I drew a blank.

"A what?"

"Oh, for heaven's sake! Have you not heard of it? Where are you from? Probably some back woods north of the border."

I grimaced.

"He's a whore, in the simplest terms. Women pay to sleep with him. Or he escorts them to special events."

She rolled her eyes again. "You wouldn't believe the looks I got when I ran into him at the Warrens' formal dinner party last spring. Call that uncomfortable. But he's a grown man, and a good-looking one, so who am I to judge? I had my own young lovers, too, after my Henry died. But they were only after me for my money and I was only after them for their sex."

I gasped. Tea splashed out of my cup.

She didn't bat an eye, looked momentarily at the stain on my shirt, and kept on. "There was a mutual understanding, if you will. We both got what we wanted."

"I thought you said he wanted your money."

"I paid for his fare home in the morning." She looked down at her cup. "We should have something stronger than this tea."

She looked at the clock. "My nurse will be here any time. She cleans me up out of these awful things between my legs. The bladder isn't what it used to be."

She repositioned herself in the chair. "Only thing worse than pissing yourself is sitting in it."

"Can I?" I'm not sure why I offered. I was not a nurse, but thought it was the decent thing to ask because I had hidden out in her house for a good, solid week.

"You *are* nuts," she said. "And no. One young gal gawking at my nether parts is more than enough. So, Miss..."

"Maggie."

"Mag-gee," she enunciated the syllables, "What are your plans now? Now that you are unemployed and red-marked? Will you go back home?"

"I'll go back to my sister's, maybe."

"You don't seem sure. What about a boy? I'm sure you must have a steady? Well, hopefully not that repugnant ass who turned you that ugly shade of chartreuse?"

"Oh no." I shook my head.

"Good. Good riddance. I hope he gets what's coming to him. The world doesn't need more high and almightys."

"Ah. No. Ma'am. No one. No matter." I felt a sudden chill and curved my shoulders.

Her eyebrow raised. "What?"

I shook my head. "Nothin'."

"You're hiding something." She turned her face to the left, eyes narrowing on me, brain scanning. I could see her thinking. "Or you're ashamed. Or both."

I bit my lip and looked down at my lap, finding I was holding my hands the same way as Mrs. Gertrues.

"What is it, child? Say it. Nothing I haven't heard before," she asked in a delicate way. Not the snappy, stand-offish, confident woman that I was talking to when I first saw her.

She reached out and touched my hand. Her fingers were warm but bony, her skin soft, her nails strong like talons, like they would latch onto you and never let go.

My eyes met hers and she looked concerned, vulnerable even, like we shared something deep on a personal level.

My fears melted away momentarily and I opened my mouth. "I'm tarnished," I whispered. I said it so low I didn't think she had heard me, but she did.

She patted my hand with her palm. She did that for a few moments.

"Did you have the child, dear?"

I shook my head.

"Well...that's lucky, isn't it?"

I nodded.

She released my hand and sat back in her chair, looking at me with new eyes. She squinted like she was assessing me. "Whatever happened, let it go or accept it. Don't be believing that you aren't good enough to be loved. Don't go thinking that you won't belong to anyone and that happiness will never come to you. If you go on believing those things, then you *are* tarnished. But, as I've learned in life, we sometimes have to shine our own silver. You may be tarnished, but with nothing a good spit and polish wouldn't look after. You could be gleaming underneath, if you let others see it. Shining like the brightest star. And that hair colour. Is that real? Or do you dye?"

"It's mine." I furrowed my eyes, ran my hand down my length of my mane, trying to tame it and looked at her. I tried to smile, feeling shy. I had never thought of my situation that way before. Never considered it for a moment till I heard what she had to say. I smiled.

A woman walked in with a fast pace, wishing 'good morning' with her brightest, sunniest smile, would have to be the nurse.

"Ah. Wilhelmina is here. Awful name. Nurse Willie I call her for short. You're late!" she barked. "I best get on with this before the staff comes. I send them away when she comes over." She leaned in in a whisper. "The lot doesn't have to know all of my secrets."

I stood up and retrieved Mrs. Gertrues' cup as well as my own. As the nurse nodded to me in her bright, white, crisp uniform, I cleared my throat and said, "Thank you, Mrs. Gertrues. It was very nice talking to you."

She nodded to me as the nurse led her away in her chair. "Remem-ber now," she sang, "What we talked about, stays in this room." Then she turned around in her chair and said in a hoarse voice, "Who was that, anyway?"

24: Hell or high water

April, 1958

I had not exactly told Sarah my plans. I mentioned in passing that I'd take a few days to come see them, but had not said when.

"What, Maggie? You have to speak up. Boys! Oh, for Pete's sake." Her little ones were screaming in the background.

She dropped the phone on the counter then and there was crying, and shooing.

"Maggie. I've got to go." The phone clicked. She hung up abruptly without saying a proper good-bye.

No matter. It was mentioned, whether she heard me or not.

It had been almost a year and a half since I had last seen Sarah and the boys. Of course, I hadn't planned on staying away that long, but our holidays never seemed to correspond with each other.

My first summer when I was away in Boston, I had a few days off and suggested to Sarah I'd come home to help her out. But she had other plans. "Nice of you to offer, Maggie, but we'd like to spend some days by ourselves. You understand."

Of course, I got it. She didn't want me hanging around. I was the third wheel.

~

On the bus trip, a mother sat opposite me with her two little ones. The older one, a boy, who looked to be about Darryl's age, had a crop of brown hair and freckles peppered over the bridge of his nose. His little sister looked about a year or so younger. She moped and cried and did not like the bus. It made her motion sick, the poor thing.

She turned this way and that on her mother's lap, vomited into a bag. The brother didn't say anything. A few times I saw him pat his sister's back. Otherwise, he stared out the window for hours, watching trees and trucks and the sky blow by, his slender arm touching the seat ahead of him.

I wondered where they were heading, or getting away from. The mother looked thin and talked in a low whisper. The girl, pale-faced and withdrawn, had her eyes closed.

It made me so lonesome for Darryl and Sarah's boys. How big would they be now?

The bus slowed, signalled to turn, and wobbled into the Greyhound depot off Chatham. We had finally arrived in Windsor, the brakes making a *ssssisssss* sound.

I flagged down a taxi, and, as I neared my sister's house, my stomach went into knots. I didn't know why I had suddenly become so nervous. I had practised all I had to say on the bus ride.

She'd wonder why I just showed up. She'd wonder if I was going back. I'll ask to stay till I have things figured out, but I'd get to that once I saw her.

The taxi pulled up to Sarah's place and I noticed right off the bat that their car wasn't home. But that could mean any number of things. Maybe they went out for a drive? Or Colin was still at work. It was only early afternoon.

I paid the taxi driver and gave him a tip and he helped me with my suitcase and set it on the curb.

After he drove away, I grabbed it and placed it at the foot of the stairs. Now I wondered if I should have come at all. What if they went away for the weekend?

I knocked on the door anyway but no one answered so I sat down on the step to wait. The sun was hot and, as it beat down, it made me feel light-headed. It had been a long bus ride and I hadn't eaten properly.

Placing my elbows on my knees and resting my chin on my palm, I contemplated what I should do next.

I took off my shoes and stretched my toes, rested my head on the railing and closed my eyes. The heat made me sleepy.

The sound of a car horn jolted me awake. Had I dozed off that fast? Momentarily forgetting where I was, I almost tripped down the staircase.

Parked in the drive was a blue sedan, and my sister was staring at me from the passenger's seat. An ice cream in front of her face.

When she had processed what she saw, her eyes widened. 'Maggie?' she mouthed.

She handed Colin her ice cream and opened the door. Out waddled my pregnant sister, arms outstretched, rushing towards me.

"Oh my God, Maggie! What are you doing here? You didn't tell me you were coming."

We held each other for a few moments and it was then I realized how much I missed her. How much I needed her. She smelled good, like the sister I remembered, of sweet perfume and freshness, of outdoors and sunshine.

She cupped her hands under my chin and looked at me, a broad smile across her face. "Well. Look at you. All grown up. Boston was good for you. A lot of makeup, though."

I blushed. "And look at you, Sarah. You never mentioned. How far along?"

"Six months." She rubbed her hand on her growing belly. "Hoping for a girl this time."

Colin got out of the car, walked over, and handed Sarah her ice cream. "Holy smokes, Maggie. You're looking good."

Sarah swatted him in the stomach. "Don't be going all pie-eyed over my sister. She probably has a beau."

I shook my head, the heat coming back to my cheeks.

"Geesh, Maggie. Sorry." She looped her hand around my arm and dragged me back to the car. "Come see the boys."

"They get my presents?"

"Of course."

She opened the back door and there were two almost-identical, little sandy-haired boys with charcoal eyes. The third, the older one, wouldn't look at me. He turned his face to the window, his ice cream already inside his belly. He licked at his fingers. The other two had theirs dripping down their arms and onto their shirts and pants.

"Boys. You remember Aunty Maggie? She sent you the colouring books and the dinkies."

The boys' eyes lit up at the words and then faded back to their ice cream. The younger two scrambled out of the back seat while the last one dawdled after them.

"You eat all your ice-cream already, Darryl?"

He nodded.

Darryl! My Darryl. I went still as I watched him lumber up to Colin. He stood beside him like he was his shadow.

"Darryl?" I asked, looking at Sarah. "Why are you still looking after him?"

She rolled her eyes, and glanced up at Colin. His mouth twitched.

I walked over to Darryl and squatted beside him, resting my palms on my knees. I reached for his hand. "Hi sweetie," I cooed. "I'm your Auntie Maggie. Do you remember me?"

He shook his head 'no' but stared at me, quiet-like, shy. He reached for Colin's hand.

I turned to her. "What's wrong with him?" I whispered.

"Oh, Maggie. If you even knew."

Colin called for his boys to come in. They were running back and forth in mad circles. He wanted Sarah and me to have a minute by ourselves.

When Colin opened the door, the two boys ran past, jabbering on at lightning speed. "You coming, too, Darryl?"

Darryl shook his head, and instead walked toward the flagpole beside the house.

I looked to Sarah. She sat down where I had been.

"What's that about, Sarah?" I asked.

"Don't be looking at me like that. We're doing the best we can under the circumstances." Her tone was curt.

I closed my eyes and took a deep breath. "Where's Joanne?" I asked, exasperated.

She sighed loudly. "Maggie. Please. You just got here. Can we not talk about this right now? Can't we just have a few minutes of normalcy?"

"Really?"

"Really."

Then I thought about the presents I had bought for Joanne's birthday. I had mailed them from the States. That would have been a few months ago now. And how they had come back "address unknown". It all made sense. "How long has he been living here?" I stared at Darryl again.

"Since you left, Maggie."

I collapsed to my knees. "Oh, Darryl. I'm sorry. I'm sorry I wasn't there for you."

Darryl's eyes drifted away from me as if I spoke gibberish like his cousins. Sarah's eyes glazed over, too.

"Sarah, you've got to tell me what's going on! Where's Joanne? Why isn't she looking after Darryl? Shouldn't she have stepped up by now? After all this time?"

I gripped the metal hand rail, really wanting to scream. And all Darryl was doing was walking around and around the flagpole.

Sarah seemed unphased and focused on finishing her ice cream. She was down to the last couple of bites, and, it seemed, was more interested in it then in the sad, shy little boy who didn't talk. She crunched away, then sat back, exposing her large, round belly.

"Are you finished?"

"I told you. I'm not going to get into this now, Maggie. Every time you bring it up, you're like a broken record. You don't want to know the truth and yet you ask. And when I try to tell you, you drift off like you're in some twilight zone."

She was starting to sound like Joanne, and act like her. She was making me angry.

"What do you want me to tell you so we can stop this nonsense?" She closed her eyes and looked up to the sky. "That Joanne's a mess? Does that make you feel any better? Is that what you want to hear?"

I couldn't answer her. Every time I tried to open my mouth, she kept inserting words.

"We've been over this a hundred times. My God, Maggie. When are you going to get it? I thought"—she paused, as the neighbour started up his lawn mower. She had to talk louder over the pulsating sound—"you'd be better after all this time. After everything that happened. You just—"

Sarah went on and on about Joanne and her circumstances, and Momma and Mary and about how I shouldn't have been left behind after she moved, and..and, how she'd never forgive herself.

I watched the neighbour pushing the mower against long blades of grass. He wore a pair of light brown trousers and a short-sleeved shirt. It was light blue. A pretty shade. He looked in his thirties, and he squinted when he walked. He walked back and forth, back and forth, pushing and pulling, cutting around the tree that was planted in the front of the yard.

I loved the smell of it. Fresh, green, crisp, and the way you could see the patterns form on the lawn from where he cut. Wouldn't Art get a kick out of this? There was something soothing about watching him do his chore, with the warm afternoon sun high in the sky.

I suddenly felt very tired. From travelling, from an empty stomach, and from my sister's voice... Everything just blended into one.

"Aghhh! What's the point?" She huffed.

"Why didn't you call me?" I asked.

"And what, Maggie? What were you going to do, exactly?"

"I would have come home."

"Home? This isn't your home," she snapped.

I opened my mouth and closed it. "Well, I, I—I would have tried to help in some way."

Sarah exhaled and her face reddened.

And I didn't want to ask, but I had to. "Where is Uncle Dan?"

Sarah picked at her fingernails. "Home."

"With?"

"Yes, Maggie. With his wife. Geesh."

Sarah was angry, I could tell. She was no longer looking at me and I felt that she was sorry I had come. She lifted a foot out of her shoe and started to massage it. "How long are you staying?"

I shrugged. I didn't know how to answer. I had thought I'd be staying indefinitely. I wanted to tell her that once I found a job, I could get my own place. If Joanne could do it, couldn't I?

"So why did Dan—?" But I didn't get the rest of the words out as Sarah answered in a sour tone.

"Martha needed him back home. But that doesn't mean anything. And don't go implying anything either. And by the way, Aunt Martha was trying to help you out by taking the baby. A baby you evidently didn't want. She thought she was doing you a favour. So don't go accusing Dan and Martha of stealing, or taking what's not theirs. They aren't like that. They have been nothing but kind and generous." She pointed a finger at me. Her eyes were wild, her mouth in a deep frown. She was practically yelling.

Colin opened the door. "Hey. What's going on out here? You two okay?"

Sarah didn't say anything else. She turned to go in, "And you are wearing way too much make-up. Who you trying to impress, anyhow?"

The words stung like a slap. Colin cocked his head, the screen door screeched closed behind them.

~

Sarah wasn't herself. I couldn't put my finger on it. She was indifferent, moody. I chalked it up to her pregnancy. Plus, having Darryl in the fold, I supposed, caused more stress.

Her boys were busy and always on the go, always wanting to be out and running. Darryl, on the other hand, seemed to be content just sitting in front of the television. He didn't say much. Nodded 'yes', or shook 'no'. He rarely, if ever, answered, especially to Sarah, who always seemed to be particularly cross with him.

Then Sarah didn't speak much to me either. She acknowledged that I was there. Asked me to get the load of laundry, or take the boys upstairs for their nap.

I did what I could, as much as I could: cooked, baked, cleaned, stayed out of the way. I slept on the couch so, once the boys were up in the morning, so was I. This meant Sarah could get more time to sleep, which I think she needed.

But even she and Colin didn't seem to be getting along. I often heard her raising her voice to him, me trying not to listen, taking the boys out if I heard them starting. Then, after hanging outside for a bit, I'd come in and see Colin sprawled on the couch with a beer, watching television, and Sarah in her room.

In a way, the atmosphere reminded me of home with Papa. This was not how I envisioned Sarah's life to be. I pictured her happier, playing with her kids and being outside: gardening, laughing, telling stories. We always talked when we were kids about having a farm together and I told her that I wanted to live with her and raise chickens. She said that was what she wanted, too.

But now, looking at her husband lying on the couch, I wondered, *Is this how she envisioned her life? Is this life better?*

I asked Darryl to help me with the supper dishes. I gave him a chair and a cloth and asked if he would dry the silverware for me. I showed him what to do, picking up the fork and running the cloth over it.

After a while, the other two wanted to help. I praised them, especially Darryl, by patting him on the back. Still, he didn't warm up to me. He felt, I believe, he was just doing what he was told. I couldn't be sure.

The phone rang and the younger boys ran like the dickens to get it. Their father hollering, "No boys! Hold on! Just wait—"

They grabbed the receiver and yelled 'hello, hello'. Colin jumped up and took it from them, their faces turning to frowns with their hands still outstretched, screaming. "Mine!"

Colin shook his head and told the person on the other end to hang on. "Sarah! Would you take these two? I can't hear a thing."

Sarah didn't budge from her room, so he looked at me.

I helped Darryl off the chair and rummaged in the cupboard for crackers. The boys needed something to get their mind off the phone they thought was a toy. Colin had his finger in his right ear, nodding.

"Sarah!" he barked. "The phone's for you."

A cranky, irritable, pregnant woman waddled out to the kitchen. "Hello," she said stiffly.

I watched her expression when she realized who it was on the other line. She rolled her eyes, put her palm on the receiver and mouthed, "You got me up for *this*?"

Colin extended his arms and shrugged, sat back on the couch. The boys ran after their father, jumping beside him and nibbling on their crackers, collapsing on his lap.

I continued with the dishes, drying, putting away as quietly as I could. It didn't seem to matter to Sarah anyhow. Half the time she held the phone away from her ear and made a face when I looked at her.

"Okay. Yeah. Yeah. Mmm hmmm." She was curt.

I looked to Colin, who wasn't paying attention.

Then she hung up and huffed, "For God's sake. Like I have to be worrying about the likes of that."

"What?" I asked.

She took a big breath. "Nothing. Just Art going on about nothing important."

"Art? I would have liked to talk to him."

"Well, next time he calls, I'll give the phone to you." She sounded so snooty. "You hear that, Colin? Next time Art calls, give the phone to Maggie."

He looked at Sarah out the corner of his eye and nodded slowly, pursing his lips together.

A few weeks had passed and it didn't seem things were getting any better in my sister's household. They had two and a half-good days followed by three bad. Colin ended up working a lot of over-time. His excuse? They could use the extra money for the new baby and for holidays. Sarah argued he was working extra so he wouldn't have to come home. That's when my name would get drawn in.

Sometimes I couldn't block out their fights no matter how I tried. It was often at night, when we were in bed. I'd put the pillow over my head or pretend I was asleep. Sometimes, their fights woke up the kids and then the boys would start crying because they wanted to go to bed with them. Some nights felt like a circus.

The next morning, I'd tell Sarah I should leave but then she'd cry and beg me to stay. Although, after the umpteenth fight I thought it best to get a job during the day, and I could take the kids in the evenings so they could have some time together, alone. But I never even had time to look.

Sarah couldn't function at the minutest tasks. She slept a lot and seemed abnormally fatigued and down in the mouth. I did what I could, more than I should, but then it would backfire because any-time Colin commented on the good meal or the clean house, Sarah would sulk, throw her fork on her plate, and leave the dinner table.

Sometimes the boys would mimic her and their father would get angry at them. They didn't know the difference, and then they would cry. Two little mouths opened wide like little birds. They would leave in search of their mother. Colin would huff then go outside, head upstairs, or make his way to the basement.

It was often just Darryl and I left at the table. Poor Darryl. He'd never turn away from a meal and ate everything on his plate.

I sat with my elbow on the table, mouth pressed into the palm of my hand, watching him eat. He paid no attention to anything around him except for his plate and fork.

Joanne. What happened? Where are you? I couldn't even broach the topic of Joanne with Sarah. Why wasn't anyone concerned about her? And wouldn't she wonder about Darryl the same as he was, no doubt, wondering about her?

So, I made a decision. Tomorrow, come hell or high water, I was going to find out the whereabouts of my oldest sister.

25: He'll listen to you

Sarah sat on the edge of the couch, shaking my arm. "Maggie. Something's wrong."

"What?" I asked groggily.

She had a substantial lean to her body, and was holding her belly. Her face looked racked with pain.

"What's wrong?" I whispered, sitting up. I was scared to talk too loud in case our voices woke the children.

""I think it's the baby," she moaned. "Will you call Colin? He's already left for work. Tell him it's the baby!"

All at once the boys came running, their eyes wide. Darryl stayed out of reach, watching from the door, and then crept away when I ran for the phone.

Abdominal cramping and bleeding. That's what the doctor said. They wanted to keep her in the hospital but Sarah wouldn't stay. The only way they'd release her was if she agreed to total bed rest.

She had screamed herself into a state, but not just today. The last couple of weeks she'd been off. Pretty much since I'd arrived.

After she got home, I peered into her bedroom and saw her lying on her side. Her eyes were open.

I didn't want to disturb her, but she heard me. She turned her head in my direction. "That you, Colin?" You could hear hope in her voice.

"No," I said softly, "just me."

I paused, waiting to see if she would say anything else. I didn't want to get her riled. "Can I get you some tea or a piece of toast?"

She shook her head, but otherwise remained still.

The doctor said she had been doing too much, and had too much stress. She needed to relax and take it easy. I closed over the door and tiptoed away.

If I could just find Joanne, I thought.

~

On Colin's day off, I made a big breakfast for everyone. The smell of bacon sizzling got the boys' attention. They ran to the kitchen like hungry little puppies.

After I poured Colin a cup of tea I scooped the boys' breakfast onto three small plates. They didn't say a word as they gobbled down their meal. I sat down after they've finished.

Colin joined me then. "Thanks, Maggie. I don't know what we'd do without you."

"It's the least I can do."

"Sarah's just so..." He stopped himself, took a sip of his tea. "I just didn't expect this."

"Expect what? Breakfast?"

He shook his head and laughed. "No."

He stared at me across the table. I always liked Colin, especially his smile. He had a crooked tooth in the front which, I thought, added to his charm, He looked thin, though, and tired. And sort of sad, too.

"You're working too hard." I said.

"You're cute, Maggie. And so patient. I wish Sarah was more like you."

I stopped chewing. Didn't know what to say. I wasn't sure what he meant, exactly.

When he got up to get more tea from the teapot he touched my arm. "Thank you." He said. His fingers felt rough on my skin. His palm, warm.

I kept my arm still till he removed his hand. Then he placed that hand on my shoulder. After the longest moment he walked to the stove to drain the pot and turned off the burner. "Any plans for today?"

"After breakfast, I have to go and sort out a few things. If you could watch the boys?" I felt like I spoke so fast.

"Yeah. Of course. Need a lift?"

"No. That's okay. I'll take the bus."

"Okay, then."

He took his tea and left the room.

I immediately started clearing plates. I didn't want to lose any time for my search for Joanne, and I needed to get away from here, too.

I was sure that Colin didn't mean any harm with what he said, that he was sincere in his thankfulness. But why was my heart beating so fast and my arm shaking?

I shook it off. Had to. Sarah wasn't well and she was pregnant with his third child. I was sure he was nervous, too, about what had just happened to her. And tired. And over-worked, like any number of men going through fatherhood.

I was sure he thought I was able-bodied. That's what he meant. He would rather see Sarah cooking his children breakfast instead of me.

I was sure that's what he meant.

~

As I sat on the bus, thoughts swirled inside my head. Darryl came first. I hoped he would stay out of trouble, that he wouldn't eat too much for lunch, that his cousins would play with him. I hoped Colin didn't play favourites, either. I didn't like that, and hoped Sarah would listen to the doctor and stay in bed. And I hoped most especially, she wouldn't argue with Colin.

My head was so full of hoping, I missed my stop.

But I remembered Joanne's street number. It was still etched in my brain, ever since I copied it from Sarah's address book the first time I came to Ontario.

I'd know the apartment complex by looking at it, too. A light-brown brick building that resembled a box of matches, and I was pleased with myself when I still recognized it so easily.

Once inside the lobby I pressed the buzzer and anticipated what I was going to say first. But after a few minutes of waiting, nobody answered.

When I was readying to press the buzzer again, I noticed the word 'vacant' beside her apartment number. I thought it odd, but pressed it again anyway. Still nothing. Confused, I checked the names on the mailboxes and after scanning, and grumbling, I realized it wasn't Joanne's name I should be looking for, but Dan's. Sarah said that he had moved back home.

Searching for his name in the directory, however, came up just as empty.

I was perplexed. Did she move to a different apartment? Or use an alias? Maybe she didn't want anyone to know where she lived? Did it get to be that bad between my sisters that they are no longer on speaking terms? Is that why Sarah is suffering so much? My heart felt heavy.

I drummed my fingers on the metal box. *Surely, Sarah would have said something to let me know*? Or, maybe not? She has been in such a state the last while.

Standing in the entrance, I waited for an answer to come to me. *Maybe if I went to her work? Maybe I'd have better luck seeing her there.*

I left the small vestibule and walked towards downtown.

It was a cool day, grey and overcast and the wind had picked up. April weather was always so unpredictable. I held my hat and walked against the wind. Although the strong gusts took away my breath, nothing was going to stop me today. The rift between my sisters needed fixing.

It had been far too long since I had seen Joanne, and when I finally saw the restaurant up ahead, I rushed toward it.

A car horn honked, and I jumped back. Without thinking, I had stepped out onto the road. Embarrassed, I waved to the driver but his face remained stern.

The street bustled with cars pulling in and out in all directions. Finally, I caught sight of her. Her slender frame and auburn hair. *Joanne.* My voice caught in my throat. It had been so long.

"Joanne," I yelled.

Her long mane whipped about her face but she didn't hear me.

Her mouth set in a serious line, like she was given some bad news. She was with a man about her age, though, and my heart warmed. *Good. That's good.*

It looked like they had been holding hands, but they had let go of one another. Her arm was adrift in the air but still connected to his by a fine thread.

I hollered her name again but she didn't hear me. She wasn't expecting to see me. She probably didn't know I was back because no one had told her. *Wouldn't Momma be so disappointed by all of this?*

"Joanne!" I raised my hand in the air, waved it back and forth.

They strode to a blue Chevy and hopped in. My heart sped. I ran after them as fast as I could to catch up. *If I don't reach them now...*

I was almost there, but the traffic intensified. I watched hopelessly as their car manoeuvred through the parking lot. *Are they intentionally keeping away? Is Joanne angry with me too?*

They pulled out on the road. I leapt forward but my fingers barely grazed the trunk of their car. Horns blared.

Only then did she angrily turn around and look.

"Joanne," I hollered one last time, "for God's sake, it's me!"

But she didn't stop, the car kept going. I stood breathless, watching as the they drove out of sight.

"Are you clueless?" a man yelled.

"Huh?"

"You're in the middle of the road."

"Sorry," I panted. Of course, I was but there was no point in explaining.

I trudged onto the curb, trying to catch my wind, and decided maybe they'd tell me where she lives at the restaurant. Didn't Joanne tell me she got a job here? Or was it Sarah who told me? It didn't matter. Today was about getting answers and I surged forward.

Inside the diner, I took a seat at the long counter on a red, upholstered stool.

The waitress saw me and came over. "What can I get you?" she asked, resting her arms wide against the counter.

"I'll have a tea to start. Please."

She nodded, started to walk away when I called her back. "My sister Joanne works here. I think it's here." I made a funny face, feeling a bit awkward and silly. I pointed to the parking lot and smiled placidly. "I just saw her leave with someone. I must have just missed her by two minutes."

She reached for the pot, flipped over my cup and poured the hot beverage, placing cream and sugar beside me. "Just a second there, hon. I have to give these customers their bill."

She scooted off to an elderly couple. The woman had short, grey hair and, although she was standing, her shoulders stooped forward. She tied a multi-coloured kerchief on her head. The man was older, round and stout, and wore a tan Fedora. He looked smart in his overcoat and hat.

I couldn't imagine my parents dining out together, let alone here of all places. *What would they even order?* What would they even think of the city? And the buses and paved roads?

Watching the couple made me think of my parents until these people noticed me gawking. Momma had said it was rude to stare so I turned my attention to the glass dome on the counter in front of me.

After they left, I raised my hand like we did in school and the waitress strutted over.

"I'd like one of those please." I pointed to the donuts.

She lifted the glass knob and placed the sugary ring on a plate and handed it to me.

"Anything else?" she asked.

I took a quick bite. "Yes. My sister, Joanne?" I mumbled. I slurped the hot tea to wash down the crumbs.

She tilted her head. "Do you mean Mary Jo?"

I rolled my eyes. "Is that what she's calling herself now?" I laughed.

"She's off for a few days, I think. I'll have to check the schedule."

"Darn." I said as I licked my fingers. "I really just missed her by minutes."

The waitress looked back at me in silence.

"What about her address? Could you tell me where she lives? I think she must have moved. I was at her place and I couldn't find her name. Unless she's with her new beau. Did you meet him? Is he nice?" I couldn't believe I had the gall and asked so many questions. Papa would be mortified. I was usually so reserved. So shy.

The waitress shook her head. "Not sure. What did you say your name was again?"

"Oh, sorry." I held out my hand. "I'm Maggie. Her younger sister. I just moved back from Boston. I'm staying with our other sister now. Sarah—"

The bell chimed.

"Sorry, love. I have to go." She nodded, looked at the food on the serving tray.

"Oh. Okay. Maybe I'll come back. On Monday, then? What time does she start?"

"Seven o'clock."

Seven. I'll have to be up with the birds.

I smiled and took another bite of the donut. *Well, I won't be here that early. But good for Joanne. She has a regular job at least, and a new apartment somewhere. My. Maybe things have finally turned in her favour.*

I arrived back at Sarah's late in the afternoon, almost suppertime, feeling euphoric. I couldn't wait to tell her the happy news, but right now, obviously, wasn't a good time. She was on the phone, in tears.

I rushed to her. "What is it?"

She held her palm over the phone. "It's...He's..." she sobbed, passed the phone to me.

"Hello?"

"Maggie? That you?" Art's throat was scratchy and worn. It never changed.

"What's wrong, Art?" I laid a hand on Sarah's shoulder. She was shaking, sitting in a ball on the chair.

"It's your Uncle Dan, Maggie. He passed on this morning."

I wanted to say something, 'I'm sorry', 'what happened?' But I didn't say anything. I removed my hand from Sarah's shoulder. I stood with my back against the wall where the phone hung. I twirled the cord with my fingertips.

"You still there?" he hacked. I could hear him smoking, breathing into the receiver.

"Yeah," I said quietly.

"I told him not to be going on that roof. He's too old to be doing that. I told him to hire someone young to help out. But your uncle was too cheap, too—"

"He fell off the roof?" I asked.

Sarah looked up at me, pinched up her face. She hobbled to the kitchen in search of tissues.

"No, no," he hacked. "He got down from the roof alright but said he felt tired so he went to bed right after. Never woke up."

"Oh!" I pictured him lying down, his arms by his side. His big nose and mass of hair askew on his forehead, Aunt Martha shaking him, hollering his name, trying to wake him up. "And, how is she?" I could barely say her name.

"Well, she's a tough old battle axe, you know, but this here she's taking pretty bad. But, Maggie. That's not the worst of it. I was telling your sister, your father's not in a good way, either. I tried telling her a few times but she seems to have her hands full."

"What do you mean?"

"Well, he's getting forgetful. Keeps getting lost. Says he's looking for the horses but he ain't had one of those in years. Well, none that I know of. Unless he has one hidden away somewhere. He had a pretty good fall, too. And whacked himself with the axe. He had a good gash on the side of his head when I went to see him. The blood still caked on his face. Like he didn't know he was hurt or forgot to wash himself. I think it best you come home and help him out. What do you say? He won't listen to me. But you—he'll listen to you."

"Me?" I asked, appalled, my eyes wide. "Why me?"

"Well, you're all that's left, Maggie. Sarah's married and got the children and, from what I understand, having another." He wheezed again. "Maybe if you just came and stayed with him for a bit, get him settled. It would be good for the both of you, I think. According to Sarah"—he trailed off—"she thinks it's a good idea, too. You'll come home for the funeral anyway, won't ya?"

"I wasn't planning on it."

"Well, someone has to represent the family and it can't be your sister."

I looked at her consoling herself, her face red and splotchy, eyes glossy and sunken. I closed mine and sighed.

"Art." I wanted to scream. I didn't feel anything towards Uncle Dan or even Aunt Martha. I hadn't since they wanted to take Darryl away. Even before that.

"I know, I know. But it's for the best, I think. Do it for your sister. You know she can't go and it would mean a lot to her, I think." Art kept talking while my insides seethed. "It's your people, Maggie, not that I'm telling you, and not that I'm—"

"Fine," I snapped.

"You let me know when you're coming then and I'll pick you up."

I hung up the phone and marched upstairs, leaving Sarah to console herself.

26: Got the woman's touch

I didn't get to see Joanne like I had planned. Sarah had booked my ticket to go home the very next day.

I stomped around my room, firing clothes in my suitcase. I didn't want to go home. I didn't want to see my father, or look after him. I had left Port Hope for a reason, and I especially didn't want to go to Uncle Dan's funeral. Art could go to that. He could represent the family.

I slumped on my bed. What was the point in arguing when there was no one to argue with? They had bought the ticket and my bags were now packed.

Colin drove me to the train. It was an odd exchange. He got out and handed me my suitcase. "Have a good trip," he said.

Trip. This wasn't a trip. I watched him pull away and I lingered by the entrance. What if I didn't get on? What if...I contemplated, where could I go?

A woman wearing a blue dress walked past me. "Let's go home, dear," she said to the teenage girl who walked alongside her. I drew in a deep breath. It was like her words told me what I should do. I held the ticket tight in my finger tips and made my way inside the building.

In one way, the train trip prepared me for the rest of my journey. It gave me time to absorb why I had left, or more accurately, why I had to leave. The phone call from Art was the cut; the ticket, the scab; and the train ride, the healing.

~

"You packed light," Art said to me.

He had another tooth missing in the front and it looked silly when he smiled. He looked much older, too, and his hair was long and thin. He stank of cigarettes and sweat. I wondered when he had last bathed.

He chewed on tobacco and the dark juice ran down his whiskered chin. Sometimes he would wipe it with the back of his hand; other times, the black fluid just dripped onto his already-discoloured undershirt. He hadn't changed a bit.

Driving home, he talked a blue streak. Asked about Sarah and her house, the kids. He asked about Darryl, too. He said Sarah sent him photos and he had those at home in his window.

I nodded and didn't say much.

Then he asked me if the cat got my tongue and slapped my leg, but I found I had nothing to say. I stared down at my hands, picking at the skin and the cuticles, then stared out the window. More trees. *My God, is that all that's here? Trees?*

As we pulled up my drive I noticed how empty the house looked and how overgrown the fields were. The roof on one of the small outbuildings had caved in, too. It was the place where we had kept the hens.

"What happened there?" I asked.

"Windstorm last fall," Art answered. "Blew down them trees. Lucky it didn't go through your roof," he added.

When I got out of the car, I grabbed my bag and noticed a large pile of wood and the axe. Piles of wood everywhere.

He saw me staring. "Lots of felled trees, or your father just cuts 'em. That's what he does with his time now. You won't run out of logs for the fire this winter. Not for a dozen years."

He laughed, his throat raspy and sharp. He started coughing, and spewed black spit onto the ground.

Art walked ahead of me and went into the house, pushing on the door. It opened with a mean creak.

I expected to see Papa where he always was, on the daybed with the fire blaring, but the room was dark and cold. Empty. The house looked like it was not lived in and had a strong odour of pee and rancid cheese. The smell made me want to vomit.

As I walked to the window to let in some fresh air, a small mouse darted across the counter and I let out a scream.

"What's the matter? Forget what a mouse looks like?" He chuckled. "If I catch one, I'll have it for supper."

I turned away in disgust.

He stuck his finger in the hole where the creature disappeared. "We'll plug that with something."

He pulled out his finger and examined it, like he thought there would be mouse residue or cheese there. He rested against the counter, and said casually, "Well, he's not here I see."

"Did you tell him I was coming?" I asked.

"Don't matter. I could tell him a hundred times, he'd still forget."

He turned on his heel. "He's probably out in the barn or down by the well. I'll go fetch him." He grabbed for the handle of the door, "You—You can...Well, it's your God-damn house. You know what to do here."

And he left.

I stared out at the woods from the kitchen window for what seemed like twenty minutes, not moving, in a trance-like state. I didn't want to be here. The place had never looked so bad. *Did it actually look like this when we lived here? When Momma was alive?*

I lifted my finger to touch the curtains. They were white when she first hung them and she was so proud of them. I remember Joanne telling us that. They had a delicate lace detail, and now it was brown, caked with cobwebs and moth holes. When I touched it at the seam, they crumbled in my fingers.

I turned and faced the stove, contemplating putting on a fire just to get the dampness out, and I hoped it would improve the smell.

But the stench seemed to be coming from my father's room, which was just off from the kitchen. It too, was dark, and as I walked toward it, the aroma overwhelming. The source of the smell was the piss pot, filled to the brim with cloudy urine, the cover on its side laying on the floor.

Gagging, I grabbed an old rag, probably one of Papa's undershirts, and lifted the ceramic cover back on.

In one slick movement, and holding my breath, I drew open the curtains and attempted to lift the heavy window. Grunting, my fingers dug into the swollen wood frame, realizing Papa probably hadn't opened it in years. When I finally raised it up, I pulled the slat from the sill to keep it propped open and quickly fled the room closing the door behind me.

It was then I set about putting a fire on in the kitchen. I bent down, remembering how to do it. Thin slats of wood, crumbled paper, and a good match. It rose to life, crackling joyfully. The whiff of smoke and wood burning raised my spirits slightly.

There was still no sign of Art or Papa even though I searched for them out the living room window. Art's car was still parked where he had left it. I scanned the barn and the fields too, but there was no sign of life anywhere.

As the warmth of the fire enveloped the room, I took a seat at the table and strummed my fingers to pass the time. Within five seconds of waiting, I started tidying up.

I brushed the crumbs off the counter and filled the sink with hot water and soap. Swept the floor and soaked the teacups, checked the fridge for food that needed to go, and threw away a number of things of unknown origin. I flung those out into the yard for the crows or the birds, or whatever other animal happened to graze by. I hoped it wouldn't kill them.

Knowing full well Papa would be angry at me for using his electricity, I turned on the lights in the kitchen anyway. It didn't matter. I was prepared for his reaction.

After I finished in the kitchen, I went into the living room, where the fire did not reach. My shoulders curved inward as I felt the dampness and the draft. I assessed every part of the house with new eyes.

The linoleum had lifted in spots, making it dangerous to walk. You could easily catch a foot and trip if you weren't careful.

Matter of fact, the whole living room appeared to be a hazard. The Chesterfield had a wire spring sticking out of its back. I placed a yellowed pillow over it in case someone sat there, although no one ever came in this room.

That's when I noticed the chair I had sent home. It was forced against the back wall, looking like it had never been sat in. I ran my hand over the stiff fabric, sighed, and kept on through to the back staircase.

The stair railing stuck out at an odd angle and, when I placed my hand on it, shook loose. Splinters of wood lay strewn on the hardwood and two of the spindles were snapped off. I could see that this might be where my father had fallen and got the gash that Art had talked about. I couldn't fathom what he was doing or why he had been here, as he rarely went upstairs.

There was a small pool of congealed blood that had dried on the floor and tiny prints ran through it. It looked like a jelly jam left out too long.

Up the stairs I went, the boards creaking under my feet. The air smelled thick and musty, like the house has been closed for all the years I'd been gone. Untouched. Uncleaned.

I wondered if I should be staying here at all. It didn't feel like my home anymore. It seemed different. Vacant and lonely.

Maybe because Art was still off looking for my father and I felt the physical absence of people in the house. No sisters to make the house warm and welcoming with their laughter, no mother to have the meals prepared. Freshly baked bread coming out of the oven. Animals in the fields. Cows to follow you with their gentle eyes, horses neighing, chickens clucking as they scurry about your pathway like they had suddenly joined in a game of children's tag.

No, I was alone with the cobwebs. Even the spiders had left their homes for other, more adequate, lodgings.

The stairwell and hall leading to the bedrooms upstairs had dark-wood panels. I slid my palm down the wall and felt the roughness of the wood, the knots that had not been planed. Irregularities and bumps that did not seem relevant in the building and the constructing.

Not like Sarah's place, with all the new technologies and building materials. The smoothness of her walls, the new fridge and stove. The modern conveniences.

Had I ever noticed these differences before?

And the walls lay bare here. In Sarah's house, she had photos of the children on hers, and framed wood scenes and clocks. Things that made a house a home.

I peeked in my room first. The place I shared with Mary. How small it looked. My room appeared no bigger than a place where elves slept. How did we both fit on that small bed?

The iron frame needed a fresh coat of paint. Much of the white looked dull and had flaked off, leaving darkened scabs.

A gray coat of dust covered the floor. The sheets and blankets were upturned, the pillows strewn, the drawers to the bureau opened like someone had been looking for something. A burglary, I thought and chuckled to myself. I touched my fingers to my lips. It felt foreign here, my laughter. We always whispered, were never allowed to talk too loudly.

Next, I turned towards Joanne and Sarah's room across the hall. The room I moved into after Joanne left and Mary had died.

It too was unmade and messy. In this room stood a two-door wardrobe with a glass panel that was supposed to be a mirror. It was so worn through we never truly saw our reflections, just a distorted shadow of ourselves. The girls used it to hang their dresses and Momma's clothes. I had felt jealous. They had a part of her in their room.

Inside the wardrobe—a few wire hangers still hung, but with nothing on them. All that lay inside was dust and more cobwebs.

Dead flies blackened the corners of the window; probably died trying to stay warm. Their bodies turned to soup.

I lingered for a while, studying the room, remembering my sisters. Imagining the low whispers they shared from across the hall, wondering what deep secrets they kept, what dreams they had.

The voices started downstairs. Art banged in, stamped his feet, spoke loud. "Looky here, John. She's got the woman's touch." His voice carried upstairs.

I didn't hear my father's voice and felt reluctant to go downstairs. I knew I wouldn't rush to him the way Sarah's boys did with her. I remained perfectly still.

Why am I here? I wished at that very moment I was back at Sarah's, or somewhere I was needed.

"Maggie? Where ya at? Your father is here," Art yelled. "Did you get lost or something?"

I walked down the stairs. The echo of my footsteps told them I was coming.

I walked past the dried-up blood and broken rail, past the living room with the unused chair, the dining room that we never used to eat in, and stood before them in the kitchen, beside the wood box. Papa lay on his dirty daybed.

"There ya are. Playing hide and seek, eh?" Art said with a laugh. It sounded scratchy, like a record player. "Getting all snuggly up in your room, were ya?" He slapped his hand on his leg.

Papa searched my face. He stared up and down the length of me, and nodded slightly. He put his arm over the top of his head and closed his eyes.

Silence ensued for a few moments until Art spoke. "Well, John, Maggie, there's a warm acknowledgement. Okay, I'll leave you to it. I'm sure you've lots to catch up on without me here."

I looked back at Papa. The only thing he needed to get caught up on was sleep and his blatant disregard for me. I bit the inside of my cheek and tightened my fingers into a fist.

"Art?" I asked, "Can I stay with you?" I made for the door.

He narrowed his eyes and then looked towards my father. Apparently, Art didn't want me either.

"There's no food here, and not even a bathroom. Why isn't there a proper bathroom at least? I need to be able to shower or bathe. Papa?"

Papa opened his eyes and moved his shoulders and grunted. My voice, not my words had aggravated him.

But I didn't stop. "Really? That's all you have to say? Well. I'm not gonna stay here unless there's at least a decent washroom. I'm not gonna be relieving myself in a bucket. I'm not a primate. I'm not barbaric. I'm not like him." I pointed my finger at my father.

Art said nothing. He kept his hands by his sides, shifted his eyes from me to the floor.

"You better tell me I can stay at your place, Art, else just take me back to the train station. Right now, and I'll find my own way back."

"Hold on, hold on!" Art seemed unnerved, his eyes furrowed, and he kept looking back at Papa, who said nothing. "What's gotten into you? You used to be so quiet," he snapped.

I opened my mouth, but he beat me to the punch.

"Okay, Okay. Easy now. Have some patience. Go and get in the car. We'll get you to the store tomorrow for some groceries. You hear that, John?" He bent over my father's frame, talking loudly, like his inability to communicate was based on Papa being deaf. "Groceries, tomorrow."

Papa barely nodded.

He looked so pathetic and skinny, his hair a swath of white where it used to be as grey as the chimney smoke. His eyes looked sunken. There was no reason why he couldn't look after himself. It wasn't my job. That was just laziness.

When we were in the car, I said, "What the hell is wrong with him, Art? I mean, he is a lazy-good-for-nothing—"

Art turned and glared. "Maggie. I don't know what's going on with you. First, you wouldn't talk and now you won't shut up."

I gasped. Folded my arms across my chest.

"You're angry."

I turned my face toward the passenger's side window, hurt by his words, and veered my body almost completely right as well. We drove for a few minutes in silence.

Art sighed. "Maggie," he said in a low, gentle tone. I didn't answer. "You're mad at me now, are ya?" I remained silent. I stayed inside my brain as we drove to Art's.

We pulled into his drive. It looked like Art had collected more in the years I was absent, too. He had a couple of cars parked in the yard, one with its hood open. The old truck he had years back was still there. So too was the old horse wagon, and a rugged fence around a small outbuilding.

"Don't tell me that's the bathroom?"

"No. No. It's for—never mind. You'll find out soon enough."

He turned off the key and the two of us sat without moving. Small dots of rain peppered the windshield.

"Art?" I mustered. "You're older than my father, right?"

"Yes, by three and a half years." He took out a cigarette and lit it, blue smoke rose from his mouth.

"Then how come?" I stammered. "How come he's so backward and you're not. I mean, you have a car and can drive, for starters."

Art took a long drag of the cigarette. "Maggie. You're asking questions I can't answer. Why don't you ask your father that?"

I didn't say anything, just huffed.

"I think, if you're asking... your father's still mad at you."

I gawked at him. "What? Why?"

"Well, you left him alone."

"Yeah, and? I'm not his wife."

"No. I know that. But you were all that he had left. He's lonely, I think."

"But he doesn't talk and doesn't communicate. I mean, he doesn't even have a phone. He doesn't write. He didn't try to get in contact with me even once all the time I was gone."

"I was his communication, Maggie. For you and your sister. Well, mostly you. You stayed in touch with me and I told him what you were doing. I told him about the children and your work and Sarah's house." He waved his hand in a circular motion as he listed all the things he talked about.

"You're more of a father than he ever was."

Art started to hack and cough. His shoulders shook as his lungs shuddered.

I waited for him to stop, and when he did, he took another long puff and opened his door and tossed out the butt.

"Your father's been through it all, Maggie. More than I ever had to go through. You forget he lost his ma and sisters in that fire when he was young. Can you imagine that? Hearing the screams and smelling the flesh burning?" He shook his head. "And then of course your own ma and his children. There's a reason that man doesn't speak, Maggie. He's been in his own hell for years."

I scratched at the fabric on my dress, picked at my fingers.

Art turned towards me, "And, Maggie, your sister is worried about you. That's another reason why she wanted you to come home, eh?"

"I know. The stupid funeral." I rolled my eyes, feeling more like a sulking six-year-old.

He opened the car door. "Come on, then, get inside. We'll talk more tomorrow. You had a long trip."

I opened the door on my side and got out.

The rain held off long enough for the two of us to get into the house, and then it came down in a whoosh.

~

We feasted on homemade beans and slices of ham. We ate in relative silence. I washed up the dishes. Art had his drink of whiskey and several cigarettes.

He told me to sleep in whichever room I liked. With every intention, I planned on sleeping in the room I used to stay in, but the dark night and the room itself gave me the prickles. Like spooks lived in there, hid in closets, waited for me to lie down only to disturb my dreams.

I slept, instead, on the chair by the fire, which Art stoked before going to bed himself.

I woke in a sweat and my tongue stuck to the roof of my mouth. I lay awake for the next few hours, listening to the unfamiliar sounds that once were recognizable to me—the ticking of the clock, the rain hitting the roof, the tree scratching the window. Hearing Art farting all night and his abominable snoring didn't help either.

My eyes wouldn't stay closed no matter how much I willed them. I tossed, I turned, I flipped and flopped.

I finally must have drifted off only to be awoken by him. Art gave me such a fright, seeing his old, unshaven face and smelling his pungent, sour breath.

"Wake up, Maggie. It's just a dream."

I let out a gasp, more from seeing him, and sat up. The blanket had fallen to the floor and I leaned over to get it.

"Jesus, Maggie. You trying to give me a heart attack?"

He waddled around in his underwear that looked like a loose, wet diaper. His legs were so scrawny and white, they gleamed like marble columns in the moonlight. He flicked on the light and I watched as he went to the cupboard and took a small glass, reached again and took out a bottle, poured amber liquid from it.

He turned to face me, holding the glass and handed it over. "Here. Drink this."

I reached for it, smelled it, made a face.

"Oh, don't be so God-damn queer. Drink it. It'll make you sleep."

I brought the cup to my lips and tipped my head back, tasting the toxic substance. It turned my tastebuds to fire and I squirmed.

He tapped the bottom of the glass, kept it tipped towards my mouth. The fluid ran to the back of my throat and down, the excess sprayed outward beyond the glass and onto my cheeks.

Gagging, I pushed the glass away, waving my hand in front of me as if that would help to quell the heat in my mouth.

Art tittered, looked in the glass and brought it to his own lips, finishing what I couldn't.

Then, out of nowhere, he struck a match and lit a cigarette, sat opposite me on a wooden chair and handed it over.

"I don't smoke."

"You should," he said, his laugh hoarse. He took three quick drags, the orange glow radiating from the tip.

He ran his dirty fingers through his whiskers, his hair a tousled mess upon his head. He wore a ratty, old, long-sleeved undershirt and wool socks that were bunched at his ankles.

He sat wide-legged in front of me and, if I had dared to look, I'm sure his manhood would have been exposed, but he didn't care. He was as content with himself in his unwashed, thread-barren garments as a king in his fine silk robes.

"Art. You need some new clothes."

Looking down at himself, he raised his hands with the cigarette still held between two fingers. "Nothin' wrong with what I got on. You women are too particular."

"That why you've never had one?" I asked, eagerly awaiting his response.

His mouth turned up at the ends, exposing his blackened gums. He nodded, chuckled with his raspy voice that I now found therapeutic, almost like an itch that needs nails to scratch it.

"Seriously, Art."

"Don't be asking questions this early in the morning, Maggie. I haven't had my coffee yet."

He dropped the butt it in the glass. It sizzled.

"You had a shot. That's stronger than coffee."

He laughed again, deflecting my answer. I knew Art would never say. "You might have made a good husband for someone."

He stood up and winked at me, licked his lip with his thick tongue and scratched his buttocks. "Going back to bed now, Maggie. You try, too," he grunted.

"Thanks, Art." I waved to him.

"Don't mention it."

And he blew a squeaky fart as he walked back to his room.

27: *Deagh thlachd*

I made fat molasses cookies and a tray of sandwiches for the wake. Art had picked up the ingredients for me. I couldn't imagine trying to prepare anything at Papa's.

"What'll we do first?" Art asked as he grabbed a cookie. "Drop these off and then go get groceries for your house?"

"What?" I said, as I turned my head. "I thought Papa was going."

Art ate the cookie, biting with his back teeth. Crumbs stuck to his lips and whiskers. "No. Be too much for him. 'Sides, he'll just get the same stuff anyway. Bread, milk."

I pursed my lips in disgust. "They any good?"

"They're a bit hard," Art said jokingly. He spewed crumbs when he laughed and I shielded my face with my arm. "Kidding. Course they good. They're molasses."

He took another bite. "Be good with the tea. You make a little extra? To keep here?"

"Of course."

"Good. Let's have a cup then we'll get going."

As we headed to Aunt Martha's, I sat motionless clutching the plate of sandwiches, swallowing, a tightness clamping down in my chest. I would have given anything to get out of going. Anything.

But it was no use. Sarah had begged me to go because she couldn't travel in her condition, Papa had made a pact years ago he would never set foot in that house again, and I didn't get time to reach Joanne. *So, here I am. The only family who can represent.* I rolled my eyes and blessed myself.

I went over in my mind how things would unfold. Contribute the food, offer condolences, leave promptly. My part would be done.

The tightness in my chest, however, was three-fold. It gripped and squeezed my lungs like I was in a well trying to get to the surface for air. I forgot about the plate, clutching the dash instead, and held it firmly in my grip. The sandwiches slid dangerously forward.

Art eased off the gas. "We're almost there."

"I know," I said mechanically.

Aunt Martha's stone chimney came into view. The land dipped then and we could see the full view of her abode. The fine house with the shutters and the drive leading towards it.

The old apple tree was leafless and grey. Its scrawny branches arched outward like the fingers of a cadaver, a skeleton hand coming through the spring soil, reaching for its next victim. *Uncle Dan.* 'It' pulled him off that roof, poked him hard in the chest and squeezed the life out of him, I thought.

By the time Art had parked the car, my fingers were tightened into deep fists, my teeth gritted, heart pumping like I had just run here from Art's.

"Come on, then. Let's get his over with," he said.

Art grabbed the bag of cookies and I carried the sandwiches. Every ounce of my body slowed as I inched forward. It felt like I was trudging through soft, knee-deep muck.

Art walked in ahead of me. He left the door ajar, signalled for me to follow. I closed my eyes and took a breath, not realizing my arm rested across the tray of sandwiches. It looked like eggs had exploded on the plate.

I walked in slowly. The first thing that hit me was the familiar scent of my aunt's house, the wood stove, and homemade bread. I felt squeamish.

I placed the dented sandwiches on the table, heard the murmurs of people from the other room, where *he* was.

Art poked his head around, "Come on now. What's taking you?"

I felt my face redden and I was hot. He reached out his hand for me to take it. Not that I ever held hands with Art. Never. That never happened.

But today, in my aunt's house on the day of my uncle's wake, the old man that took me here, perhaps sensed my insecurities or fear or hatred or discomfort, let his palm dangle for me to grip it, as if I was a seven-year-old attending my mother's wake. He waited for me on the other side of the threshold, fluttering his hand, waiting patiently impatient.

I caught a glimpse of her hair first, tied back with pins. Her scent wafted towards me, floral, motherly, soft.

Then her voice when she recognized me, "Maggie? That you, dear?" in an almost painful, child-like voice.

My voice caught in my throat. The room was stifling, my head spun. I needed air. I needed to get out. I trembled and fell to my knee.

She rushed towards me, embraced me with all of her. Held me close—so tight. She said my name, raised me to both feet, rubbed her hands over my skin, brushed my hair out of my face.

"Maggie. Oh, Maggie. You've come. You've really come."

She laughed like I had said something funny. She sniffed, wiped her nose, fidgeted, hugged me again, crushing me against her full frame. I couldn't speak and didn't want to.

Art held out the bag of cookies, flopped them in his hand. "She made these." He looked at the table and pointed to the flattened sandwiches. "And those."

"Isn't that nice, Maggie? Thank you, dear. Art. Thank you," she whispered loud to him, as if I wasn't there. "I didn't expect anyone so early. It's just the priest here, and Dan's brothers."

"We can't stay, Martha," Art interjected. "We've got things to do. Wanted to drop off these here goods."

Martha's face dropped. She kept gripping her hands, rubbing her thumb over her knuckles, caressing her palms. She smiled and frowned, wiped her eyes.

"Groceries for John. A bathroom for Maggie." Poor Art didn't know when to shut up.

"You need to go to the washroom, Maggie?" She looked at me with concern, her hand touched my back.

I flinched. I shook my head.

"No?" She looked confused. Then she just nodded and turned her head, raised her finger to her mouth like she was to say something.

She looked older. Yet she looked like my mother. I couldn't believe how much she reminded of me of her. Her mouth and sharp
nose, her dark eyes when she looked at me, particularly when they
were watery. Deep, sensory. She knew what I was thinking, feeling.

God, how I missed my mother. Tears came to my eyes.

Another car pulled in with several women. They had baskets of
flowers and more food. I got pushed forward in the rush of hugs
and sentiments.

I was moving to get out of the way when I saw him, Dan, in the
casket. His chest heaving out of it, his hands crossed against his
stomach.

One of Martha's brothers-in-law came in with the bouquet and
placed it beside the coffin. Roses. Beside their wedding picture.
There were a few other black and white photos. One of them with
their son, my cousin.

I was studying it when Martha came in and stood beside me,
grabbed my hand and led me to Dan up close. She tried to make me
touch him and I yelled for her to stop. She looked at me with shock.

"Stop it!" I said again. "I don't need to see him, let alone touch
him."

"Maggie."

Our raised voices caused alarm. Everyone came rushing over
like there was something to see. They all grimaced, mouths
pressed in a straight line, eyes searching, staring.

I jerked my arm away and tried to press through the tall bodies
but she grabbed me, turned me around.

"I know you're upset. It's okay. It's okay to cry."

"You don't get it, do you, Martha? I'm not upset about him. I'm
happy he's gone."

"What?" She pressed her hands to her face. "What are you saying?"

The murmurings started around me. Heads twitched, shook,
tsked.

"You're being disrespectful here," Uncle Dan's brother said. The
women in the kitchen whispered in each other's ears, staring at

me, pointing, figuring out who I was.

"Maggie." I heard his voice and knew his tone. "Not now, girl. Let's go." Art stood in the clearing, holding open the door.

My whole body suddenly felt lithe. I brushed past the clutter of people, nearly knocking the tray of sandwiches off the table.

We drove in silence. Art said nothing to me about my outburst. Didn't lecture or scold, or ask questions. He just steered the wheel and smoked. I found I had nothing to say anyway. I let the moment pass as the movement of the car and its warmth embraced me.

When the car stopped, I opened my eyes. I looked up, surprised. We finally had a real grocery store.

"You go in and get what you need."

"But I don't know what we need."

"Probably everything." He slammed his door, tossed his butt on the ground and walked towards the hardware store.

I grabbed a shopping cart and wished I had made a list. I was going through items in my head. What we'd need. A chicken and potatoes. He probably needed potatoes...a turnip? Carrots. Darn. I wished I had asked Art what sort of garden he had. Maybe he had all these at home?

I got milk and bread anyway. Peanut butter. Would he eat that on a biscuit? Flour, eggs. Butter. Molasses. We didn't have hens anymore. Nor cows. I found my mind drifting off. Why did Papa get rid of the animals? What did he do with his time?

I got to the checkout and saw Art. He came up to me, inspected my order. He left and came back with a bag of apples, a tin of coffee, and a bag of brown sugar. "Papa doesn't drink coffee." I inspected the items in his arms.

"Coffee's for me. So are the apples. You can make me a pie." He winked, showed me his gummy smile.

"Oh yeah. Who says?"

"Well. I've got the MacKellan fella coming over to inspect your toilet facilities." He wiggled his fingers at me. "Best have something in if he's gonna' be working there. Sweeten the deal," he said, smirking.

I jutted out my chin, assessed this news. James MacKellan a licensed plumber? I hadn't seen him in years.

I made a roast chicken dinner without the stuffing. It was edible but a bit bland. Sarah was the cook in the family. I made meals that got me by.

Papa ate all his, which signified it had to be good enough. I take that back. Papa would eat anything if he was hungry or if someone else made it.

He didn't say a word the whole time. He ate, nodded, picked at his teeth, pushed his plate away from him, showing he had finished his meal and waited for his tea to be served. He didn't ask for anything sweet so I didn't give him anything. It was just like when I was kid.

"Why'd you sell the cows?"

"Don't need 'em."

"But you used to sell the milk and whey to make cheese."

"I sell the hay now."

I nodded. We had so much unused land, Papa could make as much hay as he wanted. And potatoes. He still farmed potatoes. *Nothing better than a good potato.* I remember him saying that, never fulling realizing what he meant until you had a bad one.

He wouldn't let me use any of the potatoes I bought from the store. He went down to the cellar and brought me his. He deposited them from his hands into the sink. The dry earth still clung to them. I could smell the mud and must. They were still firm and looked like they had just come out of the ground.

It took forever to wash the caked dirt off them, however, they were the best mashed potatoes I had ever eaten—the best part of the dinner, actually.

After supper, he lay where he usually did, on the daybed. His stomach was full and he was content, like a well-fed barn cat.

I wondered if food was the only thing that made him tick.

He caught me staring. He had opened his eyes and stared back, unblinking, like he could sense me. I felt like I was being watched by an owl, or some other unknown creature of the woods. Something that could remain motionless, gazing, having an unnatural perception of its surroundings.

I had to turn away. It unnerved me.

I looked around at the dishes, at my fingers, his feet, anything but his eyes. Then, when I looked in his direction again, they were closed. His mouth slightly opened, his breathing deep and rhythmic, as if in a trance.

I scratched the back of my head and sighed.

I hadn't really thought all of this out. What were my plans? Really? Was I just going to move back here? Stay with Papa 'till he gets better? What about Sarah and Joanne and the kids? I needed to see them. I couldn't go months without them.

I drummed my fingers. There wasn't much to do now but clean up.

The evenings were getting longer but the nights were the same. Long and dark and lonely. I could never forget that. I piled the dishes together and placed them in the sink. At least Art gave me something to do. The pie. He said they'd be coming by tomorrow.

~

James didn't make eye contact. I had actually looked forward to seeing him. It had been a few years and he was one of the few people that had made a fuss over me in the past.

I met him and Art at the door before Art pushed me out of the way. Papa nodded and the three of them spoke.

"It's this here lass that wants it. Where, Maggie? Which room?"

"Joanne's and Sarah's," I said. "Here, I'll show you."

I raced off ahead of them, taking the stairs two at a time while James and Art followed. Papa remained where he was, in the kitchen. In fact, I didn't think it mattered much to him what I did with the house—whether there was a working bathroom or not. He'd probably keep using the piss pot anyhow.

James jotted down notes on his paper, took out his yellow tape and measured, chatted with Art, pointing, nodding. They started back downstairs jabbering on. It was like we were in Art's house.

I tried to inject a word or two but they ignored me, talked over me. I huffed.

That's when Art hollered for me to put the tea on.

When I put the kettle on the stove, Papa moved like a lynx from his bed to his chair, waiting for the hot beverage and a slice of the pie. It wasn't even lunch yet and everyone wanted dessert first.

James shrugged when he ate it. As if he was insulted by it. "My mom makes it better."

Now I was offended. I had painstakingly rolled and fluted the edges on the pie crust as if it was some fine piece of sculpture. The apples, tossed with not just white, but brown sugar too, cinnamon, nutmeg, a few dollops of butter here and there. The way Sarah had made it. The way our mother had made it.

I said nothing. I swallowed a bite myself to see what prompted the indifference. The apples were soft, not mushy; there was a sweet fragrance from the spices, the body of the pie itself was juicy, not sopping wet, and the crust: flaky and golden. I couldn't have done better if both Sarah and Momma were behind guiding me with their own hands. In all actuality, they were.

"Ah, it's good, Maggie. Don't be paying no attention to James. He don't know everything." Art winked at me, smiled, his face full of dessert.

I stared at James coldly. It didn't matter. It was only a pie.

But James paid me no attention, I noticed. It was like I was invisible.

I listened as Art discussed the supplies and costs and how long it would take, while I stood at the sink, waiting to be included. James had the nerve to shake Papa's hand and he and Art walked toward the door and out, still blabbering as Papa lay back down on his bed.

I fumed. *Why had I suddenly become the ghost?*

I was perturbed for the rest of the day. Agitated, moody, could snap the head of a dandelion three feet off the ground.

I didn't want to be in the house anymore, so I left on foot, headed out into the fields. I followed a worn-out path. I was surprised it still remained.

It was a cold day in late April. The north wind bit hard and clumps of snow lay in dirty patches here and there.

By the time I reached the woods, the sun had come out and I was surrounded by the warmth of fir and spruce emitting a fragrance I welcomed. It helped me come to my senses.

I kept walking. The forest guided me to a clearing where Papa planted his potatoes. The earth was rough and clumpy, with hardened rows of soil.

I remembered when we had one patch. Now, according to the sheer size of it, this was where Papa spent all his time, tilling and sowing and fertilizing. There must have been ten? Twelve? gigantic rows for potatoes. The place was massive and I felt eerily spooked, like someone was with me.

I turned to see my father standing not twenty feet behind me in the woods, watching. Did he follow me here? With his long, deer-like legs? Is this his place of solitude and I interrupted him?

I called to him, but just as fast as the wind changes direction, he was gone.

I hadn't seen Art for a couple of days and there was no sign of James, either. I wasn't sure if they were putting me on. Maybe we really weren't going to get a bathroom. I wasn't sure how much it would cost, or how much money Papa had.

Could he afford to put it in? I hadn't really thought of that.

I had a few dollars saved, which I could offer, but what was I doing? Was I planning on staying here? Indefinitely?

And as far as Papa being ill? He seemed fine to me. I hadn't seen any of the issues Art had described. He wasn't throwing up or running a temperature, to my knowledge. His appetite seemed good. The same as it always was. He could eat whatever and as much as you put in front of him. He drank tea at least fifteen times a day and didn't smoke. He did like his occasional chew, but he seemed to save that for planting and harvesting time, spitting the black tar into the soil.

Art had finally stopped by a few days later. It was Uncle Dan's funeral and he asked if I wanted to go. He wore the same shirt and pants he wore every day. The only difference was that he had had his hair slicked back with Brylcreem and he may have shaved.

"You don't even have to go into the church, Maggie. You can just stay out in the car and when the procession walks to the cemetery, you can come then."

I shook my head vehemently. In fact, I practically ignored him even when he stood in the doorway. He took out his pocket watch and clicked it open, placed it back in his front trousers, knowing full well he would be late if he waited another second more. He spoke to my father in Gaelic and my father laughed out loud.

"What?" I asked.

Art looked down. "Nothin'."

He waited a few more minutes. "Well?"

I felt like my father just then, channelling him, not saying anything, looking away. Ignore. Ignore. Ignore.

Art finally got the message and turned on his heel. Before he left, he said, "I'll give her your condolences."

My mouth slipped open. But he'd left. I'd tossed the dry cloth on the counter and blew through my tight-pressed lips. My bangs had wafted in the air.

"Good riddance," I had said. "How do you say that in Gaelic, Papa?"

"*Deagh thlachd.*" He had smirked. I knew then that he felt exactly the same as I did.

28: *Cò tha sin?*

May, 1958

James arrived in a pick-up with all the supplies, the wood, packages of nails, copper pipes. Art pulled in a few minutes later. The men spoke to one another.

My father stayed out of it, but looked annoyed. The door swung open and banged shut, the cold air came in. It was the noise he hated.

"Quiet," he bellowed, but Art and James ignored him. They kept coming in with the two-by-fours and the scent of wood. Progress.

They grunted and stammered; banged into the walls as they rounded the sharp, small corners to the upstairs with their load.

"I thought this room was supposed to be cleared out?" James hollered, directing his attention to me, albeit not in a good way.

I hadn't even thought any more of it, having not talked to, nor seen James in weeks. I had spent my time straightening up the downstairs, cleaning the things that hadn't seen a broom or a mop in years.

I ran to the top of the stairs and shuffled around the lumber, stared at the unmade bed and belongings of my sisters' room.

James walked in and pushed the bed away from the wall. The metal legs screeched across the floor. I gathered as many blankets as I could, scooping them up in my arms, and depositing them in my old room.

"This window will have to be replaced," James stated, matter-of-factly. "The pane is broken, for starters."

"Ah-ha," Art said as he bent down, assessing the state of it.

James flipped the mattress off the bed and pulled it out into the hallway, then dragged it into my old room. I wasn't sure why this bothered me so much. It had been empty all these years. I wondered what Momma would think if she were alive right now.

James barely looked at me, kept to his work. He managed to get the bed frame apart with a lot of banging and put that in my old room, too. He needed help getting the wardrobe out, but Art was not the man for the job. He was too old and scrawny, so James asked him to get the 'old man'.

I laughed.

Papa sauntered up the stairs like an old dog being called. He didn't say anything about the mess and the fuss, yet his eyes said otherwise, shifting from here to there. He stood on the threshold awaiting orders.

James grabbed hold of one end of the wardrobe and Papa bent and lifted from the other. He picked it up as effortlessly as he would lift a small child. James' face reddened and he heaved and groaned as he held his mouth tight. I was sure Papa could have moved the whole unit by himself.

They placed the wardrobe at the end of the hallway, tucked neatly out of the way. I stood looking at it, turning my head sideways as Papa moved around me and made his way back down the stairs. His part of the project was done.

Art pulled out a chair and sat on it, waiting for the work day to begin.

"That'll make a good linen closet," James said, finally directing his attention to me.

I nodded and looked at him, roused by his thoughts.

He caught my eye for a brief second before turning his attention to the room at hand. "Okay, Art. Let's get going."

"All right, boss. Just tell me what you want."

They banged all morning. Smashed, tore, hammered. They tossed riff raff and debris out of the bedroom window to the ground below.

Papa paced like a crazed cat. He didn't like the noise. He was used to the quiet and solitude of his house.

"It will be good once it's finished, Papa," I said as I prepared the soup for the men's lunch. He grumbled incomprehensibly, obviously not agreeing.

I made ham sandwiches to go with the vegetable soup and called to Art and James to come down when it was ready. I felt quite proud they would sit down to piping-hot bowls with sliced sandwiches (minus the crusts) placed on the side, a technique I had learned in Boston.

The tea was on and I poured the cups when Art and James came down, covered in white dust. They looked like ghosts and James' teeth gleamed yellow in contrast. They brushed their hair with their hands and the powder dissipated.

Papa was already at his spot at the table and Art took his usual. James stood, his hand resting on the back of a chair as he watched the older two men devour their meal.

"Aren't you going to eat, James?" I asked.

"I'm waiting for you."

"There's only three chairs," I said. "Please take it." I hadn't planned on eating with the men anyway. It wasn't my place. The workers ate first and then I'd have a bite when they were done.

"Oh," he said, surprise in his voice. He pulled out the chair and sat. "Thank you. This looks really good."

I felt myself blushing and turned around. My hands shook as I poured the tea.

Art insisted I stay a few nights at home for various reasons. Sometimes he 'had company', he said, and didn't want me there. I thought it was a ploy to get me to stay here and keep an eye on my ill father, which I thought was a lot of malarkey. Other than Papa being his usual man of few words and low grumblings, I had seen no behaviour or illness that needed to whisk me away from my sis-ter's side.

I was sleeping on the squeaky couch in the living room as the upstairs was in such a state of upheaval. Like every morning when I stayed here, I heard Papa wake. He shuffled around, talked to himself, dragged the cover off the piss pot, and then I heard the long, steady stream of water hitting the bowl. I grimaced and felt that pang and pressure of having to go myself, but it was too early to get up just yet.

I turned over and adjusted my position. The couch squeaked as I flipped. I faced inward towards the high back of the couch and ran my hand around feeling for the sharp spring, making sure I didn't make contact with it. I squiggled again to get comfortable, and the blanket fell off me.

Papa was unusually quiet. I didn't hear the kettle hissing, or the wood stove being stoked. I reached for the fallen blanket.

Then I heard it. Behind me, almost like a sixth sense. A presence that someone was there even before I felt the cold, circular, piece of metal on my exposed shoulder blade. I flinched.

"*Cò tha sin?*" he said.

"Papa?"

He cocked the rifle. He pushed it further into my back so my mouth was jammed into the back of the sofa. I couldn't move. I didn't breathe. It was my father, spooked. Forgetting I was here. That I was sleeping here.

"*Cò e?*" he said again in his deep, agitated voice.

"Papa! It's me. Maggie!" I twisted my head to see his figure standing there, the firearm held taut, his eye squinted, finger on the trigger. The blood rushed out of my body. "Paaaappaaaa," I cried, but he didn't hear me.

The barrel dug deeper and he went into a litany of profanities in Gaelic.

I turned sharply and, with my exposed hand, jerked the end of the rifle up and away from me. The gun fired and the bullet blasted through the ceiling with a thunderous crack. A spray of plaster rained down on me.

I hopped on the couch, my fingers clutching the barrel. My arm shook with the weight of it.

My father had bolted, disappeared like a rat. The sound must have startled him, too.

I wasn't sure how long I remained there—on the couch with my legs bowed, holding the rifle. Every hair on my head stood on end. I had been too scared to move, too scared to make a noise.

My knees started to knock, my legs vibrated, and then my arms trembled. Goosebumps erupted up and down my body as I stood exposed in the cool morning air wearing nothing more than a threadbare nightdress.

I stepped off the couch and placed the rifle under it, breathing hard. I was still too scared to go into the kitchen, and remained where I was until I was sure he had gone back to sleep.

I picked up the blanket and pulled it tight around me, tip toed into the kitchen. He was where he usually was, stretched out on the daybed, one hand over his head. He opened his eyes and looked at me sleepily when I stood at the entrance.

"I'm hungry," he said.

~

We stared at it like we were assessing some kind of cosmic anomaly. Art, James, and myself, our bodies twisted sideways staring up at the ceiling. James stood on the back of the couch and stuck his finger in the hole where the bullet blasted through the plaster. Small bits of white chalk sprinkled onto the couch and the floor.

Art was particularly speculative. "He wouldn't intentionally kill you, Maggie."

"No?" I rounded on him. "You did say he was still angry with me."

"Yes, I did say that." He groped his chin, scratched at his whiskers with his fingertips. Then he knelt down on the floor, stuck his head under the couch and stretched his arm out, retrieved the rifle.

"Whoa," James said, his eyes wide.

Art lifted a leg and rested his foot on the couch. He checked for any more shells.

"She's clean. Only used one by the looks of this here."

"One would have done it, Art, if he chose to." James leaned against the door frame, his arms resting behind his back.

"He never uses his rifle, Maggie. I can count the number of times on one hand in fifty years. He just forgot you were here, is all."

"And he doesn't remember aiming it at me?"

Art shook his head, tucked the rifle under his arm.

"Maybe he was sleep-walking," James interjected. "I've heard about that; well, read about it..." He trailed off. He seemed embarrassed by what logic he just offered.

I wanted to believe him. Of course it made sense. He had no memory of aiming a gun at my back and I hadn't lived here in—how many years? Plus, I had not been sleeping in my usual room but on a squeaky couch. Then all the banging and upheaval of putting in a working washroom disrupted his usual day-time naps.

"Those noises, especially in the early morning, were so unexpected, Maggie. Of course he would be spooked."

"That supposed to make me feel better?" I bit my lip. "If it was me that heard noises in the kitchen, I don't think I'd threaten anyone with a firearm." I looked toward Art and James for more input, justification. They had none to offer.

"Well. I better get started," James stated. "The bathroom won't finish itself."

He veered right toward the back steps. His back swayed as he walked upstairs.

Art, with the rifle under his arm, headed left towards the kitchen. I followed but stopped cold in the dining room. I couldn't face my father, yet. I didn't want to see him or his facial expressions, just in case he *was* lying.

I knew I wasn't his favourite. That was Mary. Maybe he resented me being here, disrupting his life and solitude. Maybe the gun was a threat to get me out, permanently?

"John," Art bellowed, which caused me to jump. Papa grunted. I could tell he was sitting by the way the bed moved, the way his shoes shuffled on the floor. He always seemed to respond to Art but never to me.

"I'm gonna take this here rifle home, okay?"

"No need. No need of that. I use it sometimes."

"When did you use it last, John?"

There was silence as Papa thought. "Must be two years by now, when we thought wolves were into the chicken coop."

"Who is 'we'?"

"Me and Mary."

"Ahhh," Art peered over his shoulder to me, made a face. "You know, John, it couldn't have been Mary, eh? She's been dead for, wha?" He looked to me again for clarification.

"Eleven years," I whispered.

"Eleven years," he repeated.

I moved in closer and saw Papa sitting on his daybed, his shoulders drooped, his hands lying by his sides. He looked at the floor, and at Art. His eyes darting back and forth.

My footsteps caused him to look up at me, then he turned away.

"You know who this here is, don't you?"

"A course. A course," he grumbled, sat back on his seat again. His mouth glowered.

"Where do you keep the shells, John?" Art hollered again.

Papa pointed with his finger, towards his room.

Art twisted his head, followed his direction and walked to Papa's bedroom. He disappeared into it in search of them. Papa closed his eyes. As Art moved things around, opened and closed drawers, the muscles in Papa's face tensed.

"Where are they, John? Oh, never mind, I found 'em."

He came out with a small box, placed it in his front pocket. "I'm gonna take this here home, John, and give it a good cleaning, all right?"

Papa nodded. He'd agree with anything Art said to him.

"I'll bring it back when I'm finished with it."

I gave Art a dirty look. "I don't want that back here," I scolded in a low whisper.

He splayed his hand out, shook it. "It won't be. But he don't know that."

The knocking started upstairs again and Papa growled, sat up, put both hands to his head. I shuffled back to the dining room.

"John! You okay, John?"

Papa didn't answer. He stood up, mumbling to himself, and rushed to his room, slamming the door behind.

Art watched Papa's door for a minute, then said to me, "Maybe he'll go back to sleep there for a bit."

I nodded, hoping it was true. By the looks of it, neither of us were getting much of it here.

I followed Art to the door. "What do you make of him talking about Mary?" I whispered.

"He's been alone here for a long time, Maggie. Whether he's just imaging it or dreaming it, I don't know. Sounds like he's not sleeping proper, with all the noise during the day, either. But there was something getting the chickens all right."

"Really? So, there was an element of truth in his story?"

Art's eyes glazed over as he stared out at our old barn. His eyes shifted back to me, then he ran his tongue over his gums and lips. "Well, it wasn't a wolf. I remember that much. It turned out to be a weasel."

"Oh." I laughed, thinking it was funny for some reason.

"But it wasn't your father's. He hasn't had chickens in years. It was the Mullhollands that lived next to our place when I was a boy. The house is gone now, fell down years ago. Anyways," Art became sombre in thought, "Bernie, the owner, had caught two weasels in his trap. Scary-looking critters. All white, looked like miniature seals with ears and really sharp teeth."

He shuddered. "They could squeeze themselves into a space that small." He pinched his forefinger and his thumb together to show half an inch. "Your father was living with us then, and I remember how excited we were because we thought we were going to shoot a big, bad wolf."

He chuckled, exposed his dark gums. "It kept your Pa's mind off things, you see? After he lost his mother and sisters. I can still see the disappointment in his face when he saw it wasn't a wolf."

Art shrugged. "I didn't understand it, myself. But for some reason, that really bothered your father. He didn't kill them, either."

"What he do?"

"He let the critters go."

"Why?"

"Thought they were spirits of the dead."

I felt a cold, almost darkening, shiver run through my body. I swallowed, looked at Art and he seemed to sense my discomfort.

"I think it's high time we get you a working phone in the house, too."

"Yeah," I said, my mouth dry, "good idea. And I'm staying at your place tonight."

29: No more piss pot

"Well? What do you think?"

I beamed when I presented the working washroom: the new tub, toilet, sink, a window that opened and shut, a cabinet with a mirror, and pull-out drawers with storage. I thought I was dreaming. "This is just like the O'Learys' house in Boston," I gushed. "I never thought we'd have one here. Ever. Sarah will be thrilled when she comes home."

Art nodded too, drew his palm over the counter like it was the hood of a new car. "Mighty fine." He stood in front of the toilet and flushed it. The whoosh of water emptied and refilled.

Papa stared in nonchalance.

"No more piss pot, Papa."

His brows furrowed.

"And no more spot cleaning." I laughed. "You can shower in here."

I pulled back the curtain to reveal mint green barker tile. "Look at it! So bright and shiny."

I turned on the taps and pulled up the metal knob. The water ceased flowing from the lower spout and out sputtered rain from the shower head. It sprayed in all directions. I closed the curtain.

"See, Papa? You stand in the tub but make sure you pull in the curtain else the water will go all on the floor."

Once again I opened the curtain, pushed down the button then turned off the tap. "See? You can go first."

Papa looked at me like I was crazy.

"Oh, go on, John. Make the girl happy." Art chuckled.

"How 'bout you, Art? You want to go next?"

"Sure. Sure."

I clapped my hands in excitement. I couldn't contain myself. "Sarah and Joanne will be thrilled."

I walked out of the washroom to the wardrobe and retrieved a towel and a fresh, new bar of soap for Papa.

"I also picked up this." It was a bottle of Prell shampoo and its colour matched the colour of our new bathroom.

"Don't bother giving him that." Art grabbed the shampoo and examined it. "One thing at a time. Just give him the soap."

"Alright," I said.

It was like trying to show a toddler how to eat his cereal. Papa didn't have a clue what to do even though I just showed him the steps. I had to do it again. I turned everything on for him and closed the curtain. Then I left the room.

"You just get undressed and go in and wash," I hollered from outside the door. I would have liked to take his old clothes and burn them, or at least have something new and clean for him to put on.

Then I thought about the shirts I had sent Papa and wondered if he ever wore them. I left Art in the hallway and barrelled down the stairs, rushing past the kitchen and into his room. I checked his drawers and wardrobe.

While I was there nosing around, I found socks that hadn't seen a foot, pants folded still with the tag, a shirt that I sent that still had the pins in it. He had almost everything except underwear.

I should have been angry that he didn't wear anything I had sent, but right now it didn't matter.

I gathered up the haul and ran back upstairs and dropped them outside the door. I told Papa that his new clothes were there and to put them on, and when he didn't answer, I opened the door and pushed them in.

I paced the hall, feeling like a father awaiting the arrival of his new babe.

When the door finally opened, I was hit with hot steam. Staring back at me was the cleanest, wettest version of my father I had ever seen. His hair stood in all directions and that's when I thought it was time for a cut.

I remembered seeing a pair of scissors, Momma's shears, that she used to use for cutting fabric for quilts down on his bureau. I took it upon myself to retrieve them.

When he came down to the kitchen, wiping his ears with the towel, I gestured for him sit on the chair. He did it without question and then I threw the wet towel around his neck like a bib.

"I'm going to cut your hair," I said in a loud voice, mimicking Art. Papa sat in the chair as instructed and placed his hands on his knees.

I combed his wet hair flat and smooth. The water beaded down his cheeks and he wiped it away. I had to recomb.

I took the scissors out of the pocket of my apron and started to cut, chopping away long uneven strands for shorter ones. I found I enjoyed what I was doing, having forgotten about Art hopping in the shower next. I kept cutting Papa's locks shorter and shorter, including his sideburns.

I stood back, assessing him, and the curls of white hair littering the floor. Papa remained relaxed and at ease the whole time I trimmed and snipped.

I caught Art in the corner of my eye, not wanting to turn around in case Papa came out of his trance.

"Well, I'll be," Art said with a laugh. "My turn next?" Art's mouth was turned into a wide smile, his eyes squinting.

"Sure. Just hold on."

I bent Papa's head forward so his chin was almost resting on his chest. I tried to cut the hair on the back of his neck as straight as I could.

When I thought I was done, I removed the towel, snapped it and dry hair fluttered in the air like butterfly tresses.

Papa wiped his face with his hand and ran his fingers over his scalp. "Good. *Tapadh leat.*"

"You're welcome." I appraised his cut. It wasn't too bad considering it was my first try, and it was considerably better than what he had before.

Papa turned and noticed Art standing behind him and stood up.

"Okay, Art," I said. "Have a seat."

As I combed and snipped Art's hair, he started telling stories of when he and Papa were boys. I appreciated hearing the tales I had never really been privy to, maybe because I was a girl, or maybe I had never been interested. Maybe because there was always work to be done and no one had time to sit and talk about such things, but today, it seemed, was a perfect day for hearing the two men in my life banter and laugh, a day when troubles, although always on the horizon, were not spoken.

~

After that, there were times when Papa would get up in the morning and simply be gone all day. At first, this didn't bother me because I could prepare the house for Sarah's arrival. She had said she would be home in the summer and we would have the christening.

My first mistake was assuming we would be having the christening at our place. Nevertheless, I scoured and cleaned, tossed out old moth-eaten or musty blankets that couldn't be cleaned, disposed of bugs and dead flies from window panes and light fixtures. Cobwebs that were so thick you thought it was some kind of string, and linoleum that I either had to pull up and scrape off with bruised and bloodied knuckles or nail down with a hammer.

I dusted end tables and moved furniture around. With Art's help, I tossed the old couch that was a hazard, with the loose spring sticking out. I tried to rid the house of any unwanted and repulsive smells, including hiding Papa's piss pot because he simply refused to go to the bathroom upstairs. Either he forgot about the new working toilet or thought the urine was being filtered back into the kitchen faucets. Either way made no difference.

In lieu of his yellow-stained, repugnant, foul-smelling ceramic crock, he made use of Momma's old stock pot that I had really liked to use for cooking carrots, but not anymore.

There were days when Papa wouldn't come home for lunch and wouldn't come home for supper either. On those days I had to remember when I last saw him, or if I had seen him at all. Had he eaten? What direction had he gone?

Then I would get Art on the line and ask if Papa was there with him. Sometimes he was, having wandered through the fields and forest on an old path that he remembered and ended up at Art's. His feet and pants would be soaked to the knees, though, as he had to cross the brook.

One time, however, he ended up on the other side of town. We weren't really sure how he got so far. Someone may have given him a ride, or he simply kept going in the wrong direction. Now I understood what Art had been talking about.

Our solution was to put a bell on the door so I could hear him leave. My duty was to make sure I looked where he was going in the morning, or at lunch, but this didn't seem to make a difference either. He drifted over the land like a piece of dandelion flower in the wind. You never knew where he was going to end up.

Most days he just ventured down to the barn, or to the potato field, or to Momma's grave. He had buried her there with the others; his parents, his siblings, and my sisters, across the field under a big apple tree. A private place just for him.

Art said Papa had built a bench there and a fence, and most times, that was where he'd find him, sitting thoughtfully, his legs spread apart, his hands clasped together, staring at what was.

He'd always come when Art found him, though. Art would say, 'Supper's ready', something of that nature, and the two would walk back, talking about the weather and about the spring planting like it was any other day long ago.

30: The names of my family

June, 1958

Aunt Martha grasped my hand firmly with hers. Then let go. Instinct told me to cast my gaze downward, to avoid, flee. Her voice caused me to look up.

"Hello, Maggie."

Although she was smiling, her face seemed heinous, cruel. Like she had swallowed something she couldn't quite keep down. Deep lines creased around her cheeks and chin, and on her forehead. Her hair seemed longer. Greyer. She had lost weight.

I forced a smile back. "Nice to see you," I lied. "How are you?"

She extended her forearms on the metal shopping cart. We were both steering vehicles. I chuckled to myself as neither of us had a license.

We were parked in the soup aisle, facing in opposite directions. It seemed strange to see her here. I never saw Martha outside her house, only at mass on Sundays. She looked so out of place.

She was elegantly dressed, as always. She wore a long skirt and matching blouse with a turned-down collar. A string of pearls around her neck and a marvellous hat. I often imagined Momma wearing such things and found myself wanting to touch the fabric.

"Fine," she said, playing with her rings. I looked for something to add to the conversation. What was on sale? The weather.

She touched my hand again. "Sarah's had another boy. She went early."

"Yes," I beamed. Sarah kept in contact with Aunt Martha regularly. I was sure she had a say in what she called him as well. "Ryan...Andrew?" I said aloud.

"I think you mean Ryan Anthony. After the Patron Saint." Her smile gleamed, lipstick clinging to a front tooth. She seemed to relish my misunderstanding, or the fact she had the information first.

"She must have changed it," I offered, looking down at my nails.

"It's a fine name. I'm sure he's as handsome as his brothers."

I puckered my lips together, nodded slowly. I wasn't sure what she wanted me to say. I just wanted to finish the conversation, if that's what this was, and to get on with my day.

"And your father, he's not well?" Aunt Martha was notorious about knowing people's business, even if you hadn't talked to her in months. Today she seemed to have all the time in the world.

I took a deep breath. "He's—"

A child cried out behind me.

I turned around to see a little boy, no more than two, wiping his eyes with his small fist. His mouth hung open as his mother scolded him, pulling him along.

"Maggie?" Martha drew me back to her.

"Yeah, fine, Martha. He's okay. We all are."

I felt rather tired all of a sudden. Drained, but I felt Aunt Martha was revving up for a big disclosure. The reason she stopped to talk in the first place.

The baby continued with his fussing and the mother seemed to have little to offer. I didn't like hearing him cry. I picked at my fingers the more distressed he became. When whines turned into wails, I had chewed my fingernail to the quick.

"Well, that's not what I'm hearing. I heard he's..." Martha continued. I missed the rest of her conversation. I listened more to the little boy behind me than her opinions on my father.

I thought she had finished so I started to push my cart away and she grabbed my arm for the third time. She had one more nugget to tell me.

"You know? Sarah will be staying with me when she comes and we're having the christening at my place. It's more suitable. The old place is so run down, and then, your father's condition. And yours. Sarah has been filling me in." Her eyes gleamed.

My mouth, however, hung open and I blinked like I had something stuck in it. "Pardon? What did you say?"

"Oh, I thought you knew all this," she said in an arrogant tone, her face turned slightly upward. She raised her hand to her chest, cast her eyelids down, "That's right, you've not been speaking with your sister. Understandably. Not since she kicked you out."

Then she waved her hand in the air, dismissing me. "Well, I've got to go. So much to do…"

My blood boiled. She was still going on and on. I couldn't stand it any longer. "And you're a manipulative, old bitch—"

It was too late. I had said it. I felt the air drop a degree between us.

Her head craned like an owl's. Her facial expression turned dark; her eyes narrowed. "What did you say to me?"

I cowered.

"You watch your mouth, young lady." She grabbed hold of my forearm and squeezed. "And what you've been telling Sarah," she scoffed. "Who's going to believe you? You're crazy. Your insanities! It's a wonder anyone has anything to do with you, let alone your sister."

She sunk her fingernails into me.

"Ow!" I cried, "Let go." I pulled my arm out of her clutches, rubbed my hand over the scratch.

She peered around to see who was listening, whispered under her breath so sly-like, "You were always ungrateful, Maggie. All I did for you and your family. You're miserable."

I finally saw her true colours. The person my father despised, loathed. Art once said, 'If she didn't get things her way, let the world look out.'

"All you did for us?" My words spilled out like a pot boiling over on the stove. I rounded on her. My voice raised. "You turned a blind eye when your husband had his way with my sister. So you could take *her* baby."

She gasped, splayed her hand to her chest, as if she was having a heart attack. Her mouth opened as wide as a seagull.

I now had the attention of the woman holding the child. She held him close to her chest, bounced and shushed him, kissed his hair all the while watching us. Listening. The baby whined but nothing in comparison to the exchange between Aunt Martha and myself.

Martha swiped at me, knocked my hand out of the way. "You shut your mouth, Maggie. You're mad! You just proved it. But what do I care? You're just as spiteful and worthless as your father. Your mother was cursed the day she met him."

"And you're alone!" I screamed.

She pushed the cart with great force, the wheels squeaking as she rounded the turn. The baby and his mother left just as quickly, and I was alone in the aisle.

My heart thumped and my whole body vibrated. I felt weak. I crouched down beside my cart, leaned into the cans stocked on shelves. Some fell out and landed with a thunk onto the floor. One rolled down the aisle. I wrapped my arms around myself, heard whispers all around me.

I didn't want to look up. I shook my head, squinted my eyes then felt a presence before me. I knew he was there to rescue me again. Art.

"What you doing down there, Maggie?"

I wiped my face and took a deep breath and a few more for good measure. My legs felt like rubber. "Can we go, Art?"

"Aren't you going to pay for your things?"

"No." I whispered, felt tears forming.

He looked thoughtfully at me for a moment. "Anything to do with why your Aunt Martha left in a huff? She didn't buy anything either."

I raised my arms in the air simultaneously and then dropped them.

"Aww, Maggie. It's got to end."

"Art," I spat in anger. "She said, she said terrible things to me. She said I was—"

"Oh, Maggie. Come on, then. Come on. Let's go."

I bowed my head as we walked out together. I walked in shame. Everyone gawked at me as I left the store.

I had argued with an old woman, my aunt. A widow. My respectable, church-going, affable, generous, can't-do-enough-for-us aunt.

Did everyone hear me? Did I say what I thought I did? Out loud?

The tears burned in my eyes.

In the car, I chewed at my cuticles. I did this for several minutes before I started pounding my legs, banging hard with my fists. Then I punched the dash.

"Hey—hey-there, Maggie! Easy now....Jesus, that woman can rile the devil."

"Did you know that Sarah is going to stay at her house? Art? And not just for the christening?" I yelled. I was livid.

"I see," Art said in a sombre tone, lighting a smoke.

"How can she stay there after—?" I huffed. "After everything that's happened?"

"You mean with Dan?"

"Of course, I mean with Dan. All the times we went there." I screeched. My throat felt raw. I slapped my forehead, pounded my feet up and down on the floor of the car.

I turned to Art. "She always loved Sarah, you know? Sarah *was* the special one. She never got in trouble. Always got to bake bread and pies and cakes and we had to...she sent us in the back room...or to the barn with him," I huffed, crossed my arms over my chest. Saying it felt like a dirty word. I squeezed my palms together. "Sarah was never made to go. It was Joanne first. And then it was Mary. Then it was Mary," I repeated, crying.

"Ahh," he said, quiet-like. "That explains Leela."

"And Papa never did anything. He never did anything about it!" Every muscle in my body strained.

"Maggie. Stop it! Listen to me." The cigarette dangled off Art's lip. The ash dropped, falling on his pants leg. He grabbed for my hand and squeezed it. "Your father did know. Why do you think he didn't go back to that house? Hmm?"

I shook my head, keeping the tears at bay.

"He threatened his life, went down with the rifle. Dan was never allowed back on the property. Of course, your mother never knew. Well, he hoped she never knew.".

"Well, he still found a way. Look what happened to Joanne! He never left her alone. Ever! Even when she moved to your house and then left for the city. Oh God. What a mess! What a mess. She couldn't even look after Darryl. She'll never come back here, Art. Why would she with that woman and those horrible memories?"

Art jammed on the brakes and the car slid on the gravel road. Rocks spewed and crunched underneath. He turned toward me; his face solemn He grabbed my arm, stared hard into my eyes. "Well, *you* did, Maggie."

I couldn't talk anymore. I bowed my head and covered my face.

"I want to show you something," he said. "I don't think you've been here for a long while. It's a little walk but the air will do you good."

We drove for a few minutes more and he parked the car on the side of the road. It wasn't too far from my house.

We got out and I followed him, single file at first. I was thankful for the solitude.

It was still morning time, at least. Spring had been dry this year, making the forest floor spongy and soft underfoot. Twigs snapped as we brushed by and the soft fir tickled our faces.

Art spoke over his shoulder. "Back in the day, your grandfather used to have sheep. He herded them here but that was a hundred years ago."

I thought about that, of animals having created their own paths, feeling their freedom, not caged in barns and wooden stalls.

I slowed my step and found myself breathing in the scent of spruce and other trees, hearing the robin's song, and turned to see Art disappearing into the foliage ahead. Despite his age, he was still pretty agile.

I had to rush to keep up with him.

We came to a wider clearing and, from there, a more defined path. The two of us were able to walk side by side, and at times we bumped shoulders. We didn't speak. The walking soothed me.

"I don't remember this place, Art."

Art looked at me, gave me a strange sort of face. "You can walk down the hill from your house, but this is nicer." He turned his attention back to the path, and kept going.

I could smell the fragrant blooms before I saw them. The tree before us was massive. It had long curving branches with sweet, perfumed apple blossoms dressed in their prettiest white and pinks. Bees hummed and danced and drank their way around the floral party. It was visually stunning with jade-green foliage, a pale-blue sky, and the weathered grey fencing.

This was Papa's special place, and he was here, of course, sitting thoughtfully on the bench he had created, staring straight ahead. He sat with his mouth slightly opened, his eyes listless. He looked more like a statue than a real man.

I'd never really thought of him as a real man. A good man. A father.

"Why are we here, Art?"

He said nothing. Instead, tapped Papa on the shoulder to let him know that we were there.

Papa looked up and gave Art a brief nod, then stared straight ahead again as if we weren't really there at all. Spirits spinning inside his ghost world.

Art took me by the arm and walked me to the bench—asked me to sit down beside my father. I did as he instructed.

It was familiar to me then. This was our family burial site. My grandfather didn't want his wife (Papa's mother) and his daughters to be taken away from him again, so he buried them there. Then, when Momma died, and then Mary, Papa had them lain to rest there, too.

It really *was* beautiful.

"Take a gander, Maggie, dear."

"Dear?" I laughed out loud. "You've never called me dear before." I twisted my face to look at Art.

He dismissed my comment. "When *was* the last time you were here?"

I looked at the crosses Papa had erected—the old wooden ones of my grandparents and the smaller stone markers for their girls. They looked as old as the hills. "A while, I guess."

"A long while, Maggie."

Papa had made a special marker for Momma when she died. A very large stone. I wasn't even sure where he got it or how he got it to rest there, under the tree, but it was pretty amazing. He had chiselled Momma's name and the date of her death on the stone. It looked like he'd spent countless hours on it. He must have spent time there even when he was supposed to be doing other things, like looking after us, or feeding the animals. He'd been there, chiselling away. He'd carved birds and swirls and included the names of my sisters, Mary and Joanne.

My eyes narrowed and my mouth twitched. I stood up, met Art's eyes. "Art?"

I looked at him for clarification. Papa kept talking to himself, making gibberish.

"Art? What's this? This is impossible. No, Art. It can't be."

Art placed a hand on my back, spoke in such a calm, soothing tone. "Maggie. You were always such a quiet thing. It was Mary that was so boisterous and full of piss and vinegar. But you never seemed to let up, eh? And all those times you were at my place and I'd come in and you'd have the ashtrays out with lit cigarettes although I never saw you take a puff, and glasses of my moonshine or tea, talking to yourself. Always talking to yourself."

He wiped his nose and shifted his weight on his other foot. I glared at the tombstone.

"Then you'd leave the baby with me, Maggie. Just up and left, saying, 'Joanne has to learn to look after him.' That's why your Aunt Martha wanted him so much. Well, for other reasons too. But she was worried you might harm him, eh? Either that, or you'd forget about him all together."

His words came hurtling toward me like a bolt of lightning. Zigzags of memories opened up and exploded. I gasped and choked. Vomit forced its way out of my mouth. I bent over, holding the cold stone.

"I thought you was good for a while because you said *she* left. Went with Sarah to help with the wedding, and you were present then and good. You were a good mother. I saw you with that boy. It was magic." He smiled at me, clutched his hat in his fingers. "But then you were in and out of it, Maggie. Running off to Sarah's first, then Boston, leaving Darryl again. Saying Joanne this, Joanne that."

270

"I-I-I saw her."

"You saw what you wanted to. Like your Pa here." Papa sat, mumbling incoherently to himself, secret whispers to invisible spirits only he could see and hear.

"I did, Art."

"Maggie!" Art's voice became more forceful. "That day you ran off to Dan's apartment."

"No. That was Joanne's!" I raised my hand.

Art placed his two hands on my shoulders and shook me. He brought his red face to mine, his eyes hard and his mouth cross, "You listen to me, now. When you snuck off to the dance to be with your sister that night... you were taken advantage of, Maggie. It was Dan all along. Your feelings about him were right all the time. And James—"

"What did James have to do with anything?"

"Who do you think took you home that night? That boy did. And he beat the hell out of the man that was your uncle. It was James who chased him away. That's why Dan ended up in Ontario in the first place. James threatened him. He was a savage on the moonshine, that James. He was just like his father that way and that's why, to this day, he'll never take a drop. He knows he has the power to kill a man. And he could have that night. For you."

Art felt around his pockets till he came out with a small tin can and unscrewed the cover. He tipped back his head. He took another swig before screwing the cover back on and placing it back in his pocket. "So—I don't want to hear no more stories of Joanne being here, or Joanne being there. She was here all along, may God rest her soul." He blessed himself. "She's with her family. Right here."

I dropped to my knees and read the names of my family.

> Mother: Mary Louise Died December 8 1946, aged 32
> Daughter: Mary Alice, Died March 10, 1947 aged 5
> Daughter: Joanne Frances, April 16, 1947 aged 16

I read the names over and over, sliding my finger across the stone, feeling the rough edges, carving it into memory.

"Art." I said, looking up. "Joanne died a few months after Momma and Mary."

"Yes, Maggie. It was a difficult year. Complications from child-birth and a weak heart. Stress, too, after having lost her mother and baby sister. I never saw so much grief since the time your father lost his first family."

He tsked. "'Spose it was one of the reasons your father's in the state he is. Who needs to remember all that?"

"But Joanne was sent to live with you."

Art sighed deep, "Yes, only for protection. She was pregnant with Dan's baby then. Your father wanted to keep her integrity. No one was supposed to know. Dan and Martha were paying her to have the babe, would call it theirs after it came. No one would be the wiser. But, a course, things don't go as planned. Joanne had the same condition as your mother, and her and the baby both died to-gether. That was the first and only time I fought with your father. I wanted her to go to hospital but he wouldn't hear of it."

"Why?"

"'Everyone would know that she was pregnant out of wedlock."

"What'd you do?"

"All I could. I got your Aunt Martha to try and help, but it was too late. Thank God your mother wasn't around for that." Art bowed his head.

"But we were."

"Aye, and look how you handled it."

I sat in a blind stupor. Tears streaked down my face. Papa kept mumbling in soft Gaelic, playing with his fingers.

"They say there's nothing worse than losing a child. Your father here lost two. And for a while there, you as well. He was worried."

Art took out his tin again, uncorked and took a quick swig.

I studied the tombstone Papa made and could picture Joanne's face then, and the fine blue suit she wore at Momma's funeral. Aunt Martha gave it to her. Then I remembered, it was the same outfit we had buried her in.

I shook my head. "Art? What's wrong with me? Am I losing my mind just like Papa?"

I suddenly felt afraid. Goosebumps erupted on my flesh. I clutched my arms and pushed myself off the ground and took my seat beside Papa. He was still in his trance-like state, staring at all that he had lost, all that he once had.

"I don't know nothing, Maggie, but I think you just had a lot of grief and nowhere to put it. Having Darryl so young didn't help either. No mother to help you or tell you what was happening. And, I couldn't call Martha, not after the last time. So I called Mabel. I didn't know about these things."

He looked horrified at the memory. "Then you kept calling it Joanne's baby. I didn't even know who the father was but we figured it out."

"How?"

"Poor James finally told me after you arrived back here. After Dan's funeral. He figured it was time. Told me it was him who found you that night and who was doing the...well, you know. They figured they paid for Joanne's and got nothing, thought they were owed, I guess you could say."

I looked down at my hands. They were shaking. I was in shock. So much to take in.

Art reached in his pockets and took out a cigarette.

"Art?"

"Hmm." He struck a match and lit.

"Darryl's my baby."

Smoke curled out of Art's mouth. His eyes squinted; his face warm. "Aye, and probably you should take him home, eh? It would do you and your old man good."

I went to him and wrapped my arms around his shoulders.

"Ahhhh. There there."

Art's belly interrupted the mood. It made a full rumbling moan. "I think it's dinner time, no?" He patted it.

"Dinner?" Papa looked up at Art and then to me.

He stood up, towering over the two of us. He bent forward, kissed his fingers and touched the four names on the stone. Then touched each of the stones and the crosses of his parents and sisters, and the three of us walked off.

31: I talk about you all the time

July 3, 1958

"This is delicious, Maggie. What do you call it again?"

"It's called scalloped potatoes."

"What's in it?" James stuffed another forkful into his mouth. He had almost completely finished his plate and we had only just sat down two minutes ago.

"You've got to slow down," I said with a laugh. "You'll end up with a sore stomach."

I cut into the ham and took a bite. I had to admit, supper tasted pretty good. "Oh, milk and flour, some cheese, salt and pepper."

"Delicious." He wiped his mouth with the napkin and pushed the plate away, placed his elbows on the table, leaned in.

"There's more."

He looked over at the pot, raised his head. "I'll wait."

"There's lots there, James. I made enough for everyone."

The lines crinkled around his eyes. "I'll just help myself then."

I smiled back at him. He was so easy to be around and I enjoyed his company, having dinners together, and spending time alone. "Where did you say Art and Papa went?"

James heaped the steaming potatoes onto his plate. "Not sure really. He said for a drive."

I nodded, pulled a strand of hair out of my face. It was sort of funny, Art playing match-maker.

James sat down again, his knee bumped mine. Although he still looked the same with his dark hair and long bangs, he was no longer the menacing boy I went to school with. He was kind and sweet, a perfect gentleman. I watched him as he stuffed another piece of ham into his mouth.

"What?" he asked.

"You know, you never really told me why you ignored me when I first came back home."

James nodded. He opened his mouth then pointed a finger in the air till he finished chewing. He swallowed. "Yeah, well, I was mad at you. You stood me up all them years ago. Just up and left. I know I did something wrong."

"Like what?" I stopped eating. I was more interested in what he had to say.

"That I embarrassed you. That time at the doctor's."

"I wasn't embarrassed, I was mortified." I could tell he felt bad because his neck and cheeks turned soft pink.

"I'm sorry," he said. "That wasn't my intention. I was just trying to talk to you, make conversation and sometimes my foot goes in my mouth."

I remained silent for a few moments, trying to think of something else to say.

When he was done eating, he crisscrossed his knife and fork on the plate.

My eyebrows raised, "Who taught you that?"

"My mother. Said we should always have good manners."

"James. You're like nobody I've ever met."

I had a few bites more, then he whisked away the supper plates, cleared them off in the garbage before setting them in the sink with running water. "I don't know any man that helps with the dishes."

"I did them a lot here, the summer after you left."

"Really?"

"Yeah, I initially came to find out where you went and what you were doing. But then I'd come and talk to your father. He was lonely, so I'd make him supper and we'd talk. Then he'd go to sleep and I'd clean up."

"Oh, I didn't know."

He took the teapot off the stove and poured us a cup. I sat at the table with my foot up on the chair, my arm resting on my knee. "Thank you," I said and took the cup in my hands.

"My mother told me to look after those you care about." He winked at me.

"Care?" In a dull whisper, I asked, "Like that time you took me home from the dance?"

He looked me straight in the eye and nodded.

"I never knew it was you, James. Never asked. Never thought I'd have to think about that again, but here it is. So, thank you. I just don't what else to say."

I swallowed, felt the tears forming but I blinked them away.

"Maggie. I'm sorry too. I wanted to make things better. Then we started working together but you left so suddenly without telling me. I never thought you'd come back. I thought my chances were over for good, so I started coming here to find out where you went. I was going to follow you but Art told me to hold off till you get things straightened. He said you needed to do things on your own for a while."

"Really?"

He nodded.

I contemplated his words, brought the hot tea to my lips, took a sip. We stared at each for a moment before our shyness made us turn away.

"Your father wished he could have been better, you know, but he didn't know how," James offered. "Once your mother died, that took the life out of him. He was sad for a very long time after and yet, life went on. Then your sisters."

I let him talk as he recalled my past. Knowing what had transpired, the details, the aftermath, yet not having to say anything about it at all, brought comfort.

"What else do you know that I don't?" I asked. I lifted my other leg so I had two feet on the chair, the teacup rested on the table. I turned it around with my fingertips.

"I know you were in denial for a long while."

I kept my eyes downcast. "Papa told you that?"

"No, Art. He was worried about you, too. And Sarah, of course. Art didn't tell your father about much of that, I don't think. But Art knew you'd come around, get things figured out."

"He did?"

"Of course. Said you were smart and had a good head on your shoulders. That you'd see the light of day when you were ready. And you did."

A genial smile grew on James' face, then on mine. My throat caught and I blushed, felt the heat in my cheeks.

"Must be something in the red hair."

I grasped my curly mane in my hand and flipped it down my back. "You used to pull it. You didn't always like it, if I recall."

"No, no. Now you're wrong. I loved it! Just had a funny way of showing it."

I made a face at him, confused.

"My old man, sorry to say, I mimicked him. I thought...you had to be rough. That's how he was. Now I know better."

A light went on in my brain. I recalled when James showed me some of his scars when I worked at the doctor's house with him.

"Anyhow, after he died, my mother told me not to be like him. She talked to me a lot. I had to adjust a few times, you know. It was in the blood," he cleared his throat.

"How is your mother?"

"She's good. My sisters are good to her. She's content now, I think."

"I'm glad."

"She'd like to meet you sometime. And Darryl, of course."

I looked up at him, my eyes blinked so fast, a lump stuck in the back of my throat again. "She knows about me? About us?"

He nodded, "I talk about you all the time."

"That"—I took a deep breath—"would be nice." My palms sweated and I took my feet off the chair. "They are all coming home for the christening. Early next week."

"I know, and I'd like to meet him."

I blushed.

"You know, Maggie, I've always liked you. I did for a very long time, just didn't know how to show it. I know it can't be easy rais-ing a child on your own. My mother did it and it was hard. Well, you do know."

I nodded and swallowed.

"I want to ask you...I want to help you raise Darryl."

He fumbled with his jacket hanging on the back of the chair and pulled out a small box. "We could say he's mine. No one needs to know. Will you?"

He knelt down.

"James?"

"I'd be honoured if you'd have me."

I gazed at the shiny band. "What about Papa? Did you ask him first?"

A smile crept across his face. "I did. Why do you think Art and John went for that drive?"

We looked into each other's eyes. He stood up and held me close for several minutes.

"We'll have a good life, Maggie. I'll always take care of you."

I studied his nose and cheekbones, lips and complexion. I knew his words to be true. I felt it deep in my core.

"Can we have chickens too? Maybe a cow and a horse?"

"You mean like a farm?" I nodded, and his smile matched my own.

Just then, the car pulled up. Art shouted from the driveway, "Smells some good in there, eh, John? Wonder what the missus has cooked up for supper?"

Gaelic glossary

a dhà – Two.
agus – And.
Bonnach (pronounced *bawn-ock*) – a variety of flatbread or quick
   bread cooked from flour, typically round, which is common in
   Scotland and other areas in the British Isles. It is usually cut or
   torn into sections before serving.
Dè tha thu ag iarraidh – What do you want?
Can sin a-rithist – Say that again.
Chan eil – No.
Cò tha sin – Who's that?
Cò e – *Who is he?*
Dè – What?
Dè tha thu ag iarraidh – What do you want?
Deagh thlachd – good riddance
Duilich – *Sorry.*
Èirich – *Get up.*
Far an do òrdagan? – *Where are your toes?*
Latha math – Good day.
Tapadh leat – Thank you.
Tha an t-àm ann – It's time.
Tha i dhachaigh – *She's home.*
Tha thu math gille? – Who's the good boy?
Thu làidir gille – You're a strong boy.

Trena Christie-MacEachern

Acknowledgements

First, this book would not have seen the light of day without Moose House Publications. Thank you for welcoming me into the fold. A huge shout out to its founder, Brenda Thompson; and to their editor extraordinaire, Andrew Wetmore, for his brilliance and fine eye, and for spit polishing my words until they shone.

To those that have helped shape this story from the rough first pages: Rosie Poirier, Brenda MacLennan-Dunphy, and Penelope Jackson. Thank you for expertise and guidance.

Thank you to Shelly Campbell for your help with Gaelic phrasing, and to Marie MacDonald for info on the down-east dances in and around Boston.

I am both humbled and proud to be associated with The Shean Poets and Writers, my writing group friends. To Anne Levesque, Verna Feehan, Brenda MacLennan-Dunphy, Virginia MacIsaac, Andrea Currie, Frank MacDonald, Eileen Rickard, John Gillis, and Renee Peters: I strive to better because of you.

To my online writing group, Rose Poirier, Gus Doiron, and Brad Donaldson: critiquing at its finest.

To Lee D Thompson of *Galleon* magazine who gave me my first publication and introduced me to Anne Levesque.

To my best mates and gal pals, who always champion and cheer me on in all my hopes and dreams in life and in writing: Debbie Green, Wanda Chandler, and Cindy Northen Fraser.

To my husband, Glen, who has been with me since the beginning of my dull first pages and drafts, and chats with me endlessly over it during our morning coffee: thank you for always boosting me up when I need it most and giving me confidence to continue. To my three amazing children: I love you more than words.

To my MacEachern family, especially Cynthia Mathieson, Marie MacNeil, and Maria Hartery, for sharing your love of reading with me.

To my dear friends who always support me: Harolyn Grant, Anna Ashford-Morton, Marcie McManus, Cheryl MacDonald, Melinda MacDonald, Sherry Spencer and Aggie VanBuuren. Thank you.

With sincere gratitude to my former teachers of JCHS, many of whom I now call friends: most especially Morag Graham and Jeannie MacDonald; and to my English Literature influencers, Alice Campbell, Barbara Downie, and the late Leo A. MacDonnell, for all those classes that covered poetry, plays, short stories, and novels. "It is not what is poured into the student, but what is planted, that counts." (E. P. Bertin)

To my four brothers, and my parents, Cecil and Margaret Christie.

Although this book is dedicated to my mother, I would be remiss not to mention her siblings, especially Aunts Josephine, Catherine, and Etta, for it was their stories I heard first as a girl. Some of my fondest memories are of listening with my cousins to their tales of long ago as they reminisced over wine, finding humour in the re-telling, their sides sore from laughing.

Finally, to Virginia MacIsaac, writer, poet, editor, wordsmith, friend, who started me on this path, a gentle guiding force who always reads and critiques no matter how many times I ask, no matter how much is on her plate. I always aim for the moon, Ginny, and you never laugh. You help me find the path to get there.

Thank you. Tapadh leat. Wela'lioq. Merci.

"We are nothing without stories." - The Wonder

About the author

Trena Christie-MacEachern (she/her) is a fiction writer, a wannabe gardener, and loves Halloween. Her short stories have appeared in newspapers, literary magazines, and anthologies. Her short story, "At the Wake House", appears in *Blink and You'll Miss It*, the second volume of short fiction from Moose House. 

This is her debut novel.

She lives in Unamak'i, Cape Breton, in the village of Judique, with her husband, Glen, and their Border Collie, Lucy.

Book club discussion guide

Here are some questions you can use for jumping-off points as you discuss *The Light of Day.*

1. What is the significance of the title, *The Light of Day*, for you? Did you find it fits with the theme of the story?
2. Would you have given another title? And if so, what?
3. Is Maggie a trustworthy narrator? If not, where did she lead us astray?
4. Do your feelings toward Maggie's father change as the book goes on? How did he seem at first, and how by the end of the book?
5. Were there any quotes or passages that stood out to you? Why?
6. How did the book make you feel? What emotions did it evoke?
7. Are there any books you would compare *The Light of Day* to?
8. Do you think John's emotions were warranted in the story? Did you like him in the end?
9. What did you think of Old Art? Would you befriend somebody like him?
10. Is there anyone who is not related to you that you look up to as a father-figure/mother-figure/mentor (the way Art was for Maggie)?
11. The story opens with Maggie as an old woman talking to Mary Ellen, her granddaughter. What is different between Mary Ellen's life and Maggie's when she was young?